ORIGINAL SINS

ORIGINAL SINS

A Crime Writers' Association Anthology

Edited by Martin Edwards

This first world edition published 2010
in Great Britain and in 2011 in the USA by
SEVERN HOUSE PUBLISHERS LTD of
9–15 High Street, Sutton, Surrey, England, SM1 1DF.
Trade paperback edition first published
in Great Britain and the USA 2011 by
SEVERN HOUSE PUBLISHERS LTD.

British Library Cataloguing in Publication Data

Original sins: an anthology of original stories from
   members of the Crime Writers' Association.
   1. Detective and mystery stories, English.
   I. Edwards, Martin, 1955- II. Crime Writers' Association
   (Great Britain)
   823'.087208-dc22

ISBN-13: 978-0-7278-6999-9   (cased)
ISBN-13: 978-1-84751-298-7   (trade paper)

Severn House Publishers support The Forest Stewardship Council [FSC],
the leading international forest certification organisation. All our titles that
are printed on Greenpeace-approved FSC-certified paper carry the FSC logo.

Mixed Sources
Product group from well-managed
forests and other controlled sources
www.fsc.org Cert no. SA-COC-1565
© 1996 Forest Stewardship Council

Typeset by Palimpsest Book Production Ltd.,
Falkirk, Stirlingshire.
Printed and bound in Great Britain by
MPG Books Ltd., Bodmin, Cornwall.

CONTENTS

FOREWORD

Detective fiction, it's generally agreed, began with a short story. In 1841, with *The Murders in the Rue Morgue*, Edgar Allan Poe introduced us to the character of C. Auguste Dupin: an amateur detective whose forensic eye and ruthless intellect could unpick the intricacies of the most grotesque of crimes. With his remorseless logic, sharp eye and hapless sidekick, Dupin set the template for almost every fictional detective who came afterwards, from Sherlock Holmes to Hercule Poirot to Inspector Morse. As the progenitor of what remains to this day the most popular branch of fiction, *The Murders in the Rue Morgue* can lay claim to being perhaps the most influential short story ever. Yet when Poe presented it to his publisher, the publisher turned it down. Thus, from the very beginning, we see the twin traits that have defined the short story ever since. On the one hand, it offers an extraordinary capacity for surprise and invention, for literary exploration and even genius. On the other, it's a tough sell.

Thanks to its precarious commercial standing, the short story has been pronounced dead so many times in recent years it could almost serve as the subject of a mystery in its own right. Publishers, commentators and booksellers have all lined up to mourn at its funeral. And yet, thanks to the dedication of some far-sighted publishers like Severn House, together with authors and – most importantly – readers, further investigation reveals that the short story perseveres. I'm very grateful to our publisher Edwin Buckhalter, and our editor Martin Edwards. In producing this volume of work by members of the Crime Writers' Association, I believe they've demonstrated that the reports of the death of the short story were not just exaggerated, but downright wrong.

The Crime Writers' Association exists to promote the enjoyment and appreciation of crime writing. We spend a lot of time talking about it, but I can't think of a better way of achieving our goal than by encouraging you to pick up this book and read it. You'll certainly find much to enjoy and appreciate: stories from some of the UK's finest writers, old favourites as well as new discoveries, all working in a spirit of invention that Poe would surely have recognised.

Tom Harper
CWA Chair

INTRODUCTION

The publication of *Original Sins* marks a new beginning for the Crime Writers' Association's anthology, with a new publisher and a set of brand new stories, some contributed by notable crime writers whose work has never before featured in the CWA's own anthology. And yet there is also a sense of continuity, since Severn House published three highly successful volumes of the CWA anthology, starting in 1996 with *Perfectly Criminal*, following my initial appointment as editor of the series; it is good to be working again with a publisher that has such a strong presence in the mystery field.

Not far short of fifty anthologies have been published under the auspices of either the CWA, or its regional chapters, since *Butcher's Dozen* appeared in 1956, under the joint editorship of Josephine Bell, Michael Gilbert and Julian Symons. Occupants of the editorial chair through the intervening years have included Roy Vickers, Elizabeth Ferrars, Herbert Harris, H.R.F. Keating, Liza Cody, Michael Z. Lewin and Peter Lovesey. It is an honour to follow such distinguished predecessors, and also a rare privilege to have the opportunity to be the first to read some marvellous stories from leading authors as well as from talented writers whose names are not – yet – perhaps as well-known.

I asked intending contributors to keep in mind, when writing their stories, the theme of 'original sins', but to feel that they had plenty of latitude in how they interpreted that theme, and I was delighted by the results. One especially appealing feature of this book, I think, is that it offers stories with characters from no fewer than five well-loved crime series – namely, Simon Bognor (whose long ago TV incarnation was sadly all too brief), Richard Thornhill and Jill Francis, Bryant and May, Charles Paris and Ian Rutledge.

We have contributions from authors who have won the CWA's Diamond, Gold, Ellis Peters, John Creasey, and Short Story Daggers, and also a number from rapidly rising stars such as Chris Simms, Chris Ewan, and Sophie Hannah. There is history-mystery, contemporary drama, police detection, black humour and much more besides. Something for everyone who likes good crime fiction, I hope.

I would like to record my gratitude not only to the contributors, but also to all those CWA members who wrote stories for the book: my only regret is that, even had this book been twice as long, there would not have been room to accommodate all of them. The CWA Committee, chaired now by Tom Harper in succession to Margaret Murphy, has been extremely supportive, and I thank Tom for his foreword. Edwin Buckhalter and his team at Severn House have done a great job in putting the book together. The crime short story is a wonderfully entertaining form, and we are confident that mystery fans everywhere will find much here to relish. If they are encouraged to try the novels of the writers whose stories they enjoy, so much the better!

Martin Edwards

DOCTOR THEATRE
Simon Brett

Simon Brett is a prolific writer for radio and television, as well as in the crime genre. In addition to the Fethering Mysteries, he is the creator of those notable amateur sleuths Charles Paris and Mrs Pargeter, while *A Shock to the System* was a stand-alone novel filmed with Michael Caine. He is the current President of the Detection Club.

'**M**artin Cheyney's been poisoned!'

Charles Paris was alone in the Green Room of the Kean Theatre in Shaftesbury Avenue when the panic-stricken Assistant Stage Manager burst in with this devastating announcement. He was having an unrewarding tussle with the *Times* crossword, wondering whether his inability to untangle the clues was due to nerves about the First Night of *Richard II* that lay ahead that evening or the two large Bell's he'd managed to sneak in at lunchtime.

He knew he shouldn't drink before a performance. While the custom might have been acceptable – even expected – for actors in the heyday of the Richards Burton and Harris, it was heavily frowned on in the Perrier-swigging, gym-toned theatre of the twenty-first century. But Charles Paris found old habits hard to break.

And it wasn't as though he had a very big part, he reasoned Jesuitically to himself. Had he been playing Richard or Bolingbroke, then OK, he would have laid off the sauce. But the Gardener, who only appeared in Act Three Scene Four . . . the odd Bell's wasn't going to do much harm to that performance, was it? Hard to go wrong with rustic exhortations like 'Go, bind thou up yon dangling apricocks' and a lot of heavy-handed comparisons of the state of England to an untended garden. And as for the court scenes, where he had to fill out the stage as a

non-speaking Noble . . . well, that wasn't going to be too
much of a challenge, was it? All he had to do was to stand
up straight.

Anyway, Charles Paris had frequently been described as
an actor who was BWP ('better when pissed'). In the 1980s
he'd done a long tour as Horatio in *Hamlet* ('stolidly supportive' – *South Wales Echo*) and not drawn a sober breath the
entire six months. But of course he'd been younger then, he'd
bounced back from the hangovers quicker.

Charles tried to remove from his mind the certainty that,
before that night's performance of *Richard II*, he'd have had
a few more swigs from the half-bottle of Bell's secreted in
his dressing room. He'd always said drinking was a habit he
could easily break, but he was becoming decreasingly sure
about the accuracy of that claim.

Anyway, no time for such gloomy introspection. If what
the ASM had just announced was true, there was a big question mark as to whether the First Night of *Richard II* would
actually take place.

'Poisoned?' Charles echoed. 'Martin?'

'Yes. He's in his dressing room in a terrible state. Len on
Stage Door's rung for an ambulance.'

'I'll go up and see if there's anything I can do.'

The girl was distraught, tears welling on her eyelids. Early
twenties, though he couldn't recall her name. Charles had
clocked during rehearsals that she was very pretty in the
short skirts and contour-hugging leggings that seemed to be
obligatory uniform for young women of her age. He used
the excuse of her distress to give her a big hug on his way
out of the Green Room, and felt uncomfortably like a dirty
old man as he hurried up the backstage stairs.

The Number One Dressing Room was on the first floor, and
of course Martin Cheyney had the Number One Dressing
Room. He was a very big name. He'd not only served his
time in ever-grander roles at the RSC and the National, he'd
also gained international recognition by playing a regular
character in a series of movies about youthful wizards. Martin
Cheyney was one of the few names big enough to guarantee
healthy advance sales in the hazardous business of putting

Shakespeare on in the West End. Couple him with the latest *wunderkind* director Andy Smoker, restrict the run to three months and you had the nearest thing to a Box Office certainty that the theatre could offer.

Most London dressing rooms are small and shabby, but the Number One Dressing Room at the Kean Theatre lived up to its billing. Though it would have been too camp actually to have a star stuck on the door, the place still left no one in any doubt about the status of its incumbent. Spread across half of the first-floor backstage, it incorporated a separate bathroom and bedroom. What's more, before the run of *Richard II* started, the Number One Dressing Room had been specially redecorated for Martin Cheyney's occupancy. The management patently wanted to keep on the right side of their lead actor.

Charles passed through the main space, where the gorgeous costumes of the King were hung on rails, and into the back room, where he found the star writhing on the bed in paroxysms of agony. Watching him anxiously from the doorway was his dresser, an infinitely reliable dumpy ageing woman called Milly. Sitting at the side of the bed was Imogen Clay, the young actress who had won her way through the rounds of a television talent contest to gain the part of Richard's Queen. She kept trying to hold Martin Cheyney's hand, but it kept being snatched away from her as another spasm shuddered through the actor's body.

The phone in the main room rang. Milly answered it instantly. The call was short. 'Stage Door,' she announced. 'Ambulance has just arrived. They'll be up in a minute.' She moved towards the corridor, presumably to greet the ambulance men.

'I'd better go,' said Imogen Clay. She bent down and managed to plant a kiss on the stricken star's temple, then moved quickly out of the dressing room. Charles Paris, along with everyone else in the company, knew that there had been something going on between the girl and Martin Cheyney. Though he had a beautiful actress wife and two adorable children whom he wheeled out regularly for magazine photo shoots, the star prided himself on his reputation as a ladies' man. And if he fancied a fling, everything was conveniently laid on for him in the Kean Theatre. It was not for nothing that the Number One

Dressing Room was affectionately known as 'the star's knocking-shop'. Over the years it had served that purpose many times and for many stars of many sexual orientations.

Charles tried to catch Imogen Clay's eye as she hurried past him, but she kept her gaze studiously averted.

He moved forward to Martin Cheyney's bed. The actor's face was screwed up with pain, but the eyes registered his new visitor. 'Charles . . .' he murmured. 'Thank God that bloody Imogen's gone.'

'Oh?'

'You have a nice no-strings bit of fun with some bloody woman and she thinks it's a full-on love affair, that you're going to break up your marriage and . . .' Martin winced and was unable to finish his sentence.

'What's happened to you? What's wrong?'

Martin Cheyney nodded towards a tall glass on the bedside table. It was empty, though some greenish vegetable residue clung to the inside. Charles recalled that the star was, like many actors, somewhat faddish about his diet and seemed to subsist on smoothies to whose ingredients he gave much thought, research and public discussion. Martin Cheyney could bore for England on the subject. Charles had often heard him chuntering on to groups of star-struck younger actors about how the right combinations of fruit, vegetables and herbs could cure all common ills. 'I'm my own doctor,' he would constantly assert. 'I haven't seen a traditional doctor for over twenty years.' Well, from the green tinge to his complexion it looked as though that record might be about to be broken.

On a shelf on the other side of the room stood the electric machine in which Martin Cheyney took great pride in mixing his own elixirs.

'Someone poisoned my smoothie,' he gasped.

'How do you know?'

'Because nothing else has passed my lips all day except for a Starbucks Americano at breakfast.' He clutched at his stomach as another surge of pain twisted his guts.

'Would it be easy for someone to get poison into the smoothie?'

'I'm not in the habit of locking my dressing-room door,

Charles. The top was off the smoothie maker. I'd put in oranges, blueberries, celery and kale. I added the other ingredients and the ice later, just before I liquidised them.' He froze and fought for breath as he suffered another convulsion. 'Anyone could have put anything in there.'

'When?'

'You know we were called for notes at two. I got into the theatre about one and was in the Green Room till we were called on stage.'

'But who might have . . .?'

Charles neither managed to finish the question nor get an answer. The ambulance men came into the dressing room and took over.

He lingered on the landing, as if ready to offer help, but his services weren't required. Once the ambulance men had manhandled the stretcher loaded with the gasping Martin Cheyney down the narrow stairs, he moved back inside.

Charles Paris reckoned he was too old to be part of the smoothie generation. To him the very word conjured up the image not of a liquidised fruit drink but of a slick lounge lizard – and he'd met a good few of them during his long career in the theatre.

He looked again at the glass by the side of the bed and then turned his attention to the smoothie maker itself. The smell that rose from the debris round its slicing blade was like something scraped up from the bottom of a duck pond. Charles Paris's nose wrinkled. He'd prefer a large Bell's any day.

A few shreds of vegetable matter had survived the electronic pulping. There were some orange pips, a few filaments of celery . . . and some scraps of skin from what must have been the blueberries Martin Cheyney had referred to.

Except that, rather than blue, the scraps of skin appeared to be black.

To his surprise, because it had been more than fifty years ago, Charles Paris found himself remembering the stern words of his grandfather showing the young boy round the large family garden in Pinner. 'Now I know it's very tempting, Charlie, but I don't want you stealing any fruit from the fruit cage, none of the strawberries or raspberries or redcurrants

or blackcurrants. Do you understand, Charlie? Grandpa'll be
very cross if he finds out you've done that. And even more
important – don't you ever try eating the berries from *this*
plant. If you eat these, you'll get a very bad tummy ache
indeed, Charlie boy.'

And his grandfather had pointed out to him the *atropa
belladonna*, commonly known as 'deadly nightshade'. In his
mind's eye Charles could still see the shiny round black toxic
berries.

Charles Paris was thoughtful as he climbed the stairs to the
second floor where the smaller dressing rooms clustered.
These were tiny compared to the lavishness of the Number
One Dressing Room, but at least they were single occupancy.
Nobody had to share. These were the dressing rooms for the
supporting actors – Bolingbroke, John of Gaunt, Aumerle
and so on.

(Charles Paris, by way of contrast, found that his role as
Gardener entitled him to share a long, low garret under the
leaded eaves of the third floor, which was also peopled by
those members of the *Dramatis Personae* who appear under
the heading: 'Lords, Heralds, Officers, Soldiers, Gardeners,
Keeper, Messenger, Groom, and other attendants'. Bagot and
Green, two of the 'Servants to King Richard' – in fact two
of his favourites – also roosted in this crowded communal
space. The third favourite, Bushy, however, for some reason
had a dressing room to himself on the floor below.)

Charles reckoned his next port of call had to be Imogen
Clay. The entire *Richard II* company was convinced that she
and Martin Cheyney had been having an affair, though what
the star had said to Charles implied that anything of that sort
might be over. Which news would probably not have been
music to the ears of Imogen Clay. And hell notoriously hath
no fury . . . etc., etc.

Charles paused for a moment on the landing outside her
dressing room and marshalled what he knew about Imogen
Clay. The main impression he had of the girl was that she
was incredibly ambitious. She had trained at a little-known
drama school and was doing no better than any other jobbing
actress just out of her teens until television catapulted her

to fame. Every West End show these days, it seemed to Charles, had to have its televised 'Search for a Star' component, and the one from which Imogen Clay had benefitted was called *Queen for a Play*.

For six weeks the British public had gawped at the trials, tribulations, tantrums and hysterics of the young contenders as they were put through ever tougher, but entirely pointless, theatrical exercises. The show was presented by a Geordie comedian with an ego-shrivelling line in vicious repartee, and other familiar television faces were brought in to act as 'mentors' for the hapless aspirants. There was much saccharine interviewing of their parents, who insisted that Such-and-Such's talent had been clear at age three when she'd done her hilarious impression of a teapot. She would therefore make a perfect Queen for Martin Cheyney's King.

To add an unthreateningly camp component to the programme's mix, Andy Smoker was part of the judging process, because of course it was his production of *Richard II* for which the untried Queen was being sought. He squealed, flapped his arms around and fluttered his eyelashes in a way that delighted the audience at home. And when the contenders were whittled down to the final two, the popular star of stage, film and television Martin Cheyney himself appeared in the final programme to have the casting vote in the casting.

The actress who had best negotiated all the hoops and been awarded the coveted role of Queen to King Richard had turned out to be Imogen Clay. Charles Paris was yet to be convinced of her acting talent, but there was no doubting the girl's resilience and ambition.

He tapped gently on her dressing-room door and received permission to enter. Imogen Clay sat in front of her mirror, reading. Charles was struck again by how exceptionally pretty she was. She wore tight expensive-shabby jeans and a red T-shirt which left one shoulder bare. Her short hair was natural blonde and she had a face the camera loved. On screen she looked somehow fuller, more voluptuous. Close to her reality, Charles was aware of the thinness of her lips and the hardness in her deep-blue eyes.

She looked up from her book. 'What do you want?'

'I was just worried about Martin. Wondered if you knew anything about how he got ill . . .?'

The girl shrugged. 'I went to his dressing room at three. He was already gasping and choking when I got there.' Given that she was supposed to be having an affair with Martin Cheyney, she seemed callously unaffected by his suffering.

'Was Milly there?'

'No.'

'Why were you going to see Martin?'

Imogen Clay didn't reply, she just turned her hard blue eyes on him. Their message seemed to be: if you can't work that out, Charles, then you're stupider than I thought you were. The implication was that Imogen and Martin definitely were having an affair, and that she had gone to his dressing room at three for a prearranged sexual encounter between Andy Smoker's note-giving and the First Night of *Richard II*.

'You know he was saying he was poisoned?'

That got no more than another shrug by way of response. 'Given all that muck he liquidises into his smoothies, I can't say I'm that surprised.'

Reconciling herself – without great enthusiasm – to the fact that Charles wanted to have a conversation, Imogen Clay closed her book and put it down on the neat table in front of her mirror. To his surprise, he saw that she had been reading *The Tree and Shrub Expert* by D.G. Hessayon.

'I didn't know you were interested in gardening,' he said.

'I would imagine there are quite a lot of things you don't know about me, Charles.' The actress gave him another of her hard stares. 'A state of affairs which I am quite happy to allow to continue.'

'It just seems an unusual book for someone of your age to be reading.'

'You reckon? Then you probably don't know there's a new series of *Celebrity Gardening* coming up?'

Charles had to admit she was right. He didn't bother saying that the programme title managed to combine two of the subjects that interested him least in the world.

'Well, my manager reckons, on the back of my *Queen for a Play* profile, with the publicity surrounding this

Richard II show and the kind of fan base I'm getting on Facebook, I'd be a shoo-in for *Celebrity Gardening*.'

Thinking back wistfully to the days when actors just used to act, Charles Paris asked, 'But do you know anything about gardening?'

'How difficult can it be?' She gestured to her book. 'I can learn it up.'

'Do you have a garden?'

'My manager can arrange one for me.'

There was a silence. Then Charles suddenly asked, 'Do the words *atropa belladonna* mean anything to you?'

'Is it a kind of pizza?'

Now of course the girl could have been playing a very elaborate double bluff. But Charles didn't think she was that good an actress. He inclined more to the view that she really had never heard of *atropa belladonna*.

'No, it's a sort of herbaceous shrub. You'll probably come across it in that book. It's also called "deadly nightshade".'

'Is it?' She leant across and jotted the information down in a small notebook on her table. Nothing was wasted in the life of Imogen Clay. If knowing the folk name for *atropa belladonna* might improve her chances of appearing in *Celebrity Gardening*, then it became a relevant piece of career-building.

'Martin didn't look too good when he was taken off to the ambulance,' Charles observed, in a manner calculated to sound casual.

'No,' Imogen agreed without much interest.

'If it's really serious . . . I mean, if he were to die . . . I imagine that would have quite an effect on you.'

The girl looked up at him, not face to face, but making eye contact in the mirror. 'What do you mean?' Then her puzzlement cleared. 'Yes, of course. There's bound to be publicity.' She clearly wasn't averse to the idea. 'Hm, because we had been seen together a few times. The *Daily Mail* and the *Sunday Telegraph* both ran stories hinting there was something going on between us. But if Martin actually dies . . .' The idea was appealing to her more and more. 'Yes. I mean, of course I'd deny it absolutely. I wouldn't want to cause pain to his wife and children, but there are ways of denying things which leave nobody in any doubt as to what was really going on . . .'

Charles thought it was time to break into her enchanting vision of burgeoning self-publicity. 'Martin also implied,' he said sharply, 'that someone might have poisoned him.'

'Oh?' Evidently this was a new idea to Imogen Clay.

'Someone who had a grudge against him, someone who felt he had treated them badly.'

'Well, don't look at me, Charles.'

'Martin did imply to me that your affair was over.'

'So? Do you expect me to be heartbroken and collapse into a little wet heap? Look, I'd got everything I was going to get out of a relationship with him. I'd been seen out with Martin, at the Wolseley, at the Ivy – though going out for dinner with someone who takes their own smoothies with them is perhaps not the perfect date. Still, don't knock it. The gossip-mill had started up, it's raised my profile very nicely, thank you.' She grinned a small self-satisfied grin. 'There are plenty of men out there who'd get turned on by the idea of shagging someone who'd shagged Martin Cheyney.'

'Particularly if he's by then the *late* Martin Cheyney?'

'It wouldn't hurt.' She began to see other benefits in the situation. 'Then again it does simplify the business of actually ending the relationship. None of those awkward loose ends. And it'll give me the opportunity to do a bit of the emotional stuff for the press. You know, "Martin was such a *dear, dear* friend . . . He was a kind of *mentor* to me . . . so much more than a *dear, dear* friend" . . .'

Before Imogen Clay got too carried away in her imagined interview to the world's press, Charles reckoned it was time to leave. As he moved to the door, he asked, 'So you can't think of anyone who might have wanted Martin dead?'

'I've done *Midsomer Murders*,' the girl replied, 'and *A Touch of Frost*, and in both the episodes I did the detective said, in more or less exactly the same words, "To find out who's done the murder, the first thing you have to ask yourself is: who stands to benefit from the death?" Well, in Martin's case it's pretty obvious, isn't it?'

'Not obvious to me yet.'

'Oh, come on, Charles, join the twenty-first century.

Tonight is the First Night of a production of *Richard II* which has already had a huge amount of publicity. If Martin dies, the publicity will be even greater. And the person who'll benefit from all that publicity is . . .?'

'Still not there.'

'Charles, the play is called *Richard II*. Martin is not going to be playing Richard the Second. But somebody else is.'

'You mean his understudy?'

'Well done, Charles. I thought we'd never get there.'

And he left Imogen Clay to her dreams of perpetually increasing celebrity.

Charles Paris knew the *Richard II* understudy schedule inside out. Because of his advanced years, he himself was understudying John of Gaunt, a role currently occupied by the infinitely vain actor George Burkitt, with whom he'd worked many times over the years. Charles felt pretty sure, if called upon to stand in, he knew the famous 'silver stone set in a silver sea' speech, but his hold on the rest of John of Gaunt's lines was a little more tenuous.

There had even been a couple of half-hearted understudy rehearsals conducted by Andy Smoker's much-ignored Assistant Director. But, as ever in the run-up to a West End First Night, such precautionary activities had taken second place to the greater imperative of getting the show to open with the cast whose names appeared on the playbills.

So Charles knew that the actor understudying Martin Cheyney was Hal Westmacott, a good-looking boy playing one of the King's favourites, Bushy – the one who, unlike his fellows Bagot and Green, had a second-floor dressing room to himself.

Charles tapped on the door and was greeted by a preoccupied 'Yes?' from inside. He entered, to find Hal Westmacott, like so many young actors these days, poring over the screen of his laptop. Charles Paris had never really got into computers. His wife Frances and his daughter Juliet kept urging on him the benefits of the new technology, but he remained as semi-detached from it as he did from his marriage.

He had eventually succumbed to a mobile phone, though. It was impossible these days to conduct a career as an actor without one. Details of rehearsal calls and so on were all sent out in messages and texts from the stage management. And it was impossible to conduct any kind of sexual relationship in the twenty-first century without frequent use of the mobile. Some actors maintained that they'd be lost without their phones because they never knew when their agents might call with urgent summonses to attend auditions. Charles Paris, whose agent was the notoriously lethargic Maurice Skellern, did not suffer from such anxieties. Maurice never called about anything.

But Charles could manage his bog-standard mobile fairly well. He only used it for making and receiving calls. Its other functions – the ability to take photographs and so on – were untouched. And Charles did the minimum of texting. His fingers seemed too big – and in the mornings often too shaky – to home in on the right tiny key to form a coherent message.

As his visitor entered the dressing room, Hal Westmacott closed his laptop. Not quite quickly enough, though, to prevent Charles Paris from seeing that he had been googling the name 'Hal Westmacott'. Wonderful how computers had opened up whole new broad pastures for thespian egos to gambol in. Googling their own names was for actors the equivalent of authors checking their Amazon sales rankings on an hourly basis.

The young man looked up at him. He was tall, slender, with greenish eyes and a high forehead, over which flopped a drape of dark-brown hair. As well as the laptop on his dressing-room table was an open and heavily annotated paperback copy of *Richard II*. 'What can I do for you, Charles? Have you come to congratulate me?'

'Congratulate you on what?'

'Oh, don't play dumb, sweetie. This is my big breakthrough. I'm going to be giving my Richard tonight . . . due to the indisposition of that distinguished theatrical name and all-round shit, Martin Cheyney.'

Charles knew that news travelled fast backstage, but he was surprised that Hal Westmacott had already been given the go-ahead to step into the sick man's shoes.

'Is it definite that Martin won't be able to do it? I'd have thought they'd wait to hear from the hospital when he's been checked out.'

'Andy assured me that I was going on tonight,' said the delighted understudy with some smugness. 'And if the director says something's going to happen, then it's going to happen.' He looked round his dressing room. 'Andy's always been very generous to me.'

'Are you saying Andy arranged for you to be in here, rather than stuck up in the communal dressing room with Bagot and Green?'

'Bagot and Green and you, Charles. Don't forget *you*. I was lucky. I did just happen to mention to Andy that I don't like mixing with the riff-raff.'

There was no point in rising to the insult. Charles Paris had been the butt of many worse during his long career. Besides, he was more interested in investigating the poisoning of Martin Cheyney. 'Rather convenient for you then, isn't it – Martin's illness?' he asked, quoting a line from *The Milkman Delivers Murder*, a creaky old thriller in which he'd played the Inspector who appears in Act Three ('I've seen mahogany sideboards that were less wooden than Charles Paris.' – *Northampton Chronicle & Echo*).

'Good luck generally comes to those who deserve it,' came the complacent reply. 'Though of course you can help things along,' Hal Westmacott went on, 'by making your own luck.'

'Are you saying you made your own luck in this instance?'

'What do you mean by that, Charles?'

'Martin Cheyney reckons he was poisoned.'

Hal's response was much the same as Imogen Clay's had been. 'No great surprise, given all that liquidised pondweed muck he lives on.'

'No, he meant that he had been deliberately poisoned. That someone had poisoned him.'

'Oh, really?' Either Hal Westmacott was a very good actor or this was a new idea to him. But then again, unlike Imogen Clay, Hal Westmacott *was* a very good actor. Charles had seen enough of the young man's range during rehearsals to think that he would probably make a very good fist of Richard the Second that evening.

'Poor Martin,' Hal went on. 'Never the most popular soul around the company – nobody with an ego that size could be – but I wouldn't have thought he'd have built up enough resentment for anyone to want to do away with him.' Then he had a new, rather comforting, thought. A small smile crept across his face as he murmured, 'Unless, of course . . .'

'Unless, of course, what?'

'Ooh, no, I don't think he would . . .' He played with the new thought, enjoying teasing it out. 'Though I suppose it *is* just possible . . .'

'What are you talking about, Hal?'

'Charles, it wouldn't be right for me to spread suspicion about another member of the *Richard II* company, now would it?' But Hal Westmacott was far too caught up in the galloping thoughts to succumb to anything so boring as discretion. 'How do you think I got this part, Charles?'

'The same way as most of us did. The Casting Director put your name on a list, you were called and auditioned by Andy, he decided you were the best person to play Bushy.'

'Yes, that's more or less how it happened. But Andy was *very* insistent that I should be in the company.' Charles Paris thought he understood the implication and looked to Hal Westmacott for confirmation. 'Yes, my fatal charm. I'm afraid Andy Smoker took a shine to me in rather a big way. He's been trying to get inside my knickers ever since we started rehearsal.'

'But I didn't know you were gay.'

'I'm not.' The young actor was mildly offended by the suggestion.

'The rest of the company think you're having it off with that Kelly-Anne, you know, the one who's playing Lady attending on the Queen.'

'Oh dear. It's so difficult to have any secrets in the theatre, isn't it?'

'So you and Kelly-Anne are . . .?'

'A mild flirtation, no more. A flirtation that, it has to be said, does involve frequent exchange of bodily fluids, nothing more serious than that, though.'

'But since everyone in the company knows about it, Andy must know too, so he must realise his advances to you—'

'Oh, don't be so old-fashioned, Charles. Of course Andy knows about Kelly-Anne and me, but I have made it clear to him that I'm not a one-woman man . . . nor indeed a one-man man. You have to be flexible in this business. I'd have thought, given the amount of time you've been around in it, you would have known that.'

'Yes, but—'

'Charles, Charles . . . Right now Andy Smoker is an extremely hot name in the theatre. He can do me a lot of good. In fact he already has done me a lot of good. Thanks to him, I will be playing Richard the Second in a First Night that's going to get saturation media coverage. I think Andy may reckon he deserves a little thank-you from me for that. And I think it might be churlish of me to deny him that little thank-you.' The green eyes looked straight into Charles's. 'We all need help on our passage through life, and it's up to us to choose which passage we take advantage of.' The innuendo was quite deliberate and, in case Charles might have missed it, was punctuated by a snigger.

'Are you suggesting that Andy Smoker might have deliberately poisoned Martin Cheyney to, as you put it, "get inside your knickers"?'

The young actor preened in front of his mirror. 'He *is* very besotted with me, you know.'

'But surely—?'

Charles Paris was interrupted by a knock on the dressing-room door. It was Martin's dresser Milly. She looked as if she might have been crying. Over her arms were draped her first load of resplendent costumes for Richard the Second.

And to confirm the understudy's elevation, the dressing-room speaker at that moment crackled into life. The Stage Manager announced that, due to the indisposition of Martin Cheyney, the part of Richard would be played that night by Hal Westmacott. The entire company was required onstage in ten minutes to do a quick top-and-tail rehearsal with the revised casting. And strict secrecy about the news was to be observed. The Company Manager didn't want the news of Martin Cheyney's replacement to be leaked to the press any sooner than it had to be.

*   *   *

The top-and-tail rehearsal took longer than expected. Hal Westmacott's assumption of the role of Richard meant that his part of Bushy had to be taken over by one of the Attendants with whom Charles Paris shared the upstairs dressing room. And that Attendant's part had to be filled by one of the male ASMs. A great deal of Andy Smoker's elaborate choreography of the large-cast scenes had to be run through and reorganised. The top-and-tail rehearsal even threatened to run into 'the half', that sacred time thirty-five minutes before a performance is due to start, by when all of the actors were contractually obliged to be in the theatre ready. And that particular night being a First Night, the show went up at seven, in theory to give newspaper critics time to file their review copy, so the time pressure was even greater.

As a result of all this confusion, Charles Paris did not get a chance to confront Andy Smoker until very near to curtain-up. 'Beginners' had been called over the tannoy, and that meant most of the company. Act One Scene One of *Richard II* opens with the entrance of 'KING RICHARD, attended; JOHN OF GAUNT, and other Nobles.' In that scene Charles was an 'other Noble'.

Dressed in his 'other Noble' costume, a bright tabard over heavy chain mail, he descended from the third floor and on the second landing met Hal Westmacott, glorious in his regalia, being escorted from his dressing room by Andy Smoker, who had a more-than-avuncular arm across the understudy's shoulders.

'You'll be great, Hal,' the director was saying. 'From the moment I heard you audition, I knew you'd make a better Richard than Martin. He's got so stylised these days. And he just doesn't take notes – thinks he knows better than I do how to play the part. You're going to become a star tonight, Hal – a very big star indeed.'

'I can't thank you enough for giving me the opportunity, Andy,' said the young actor magnanimously. 'I can't believe the way you've organised it all.'

'Well, you know why I have, don't you, Hal?'

'Of course I do.'

'And I'll get my reward, will I, after the First Night party?'

'You'll get your reward, Andy.'

The men's hands clasped. Had there not been other actors making their way down the stairs to the stage, Charles Paris thought they might have kissed.

Still, what he'd heard was enough for him to challenge Andy Smoker. The director had virtually admitted to causing Martin Cheyney's illness. If the poison proved fatal, he had virtually admitted to committing murder. Time for a confrontation. Charles Paris stepped closer to the pair and tapped Andy Smoker on the shoulder.

They had reached the stage level. The director turned to see who had touched him, but before he could say anything to Charles, the door from the Green Room burst open to reveal a very fit-looking and extremely angry Martin Cheyney.

'Get out of my bloody costume, you little turd!' the star roared at his understudy. 'I'm going on!'

The First Night of *Richard II* at the Kean Theatre in Shaftesbury Avenue went extremely well. The audience demographic was slightly younger than was usual for the West End, proving the value of the television publicity from *Queen for a Play*. The youngsters who cheered and whistled at Imogen Clay's first appearance as King Richard's consort clearly hadn't been to a Shakespeare play before.

Charles Paris managed to stand up straight in his various appearances as 'other Noble', and his scene as the Gardener went very well. Though he tried not to admit it to himself, he was actually very nervous before it started, but once he'd got out his first line – 'Go bind thou up yon dangling apricocks' – he was away. He felt the audience being moved as he told the young Queen the news of her husband's deposition. It was moments like that that reminded him why he had become an actor, and he felt warmed by the knowledge that his wife Frances was in the audience.

And it was only at the curtain call Charles Paris realised that, because of the excitements of the afternoon, he'd done the whole show without recourse to the half-bottle of Bell's in his dressing room. So maybe that was a kind of good news.

Rising to the standard set by their star, the other actors also triumphed. And if anyone noticed a rather petulant expression on the face of Bushy . . . well, Bushy, Bagot and Green were meant to be petulant characters, anyway.

For Martin Cheyney as Richard the Second the evening was a triumph. The audience gave him a standing ovation and called him back for ten solo calls.

The First Night Party was held in the Rose Langton room of the Century Club on Shaftesbury Avenue. Charles Paris's wife Frances was looking stunning, and it was one of those many occasions when he couldn't imagine why he hadn't been more efficient in staying properly married to her. He knew that in the past other women had been part of the problem, but . . . He must really work on getting the two of them permanently back together.

At the party Frances had met the agent of one of the actors, who turned out also to be a member of her book group in Muswell Hill, so while the two women talked, Charles looked around the milling throng, all of whom were glowing with the undoubted success of the evening.

Only Andy Smoker appeared out of sorts. In spite of constant flamboyant hugging accolades from actor friends, theatre management and sponsors, his eye kept moving disconsolately across to the corner where Hal Westmacott was making extremely unambiguous advances to Kelly-Anne, the young actress who played the Lady attending on the Queen.

As Charles looked towards the couple, an extremely excited Martin Cheyney crossed his vision. The star was loudly toasting everyone with what was clearly not his first glass of champagne.

Charles managed to get close enough for a whispered word. 'Are you all right, Martin?'

'All right? What do you mean?'

'The last time I saw you you were being rushed off to hospital in agony.'

'Oh, yes. I'd forgotten about that.' And he sounded as if he genuinely had. 'Yes, bloody painful it was,' he said quickly, to assert the genuineness of his suffering. 'But it went as soon as I got to the hospital.'

'Well, it didn't seem to affect your performance tonight. Bloody brilliant.'

'Bless you, Charles. We do our humble best.' He raised his glass. 'To Doctor Theatre!'

Charles echoed the toast. 'Doctor Theatre' was the term actors use to explain the way they can be feeling terminally ill moments before they step on stage, then make their first entrance, forget their illness for the duration of the play, and give the performance of their lives.

Martin Cheyney hadn't been poisoned, Charles reflected. The pain had all been in his mind, First Night nerves. And as he turned back towards his wife Frances, Charles Paris felt glad that he hadn't actually got as far as accusing any member of the *Richard II* company of murder.

BEASTLY PLEASURES
Ann Cleeves

Ann Cleeves has created no fewer than four series of mysteries. Her early books featuring the birdwatching couple George and Molly Palmer-Jones were followed by novels about Inspector Stephen Ramsay, and then by the creation of Vera Stanhope, who has now been brought to the small screen in a series starring Brenda Blethyn. The first book of her Shetland Quartet, *Raven Black*, won the CWA Gold Dagger, and introduced Jimmy Perez.

When I failed my A levels my parents weren't sure what to do with me. But then they've never been quite sure what to do with me. I emerged into the world yelling, fighting to make my presence felt, an alien creature to them, and so I've remained. They are gentle souls, considerate and unworldly, and they consider me a monster. I tell myself that it isn't entirely my fault: my parents were older than most when I was conceived and I am an only child, carrying the weight of their expectations. In a different family, in a freer, less ordered household, I might have been respected, even admired. As it is, they regard me with dismay and anxiety. How could someone so unconventional, so physically lovely, belong to them? I am the dark-eyed, shapely cuckoo in their nest.

Of course I set out to fail the exams. It was a challenge: to complete the paper and still achieve so few marks that I'd fail. Almost impossible these days. And harder, I might say, than getting the four As for which the dears had been hoping. All my life I've been bored. I have only survived by playing games. I don't intend to hurt people.

But of course I had hurt *them*. We sat in the garden discussing my future. They looked grey and disappointed and for a very brief moment I wished I'd passed the bloody

things so that for once they'd have something to celebrate
in me. It was very hot. There was a smell of cut grass and
melted tar. In the distance the sound of a hosepipe running
and a wood pigeon calling.

'You do realise,' I said, 'that I could have passed them if
I'd wanted.'

'Of course.' My father looked at me over his glasses. He
was a senior social worker and thought he should understand me.

'You've always been a bright girl.' My mother wore floral
print dresses, which might have been fashionable when she
was a student in the seventies. She illustrated children's books
– cats were her speciality, though I'd never been allowed
pets because she was allergic to their fur.

'We've decided,' she said, 'that you should go and work
for Uncle George.'

George wasn't a real uncle, but a distant cousin of my
father's. I'd only met him once at my grandmother's funeral
and remember him as a rather glamorous figure, with the look
of a thirties movie star. During the service he shot several
admiring glances in my direction, but even then I was used
to men staring at my body and I took no notice. Vanessa, his
wife, was pale, draped in purple chiffon. My parents spoke
of the couple occasionally but in no detail. George was a busi-
nessman and of course they disapproved of that; I had been
brought up to believe that money was grubby and something
to be ignored. George and Vanessa lived in London and that
alone gave me a frisson of excitement. In the big city there
would surely be scope for new adventures and I'd find a way
to keep boredom at bay.

It seemed anyway that I would have no say in the matter.
With an uncharacteristic decisiveness my parents told me
that everything had been arranged. I would leave by train
the following morning. I would become Uncle George's assistant and return at the end of the year to re-sit my A levels.
Working for a living might give me a sense of responsibility.
The next day they took me to the station. They stood on the
platform waving me off, looking at once sad, guilty and very
relieved.

Uncle George had a house in Camden, between King's Cross

and Regent's canal. He was waiting for me at Paddington and in the cab he talked, not expecting any reply.

'Our neck of the woods has certainly gone up in the world. One time you'd only find whores and bag ladies here. Now we live next door to the *Guardian* and a major publishing house.'

I said nothing. I was aware of him sitting beside me. He smelled of sandalwood and something else I couldn't recognise: a chemical, almost medical scent. It occurred to me that for the first time in my life I was nervous. We stopped in a street that seemed industrial rather than domestic in character. George took my hand to help me out and held it for a little longer than necessary. I recognised him as a kindred spirit then, someone for whom the normal boundaries, the conventional rules of everyday life, had no meaning.

He pushed open arched double doors in a high brick wall and I followed him into a cobbled courtyard. The rest of the neighbourhood might have been gentrified but this felt like stepping into a scene from Dickens. There was an L-shaped warehouse or workshop, with grimy barred windows. On the nearest door a sign said 'showroom' though from outside there was nothing to indicate what was being shown. I was suddenly curious about what George's 'business' might be. My parents had never discussed it, even when they told me I was to be his assistant.

To our left was a tall, narrow house, Victorian Gothic, with stone steps leading to another arched door. George took a brass key from his pocket and unlocked it. It was late afternoon, gloomy for midsummer with the threat of thunder. I could see nothing of the room inside and paused for the moment on the threshold. George switched on a light and suddenly we were in a different continent. Or even in a different dimension of being. Organic rather than concrete. It was as if we'd been swallowed by a whale or sucked into the belly of a huge beast.

It was an entrance hall with a grand staircase leading away from the centre. But there were no hard edges. The walls were covered with animal skins – zebra and different kinds of deer. On the floor were fur rugs, the fur deep brown in colour, dense and very soft. So many that there were only glimpses of polished wood. I stood in astonishment, then couldn't help reaching out to stroke the nearest wall. The skin was smooth and surprisingly cool to my touch. George nodded approvingly.

'You obviously have a feel for the work,' he said. He set my rucksack next to an umbrella stand made from an elephant's foot and led me on to meet Aunt Vanessa.

He explained more about the business over dinner. We ate steak, very rare as I like it, and drank strong red wine. My parents are practically vegetarians, so the meal alone made me feel I'd moved into quite a different world.

'My great-grandfather founded the company,' George said. 'He was a big game hunter and saw the opportunity. All the ex-pat British wanted trophies, a record of the things that they'd shot. And it reminded them of Africa when they came home. A memory of the glories of Empire.' He gave a little sigh.

'But surely that sort of thing is outlawed now. Do people shoot game any more? I thought all animals were protected.' My parents were members of the Green Party.

'The business is certainly different.' He sighed again. 'Taxidermy isn't what it was. We have to work with museums now. But I still have private clients, at home and abroad. Of course discretion is essential.' He gave a sudden wolfish grin. 'Occasionally we operate on the very edge of the law.' And I saw that was how he liked to operate. He was a game-player too. A risk-taker.

Throughout this conversation Vanessa was almost silent. Her skin was the colour of a white butterfly's wing. How could she eat red meat and drink red wine and stay so pale?

Over the next few weeks I learned more about the business. Only two other people worked in the echoing workshop. All the rooms in the attic were unused, though once there'd been several dozen employees. A serious young man called Harry prepared skins for museums. These were all birds and animals that had died of natural causes or had been killed accidentally. When I first met him he was stuffing a pine marten that had been knocked down on a road in the Highlands. He'd constructed a wire frame and wrapped it with wood wool, before stretching the skin of the animal over it. The marten was a rare and beautiful creature, he said, and most people would never have the opportunity to see it living. He was evangelical about his craft and explained that his exhibits had brought an understanding of natural history to visitors to the museums.

The other employee was Arthur, an elderly man, who'd been in the place since George's father's day. He worked with vats of chemicals and very sharp knives in his own room in the basement. He dealt with the specimens imported from overseas. Only George was made welcome there. Arthur regarded me with suspicion and seldom spoke. Vanessa looked after the showroom but few customers turned up by chance. Most of George's personal clients slipped in to his office unannounced. I never saw the victims of their slaughter arrive but the completed objects – polished ivory tusks on brass plaques or mounted wildebeest heads – were returned to them in an anonymous transit van. I had no moral problem about these transactions. The extinction of a great African mammal would have no real impact on me, and I'd always considered that laws were for breaking. Besides, it was clear that most of George's income came from these illegal commissions. Harry, of course, would have been horrified, but Harry was engrossed in preparing his museum exhibits and never quite understood what was going on.

As I got to grips with the process of preserving skins, descaling tusks and preparing heads for mounting, my relationship with George developed in an unexpected and tantalising way. I had assumed that he would want sex with me. All men did. Harry certainly blushed every time I came within yards of him and even the elderly Arthur watched my legs through narrowed eyes as I walked away from him and breathed more heavily when I approached. George, however, seemed impervious to my charms. There would have been no sport in seducing Harry, but George became a challenge. I wore more provocative clothes, allowed my breast to brush against his bare arm when we worked together. Still there was no response. The more that he ignored me, and the longer he made me wait, the more I wanted him. He became an obsession. I dreamed about him at night and woke up thinking about him. He was a married middle-aged man who smelled of sandalwood and borax, but still I wanted him more than I had wanted anything in my life.

It happened quite suddenly when I was least expecting it.

By now it was October, damp and misty, with sodden leaves on the canal path and in the Bloomsbury squares where occasionally I wandered when I felt the need to spend some time away from the business. There were no wild London adventures. I spent my evenings with George and Vanessa or alone in my room. I had begun to study for my exams. I wanted to cause a sensation: to jump from the lowest A level marks the school had ever known to the highest, and realised that even for me that would take some effort.

Harry and Arthur had just gone home and Vanessa had closed the showroom and walked over the courtyard into the house to prepare dinner. George put his hand on my shoulder, startling me. Since that first day in the taxi he hadn't touched me.

'We've had a new acquisition,' he said. 'Would you like to see it?'

Of course I said I would. I'd have agreed to anything he asked at that time. He took my hand and led me upstairs to the empty rooms at the top of the building. There was no corridor – one cavernous space led directly into another. Each was lit by a bare bulb. In the shadows were piles of sacking, the occasional moth-eaten skin, odd tools the function of which I could only guess. As we moved further into the attic, I felt my heart rate increase. I was almost faint. At last we arrived at the furthest door. George asked me to close my eyes. I did as he asked immediately. He stood behind me with his hands on my shoulders and walked forwards with me. I felt his body against my spine and my buttocks. With my eyes tight shut I lost all sense of balance and would have stumbled if he hadn't been holding me.

'Now! Open them!' His voice was unsteady with excitement.

It was a tiger. The animal had been skinned where it had been killed in India and the soft tissue of the head, the eyes and the brain removed. That was standard procedure. George had unrolled it and laid it out on the dusty floor for my inspection. In the small, dimly lit room the colours glowed like fire.

'Well?' he demanded.

I thought he'd set this up for me. He'd acquired the tiger just for this moment. It was a token of his admiration. Then he added, 'Do you know how much money this will make

me? The risk I'm taking by having it here?' And I saw I
wasn't the object of his excitement at all.

'It's magnificent.' But I couldn't take my eyes from the
holes where once the eyes had been. I imagined the skin
covering muscle and bone.

'So are you,' he said. 'You're magnificent too.' And now
all his attention was focused on me and I pushed away my
doubts. He made me wait a little longer while he looked at
me at arm's length. He ran his fingers over my head and
across my shoulders then lightly over my breasts, exploring
me as I had touched the skins on his wall on my arrival at
the house. He undressed me and laid me on the tiger skin
and that was where we made love.

He must have realised that we might be interrupted. Perhaps
for him that added to the thrill of the encounter. If I'd thought
about it I'd probably have been excited by the possibility of
discovery too. George had turned no locks. In fact Vanessa
must have seen us as soon as she arrived at the top of the
stairs, through the string of open doors across the empty
rooms to the small chamber where George had laid out the
tiger.

We weren't aware of her until it was all over. She could
have been watching for some time because she was in the next
room when we saw her, motionless and silent. I still don't
know if she'd guessed what would take place or if she'd come
looking for us with an innocent message about dinner or a
phone call. Her face was still white except for two perfectly
round red patches on her cheeks. In her hand was a knife she
must have snatched from the pile of tools on her way through
the attic. George pulled on his trousers and stood up, his hands
upturned in supplication.

'Vanessa. I'm sorry.'

I saw that he had a small paunch, like a young mother's
bulge in the early months of pregnancy. It hung slightly over
his belt.

Her face became suffused with red and she lunged at him
with the knife, hit him at the top of the paunch and pushed
it home. I heard the sound of shattering bone and soft flesh.
Then the knife was in the air, spattering blood over the tiger
skin. She stabbed him again and again until she was sure he

was dead. I slid away from her, holding my clothes to my body.

At last she stood still. 'I don't blame you,' she said, looking down at me, her face still flushed. She looked more human than I'd ever known her; it was as if someone had blown life back into a ghost. 'You're not the first of his playthings.'

'What will you do now?' I struggled into my clothes.

'I suppose I should phone the police.'

'No!' I was horrified at the thought. Perhaps I was more conventional than I'd believed. The idea of this story becoming public knowledge, of my parents reading about it in the Sunday newspapers, was more than I could bear. And it was clear that I'd meant very little to George. Rather than acquiring the tiger as a gift for me, he'd used me to make his experience of the beast more intense.

'What then?' Vanessa turned to me now as if I were a co-conspirator, as if we'd planned this murder between us.

'In this place there must be a way to dispose of a human body.'

'Oh, I don't really know. I've never been involved in that part of the business.' We caught each other's eyes and began to laugh. There was something deliciously ludicrous about the whole conversation.

'I know,' I said. 'I know what to do.'

We rolled George's body in the tiger skin and carried him down to Arthur's basement. I've always been a quick learner. The skinning was less complex than I'd expected – I'd watched Harry working often enough and it wasn't as if we needed a perfect specimen for the purposes of taxidermy. We weren't planning to preserve Uncle George. That would have been macabre. The bones and pieces of attached flesh went into the bin with the other biological waste for disposal by Camden Council and the skin dissolved very quickly in one of Arthur's buckets. The tiger skin, spattered with blood, was a trickier problem. It had already been rubbed with borax and was partly preserved. In the end we cleaned it as best we could and hung it on the wall in a small room at the back of the house. The stains hardly showed in the dim light and there were other skins of endangered species there. If challenged, Vanessa would say that it was ancient. The man who had shot it could hardly go to the police to make a complaint.

I left London by the last train home, having told my parents that I felt uncomfortable in the presence of Uncle George, implying that he'd made unwelcome advances. They weren't surprised; he must have had that sort of reputation and they seemed almost pleased that I'd decided to return to them. Vanessa drove me to Paddington and we made plans on the way. She was quite a different woman now, full-blooded and decisive. She said she'd tell the staff that George and I had run away together. And then she'd sell the house and the workshop. Even in this climate, the area had changed so dramatically that there'd be a market for all that land, so close to St Pancras and the Eurostar terminal.

A few weeks later I re-sat my exams and achieved marks that brought tears of joy to my parents' eyes. 'We always knew you were a *good* girl,' my mother said. I had decided to read politics at university. I thought I had all the necessary qualities to be an effective politician.

I moved into my little room in Oxford almost a year after Vanessa had stabbed her husband. From my suitcase I took a small wooden box. Inside was a perfectly preserved part of George's anatomy. A memento of those months in London, as potent for me as the tiger had been for him. The exhibit was surprisingly small. In the end, that day, I hadn't resisted the temptation to practise my skills at taxidermy. In more than one sense I had stuffed Uncle George.

CLUTTER
Martin Edwards

Martin Edwards is the author of eight books featuring Liverpool lawyer Harry Devlin, as well as of the Lake District Mysteries, most recently *The Serpent Pool*. His stand-alone mysteries include *Dancing for the Hangman*, a novel about Dr Crippen. He has written many short stories, and 'The Bookbinder's Apprentice' won the CWA Short Story Dagger in 2008.

'You will be aware that your grandfather died in, ah, rather unusual circumstances?'

I bowed my head. 'We can only hope his last thoughts were pleasurable.'

Beazell raised bushy eyebrows. 'At least his, um, companion, did her best by calling an ambulance. And she tried to administer the kiss of life herself. To no avail, sadly.'

'I gather there was no suspicion of . . . foul play?'

'Goodness me, no. The doctor was emphatic, and of course a second opinion is required for a sudden death. There is no doubt the poor fellow died of a heart attack, brought on by excessive exertion. Your grandfather was seventy and unfit, he'd led a sedentary life, and frankly, cavorting with a nineteen-year-old foreign woman was the height of folly. I recall advising him . . .' Beazell cleared his throat. 'Well, that wasn't why I asked you here this afternoon. The important question concerns his last will and testament.'

Beazell was a lawyer with a shiny suit and a glass eye with an inbuilt accusatory stare, as if it suspected me of concealing a dark secret. His offices occupied a single floor above a kebab house in a back street in Manchester, and the posters in the waiting room spoke of legal aid, visas for migrant workers, and compensation for accidents. I was unsure why Rafe (as my grandfather liked me to call him) had entrusted his legal affairs to such a firm. Beazell's services must come cheap, but Rafe was by no means short of money. Certainly, though, the two men had one thing in common. Beazell's floor was stacked high with buff folders bulging with official documents, and fat briefs to counsel tied up in pink string. He'd needed to clear a pile of invoices from my chair before I could sit down. Rafe, too, gloried in detritus; perhaps he regarded Beazell as a kindred spirit.

'I don't suppose wills are ever read out nowadays?' I said. 'And presumably there's nobody apart from me to read it to?'

'My understanding is that you were his only close relative.'

I nodded. My grandparents divorced a couple of years after my grandmother gave birth to their only child, my father. She had a stroke a month before my parents married, and they, in turn, succumbed to cancer and coronary disease respectively shortly after I left school and took a job as a snapper for a local newspaper. My mother was an only child, and her parents had died young. I was alone in the world – except for Hong Li.

'I saw very little of him, I'm afraid, even before I moved overseas. But we got on well enough. He had artistic inclinations, as you must know, and he encouraged my interest in photography.'

Beazell exhaled; his breath reeked of garlic. 'Artistic? Candidly, I never thought much of his sculpture. However, he told me that, in his opinion, you were a man after his own heart.'

'That was kind of him,' I said, although Beazell had not made it sound like a compliment.

'The will is straightforward.' The lawyer could not keep a note of professional disapproval out of his voice. 'He left you the whole of his estate.'

My eyes widened: I had not known what to expect. 'Very generous.'

'There is, however, one condition.'

'Which is?'

'The will stipulates that you must live in Brook House for a period of five years after his death, and undertake not to dispose of any items of his property whatsoever during that time. You are, of course, at liberty to enjoy full use of your own possessions, upon the proviso that you retain all of your grandfather's.'

The glass eye glared. Presumably Beazell thought my own possessions wouldn't amount to much, and he was right. Since coming back to England six months earlier, I'd rented a one-bedroom flat in Stoke-on-Trent and although I was by nature a voracious hoarder, I'd had little opportunity to accumulate belongings on my travels. Even so, the flat resembled a bomb site. My chronic reluctance to throw anything away was the one thing which provoked Hong Li to outbursts of temper.

'But I would lose the whole caboodle if I didn't agree to live there and keep his things?'

'In the event that the condition of the bequest fails to be satisfied,' Beazell said, refusing to recognise 'caboodle' as a legal term, 'the estate passes to charities supporting the homeless.'

I'd never thought of Rafe as a charitable donor. He must have expected me to toe the line. 'Is that legal? To force someone to live somewhere, I mean?'

'There is no compulsion, the choice is yours.' Beazell swivelled in his chair. 'I may not specialise in the drafting of wills, but I can assure you that challenging your grand-father's testamentary provisions would be a costly exercise, and litigation is always fraught with uncertainty.'

'What field do you specialise in, may I ask?'

'Criminal law.' As if to remind me that his time was money, Beazell consulted his watch. A fake Rolex, I suspected, possibly supplied by one of his clients. 'Indeed, I am due to appear at the magistrates' court in half an hour. Perhaps you would advise me by the end of the week whether or not you will undertake to accept the condition of the bequest?'

'No need to wait,' I said. 'My grandmother was right. I once heard her say that whatever Rafe wanted, he got. I'll take the house, and all his clutter.'

'This is an adventure,' Hong Li said, as we turned off the motorway.

'I hope you'll like the place . . .'

She fiddled with the silver bracelet I'd given her after our

first night together. 'I'm sure I shall love it. Life in the
English countryside! I can't believe this is happening to me.
Six weeks ago, I was working shifts in a chip shop in Stafford
for half the minimum wage, now . . . my only worry is, how
will the people in the village take to me?'

'Rafe never worried about other people, and you shouldn't,
either. Besides, the village is little more than a shabby pub
and half a dozen cottages a mile's walk from Brook House.'

'Sounds idyllic.' Her voice became dreamy. 'So tell me
more about Rafe.'

'My grandmother never had a good word to say about him.
According to her, he didn't really want a wife, but a servant
at his beck and call. He and I didn't even meet until after my
parents died. What I'd heard about him made me curious.'

'He sounds rather sexist.'

'I prefer to think he was just a product of his time. Neither
Grandma nor my father talked much about him. They blamed
him for the marriage breakdown, though I never found out
precisely what caused it. It was as if they wanted to airbrush
him out of our lives. I could understand their bitterness. Even
so, the degree of their hostility seemed unfair.'

'You like to see the good in people.'

'Why not? I wanted to find out what he was really like.'

'And did you?'

'Sort of. He was a small man, bald with dark gleaming
eyes, rather charismatic. Yet I found him almost . . . scary.
When we talked, he always seemed to be enjoying a private
joke. He inherited the farm from a bachelor uncle when he
was in his twenties, but he had no interest in farming. He sold
off the bulk of the land and lived on the proceeds for the rest
of his life.'

'After your grandmother left him, he never married again?'

'No, but he cohabited with various women he called housekeepers. He had a rather old-fashioned attitude towards what
he liked to call the fair sex.'

Hong Li raised her eyebrows. 'Actually, you're not exactly
a new man yourself.'

I chose to ignore this. 'The first time I visited him, someone
called Ramona was looking after him. Paraguayan and voluptuous, with a low-cut top and a spangly brooch on her bosom.'

'So he didn't recruit her simply for her housekeeping skills?'

'Even he described her as sluttish, though he made it sound like high praise. The house was such a mess that it would send anyone who was remotely house-proud into a tailspin. He never believed in putting things away – he used to say he liked to have everything handy. Every cupboard and every drawer overflowed. Shelves buckled under the weight of books, ornaments and knick-knacks. The floors were covered with his things. I suppose it's no real wonder that his marriage fell apart.'

Hong Li frowned. She'd come from Canton to England three years ago, and she wasn't supposed to have stayed here so long. The immigration laws are draconian, they don't give such people a hope of staying if they play by the rules. So they lurk in the twilight, taking work where they can to make ends meet. We met when I called in her shop for a bag of chips, and was smitten at first sight. Hong was not only a perfect model for any photographer, she also spoke better English than most people born and bred here. I felt a yearning for a passionate woman, and my only complaint was that her passion extended to tidiness. She was worse than my grandmother, whose mantra was 'a place for everything, and everything in its place'. Hong enthused about feng shui, and tried to persuade me there was more to it than an aesthetic approach to interior design. Given half a chance, she would chatter for hours about discovering correlations between human life and the universe, and energising your life through positive *chi*. For her, clutter was a metaphor for negative life circumstances. She wouldn't have suited Rafe, that was for sure.

'When did you last visit Brook House?'

'Four years ago, before I left for France. Ramona had moved on, and he'd installed a Thai girl he'd met through the Internet. She wore thick spectacles and seemed very earnest, but he hinted that when she let her hair down . . .'

'I really don't think I would have liked Rafe,' Hong said.

'But he was generous to a fault. He paid to bring these women to England on extended holidays, and looked after them well. He was just . . . idiosyncratic, that's all.'

'It did him no good in the long run,' she said. 'What about the girl he was with when he died?'

'From Turkey by way of Berlin, according to Beazell. Poor kid, she called the emergency services when Rafe keeled over, and her reward was to be put on the first plane out of Britain.'

Hong murmured, 'You won't tell anyone about my situation, will you? I know I must get things sorted. I want to have the right to live in England, but it takes time to tick all the boxes.'

'No need to worry,' I said in a soothing tone, hoping she wasn't about to drop another hint about marriage. I might have promised to live in Brook House, but there's a limit to how many commitments a man can take on. Hong Li was the most accommodating model I'd worked with in ages, and I understood why, after the long and difficult journey from Canton, she felt a need to create order out of the chaos of a life in the shadows. But sometimes chaos is impossible to avoid. 'There's no way the authorities will come looking for you here.'

'This is such a weird place,' she said that evening, as we lay together on the sofa, in front of a roaring fire.

'I was afraid you'd loathe it,' I murmured.

'Because of all the rubbish?'

There was no escaping Rafe's clutter. Since my last visit, he had spent another four years accumulating stuff. You could barely move in any of the downstairs rooms for junk. It wasn't only the discarded lumps of stone, the incomplete bits of sculpture that he'd abandoned whenever he chiselled off one chunk too many. He collected indiscriminately. Stacked next to the sofa was an early run of copies of *Playboy* from the 1950s, side-by-side with a pile of P.G. Wodehouse paperbacks and a dozen bulging postcard albums. He'd indulged in philately for years, but seemed to have become bored with the hobby recently, since countless unopened packets of gaudily coloured stamps from all four corners of the world were stashed away in cupboards and in between the elderly encyclopaedias crammed on groaning shelves.

'I know you can't bear mess.'

'Come on, sweetheart. Mess is too mild a word, you must

admit. There's so much negative energy here. We really have to start clearing up tomorrow.'

'It won't be easy. It's a big house, but there isn't much room left to put all this stuff away.'

'We drove past a waste disposal site on the way here.'

'You can't be serious,' I protested. 'Remember the terms of his will?'

Hong shifted on the sofa, edging away from me. 'You don't have to take everything so literally.'

'It's a legal requirement. You wouldn't want me to lose my inheritance, would you?'

'Nobody would notice if you carried out a bit of . . . what's the right word? Rationalisation?'

'Don't you believe it. Councils hide cameras on wheelie bins these days, they spy on folk who put electrical goods in containers meant for cardboard, it's scandalous.'

'Out here in the middle of nowhere? You're making feeble excuses.'

'Not in the least. It's a nightmare to dispose of anything. So easy to infringe some by-law or environmental regulation.'

'That evening we first met, when I told you my story, you said laws were made to be broken.'

'It was a figure of speech.'

'Look!' She ran her finger along the arm of the sofa, showing me the dust. 'Dirt interrupts the flow of natural energies. And the springs in the sofa have gone, it's so uncomfortable, we really must replace it.'

'But it's flammable. Even if I wasn't bound to comply with Rafe's will, it would be impossible to chuck it out without a fistful of licences and bureaucratic permissions.'

She sighed. 'This house needs some positive *chi*.'

I put my arms around her, not bothering to argue. Better prove that I had all the positive *chi* she needed.

Brook House stood on a winding lane in a quiet corner of Lancashire, surrounded by tumbledown sheds packed with misshapen sculptures and rusting cars that Rafe had driven into the ground and then abandoned. A preliminary reconnaissance indicated that he'd never got rid of a single thing. There wasn't another house in sight, which suited Rafe, who was not gregarious by nature. It suited me, too. The land that once belonged to the farm was now occupied by a business that hired out machinery. A row of huge skips lined the horizon, but as I'd made clear to Hong, it would be unthinkable to use them as a dumping ground for Rafe's possessions. It wasn't simply about complying with legal niceties; to flout his wishes would be a betrayal.

I've never cared for an excess of noise and chatter, but it was bound to take Hong longer to adjust to a new life. She came from a large family, and loved to socialise. Unlike me. During my years in Europe, I'd had a number of relationships, but none of them worked out. At least I'd got the wanderlust out of my system. When I admitted I was an old-fashioned chap at heart, and felt it was time to settle down, Hong took it as a precursor to tying the knot. Which was not what I meant at all.

'Lucky that girl was with him when he had his heart attack,' she hissed, glaring at a tower of boxes full of Rafe's correspondence from the past thirty years. 'If he'd died alone, it might have been weeks before his body was discovered. Imagine being buried under a load of magazines, broken toasters and old shirts. Do you have any idea how many ancient sinks are outside the kitchen? Not one, but two!'

'Let's recycle them,' I suggested, in a spirit of compromise. 'They make ideal planters.'

'And this whole house smells,' she complained, throwing open the windows in the living room. 'Musty books, old pairs of underpants. It's unhealthy.'

'Hey, we'll freeze if you're not careful,' I said. 'Let me build up the fire.'

'With some of those old yellow newspapers in the scullery?'

'No way. They go back twenty years. Some of them might be valuable.'

'You must be joking. And what about this?' With a flourish, Hong produced a tin box and fiddled with a small key to open it.

'You found the key!' Extraordinary. Two whole drawers in the sideboard were packed with keys of all shapes and sizes, none bearing any tag to indicate to which lock they belonged.

'It took an hour and a half of trial and error, and now I've broken in . . . well, see for yourself.'

She lifted the lid of the box to reveal half a dozen locks of hair. Red, fair, and black, wavy and straight.

'Who do you think they belonged to?'

'Old girlfriends, some of the housekeepers, who knows? Rafe must have had a sentimental streak, hence not wanting me to dispose of his clutter. I guess he kept snippets of their hair long after they'd moved on.'

'They spook me.' She pulled a face. 'For pity's sake, be reasonable, sweetheart. We have to clear this crap out, it makes me ill just to look at it all.'

I picked up one of the dark strands of hair. 'I bet this was cut from Ramona's head. It's precisely her shade.'

Hong shivered. 'Creepy.'

'You don't understand. They are keepsakes. It's touching that they meant so much to him.'

As I spoke the words, I knew instinctively how Rafe had felt about his souvenirs. Our possessions define us. Throw them out, and you throw away your history, your personality, the very life that you have lived. When we are gone, our possessions remain; they give our loved ones something to remember us by.

'You're right,' she muttered, 'I don't understand.'

The next day I continued to sift through the endless clutter. Hong set out for a long walk, much to my relief. I'd been afraid that she might embark on a clear-out when I wasn't looking. I dropped in on the pub for a snack lunch, and found myself chatting to the Russian barmaid. Anya was a pretty student, on a gap year. Something prompted me to ask for her phone number, and she wrote it down for me with a coquettish smile.

When Hong returned late in the afternoon, she was sneezing and out of humour. I pointed out that opening windows on a damp winter's day had been unwise, and she stomped off to bed with a glass of whisky and a paperback of *Zuleika Dobson* that she'd found under a pile of coffee filters in a kitchen cupboard. She was a voracious reader of English fiction, one of the reasons why she had mastered the language, and I said she ought to be thrilled to live in a house containing as many novels as a public library. She sniffed and headed upstairs without another word.

As the bedroom door slammed, I picked up the phone, and dialled Beazell's office.

'How did you come to meet my grandfather?'

The solicitor hesitated. 'Why do you ask?'

'You're a criminal lawyer. Did Rafe do something wrong?'

'Certainly not.' Beazell sounded as if I'd impugned his integrity. 'Innocent until proven guilty, that's the law of the land.'

'But he was accused of something?'

'He was a man of certain . . . tastes, shall we say? His lifestyle was by no means risk-free, his untimely demise is evidence for that.'

'What happened?'

Beazell sighed. 'He is dead now, so I am not breaching a confidence. A young Filipina accused him of whipping her black and blue. She claimed he was a sadist. He insisted that the, um, acts in question were consensual.'

'Was he prosecuted?'

'A summons was issued, but the complainant dropped the charges and refused to testify. The case collapsed.'

'A change of mind? Or did he buy the girl off?'

'I will not dignify that question with an answer.' I pictured Beazell puffing out his sallow cheeks. 'Suffice to say that I gave my client certain advice as to his future conduct. He went to his grave without a stain on his character.'

I put the phone down and stared at the contents of the casket I'd discovered under Rafe's bed after returning from the pub. It wasn't covered in as much dust as the rest of his possessions, and I suspected that he regularly inspected its contents. When I grew frustrated after trying a couple of dozen keys in the lock, I took a hammer he'd kept in the dining room and smashed open the lid. Inside the casket were photographs, some of which I recognised. A portrait of Ramona was among them, another showed the girl from Thailand in the nude.

But it wasn't the photographs that made me catch my breath, but the spangly brooch that once adorned Ramona's prominent chest, the little round spectacles worn by the Thai girl, the heart-shaped locket containing a picture of a Slavic woman. Hooped earrings which I recognised from another woman who posed for one of Rafe's photographs. And a whip streaked with dark blotches.

In my head, I heard my grandfather's silky tones. A conversation I'd forgotten until this very moment.

'You may consider it strange that I surround myself with so much ephemera, but the most precious of my possessions make me feel more *real*. Tangible reminders of the life I've lived, and those with whom I've shared it. Memories of the highs and the lows, the ups and downs. These are things to be cherished, not tossed away as if they never mattered.'

'I think I understand,' I'd said, although until now, I had not.

He'd smiled and said, 'Well, well, my boy. I believe you do.'

When Hong came downstairs, she was in a mood to conciliate. The whisky had brightened her eyes, and made her voice rather loud.

'We don't need to clear out much,' she announced. 'Just the bare minimum. Enough to enable us to turn this place into a decent home.'

'You know,' I said, almost to myself, 'I think I've finally found somewhere I can be myself.'

As she squeezed my hand, her bracelet brushed my wrist. 'We don't need to clear out everything.'

'Tell you the truth,' I said. 'I really don't want to clear out anything at all.'

Her pleasant face hardened. The smile vanished, and for an instant I saw her face as it might look in forty years' time.

'We have a perfectly good incinerator outside the back door,' she hissed. 'Why not use it?'

I gave a long, low sigh, as I surrendered to the inevitable. Rafe was right, I was a man after his own heart. I patted the mobile in my pocket. Anya's number was safely stored.

'All right.' I ran my fingertips along her silver bracelet. I must no longer think of it as a present, but as a souvenir. 'Tomorrow, I will.'

THE FEATHER
Kate Ellis

Kate Ellis has created two series detectives: Wesley Peterson, who
appears in books set in a fictionalised Dartmouth, and Joe
Plantagenet, a cop based in a fictional equivalent of York. Her
interest in history and archaeology is reflected in the sub-plots of
many of her novels, with mysteries of the past often mirroring
those of the present. She has also written a historical crime novel
set in Liverpool, *The Devil's Priest*. Her most recent Wesley
Peterson novel is *The Flesh Tailor*.

The piano in the corner of the parlour hadn't been used
for over three years – not since Jack first left for
France. Nobody had had the heart to lift the lid since
we received the dreadful news because the very sight of those
black and white keys brought back memories of how he used
to sit there and play.

Jack had known all the latest tunes and I can see him now,
turning his head round and telling us to join in. 'Come on,'
he'd say. 'I'm not singing a solo.' And when he sang, unlike
me, he'd always be in perfect tune. Our Aunty Vi used to
say he should be on the stage.

I stood in the parlour doorway and stared into the room
with its big dark fireplace and its heavy oak furniture. It looked
as it always had done, polished and spotless. The best room
that we only used on Sundays. Sometimes I wondered what
was the point of having a room you only used one day a week,
but that was the way things were done in all the houses round
here. Except when Jack had played the piano and sent a ray
of sunshine into the solemn, polish-scented gloom.

'Ivy, what are you doing?'

My mother's voice made me jump and I swung round,
feeling guilty. I'd been daydreaming again and in our house
daydreaming was regarded as a major sin.

'I was just on my way to the wash house.'

'Well go on then. Don't leave your sister to do all the work while you stand around thinking of higher things.'

I knew from the way she snapped the words that she wasn't having a good day. Perhaps Mondays were the worst. We'd had the telegram from the War Office on a Monday when our hands were wet and red from the washing.

'I'm going next door to take Mrs Bevan some soup,' she said, nodding towards the jug she was holding; our best jug covered with a clean white cloth.

She'd been taking soup to Mrs Bevan for the past week, even though our neighbour had a daughter to nurse her in her time of sickness. In my opinion Mrs Bevan didn't deserve our kindness but Mother was like that to anyone who was ill or had fallen on hard times. When Dad was alive he'd called her a saint.

As she adjusted the cloth, I caught the salty aroma of the soup and I suddenly felt hungry. But it was washday and there was work to be done.

I spent the rest of the morning helping Rose in the wash house and when Mother didn't appear to supervise our efforts like she usually did, I began to worry. My sister, however, didn't seem at all concerned and I guessed she was relieved that Mother wasn't there to scold her for her clumsiness. But when an hour passed and Mother still hadn't returned, even Rose began to feel uneasy.

'Perhaps Mrs Bevan's taken a turn for the worse,' Rose said. 'Betty Bevan wouldn't be much help in the sick room. She's never liked getting her hands dirty.'

I shared Rose's opinion of our neighbour's daughter who had obtained employment as a lady typist and considered herself above the menial work necessary to run a household if one could not afford servants. Betty Bevan had always been an impractical girl with ideas above her station and I knew she wouldn't be able to cope on her own if Mrs Bevan was really poorly. But the thought of Mother pandering to her whims made my blood boil with anger.

As I put a sheet through the mangle, I noticed a feather on the cobbled floor, wet and curled. A white feather, prob-ably from a pillow or eiderdown. I stared at it for a few moments, then I kicked at it and the dirt from my boot stained it the same dirty grey as the stone floor. I was about to pick it up when Mother appeared in the doorway. She was wiping her hands on her apron and, from the look of distress on her face, I knew something had happened.

Rose and I waited for her to speak.

'She's dead,' she said after a few moments, speaking in a whisper as though she didn't want to be overheard. 'Mrs Bevan's dead.'

I bowed my head. Another death. Our world was full of death.

Mother laid Mrs Bevan out. Betty hadn't known what to do and, besides, she hadn't stopped bursting into tears since it happened, twisting her silly scrap of a lace handkerchief in her soft, well-manicured fingers.

I gathered that Betty was planning a rather grand funeral, Mrs Bevan having paid into an insurance policy to ensure that she had a good send-off, and she told Mother proudly that the hearse was to be the undertaker's best, pulled by four black horses with black glossy plumes. Normally Mother would have relished the prospect of seeing such a spectacle outside our terraced house, but when she returned home she seemed quiet and preoccupied. I knew for certain that it wasn't grief that had subdued her spirits for she had never regarded Mrs Bevan as a close friend. Something else was preying on her mind and I longed to know what it was.

I was to find out later that day when a police constable arrived along with the doctor. Mother had summoned them and they were making enquiries into the cause of Mrs Bevan's unexpected death.

Rose told me in a whisper that Mrs Bevan's body had been taken to the mortuary to be cut up. The intrusion seemed to me obscene and I shuddered in horror at the very thought. Even Jack hadn't had to suffer that indignity. He had been trundled off on a cart and buried near the battlefield. A soldier known unto God. It was said that poppies grew where he fell, taking their scarlet colour from his innocent blood. Perhaps one day I would see those grim flowers for myself.

Mother would not tell my sister why she had alerted the police. She set her lips in a stubborn line and resisted all Rose's attempts to wheedle the truth out of her. But when she had first returned from the Bevan house she had asked my advice so I knew exactly why she had acted as she did.

I recalled her words, spoken in a whisper so that Rose would not hear.

'There's something amiss, Ivy,' she said. 'And that Betty was acting as if she didn't give a cuss until she saw me watching her, then the waterworks started.'

'What do you mean, amiss?' I asked.

'That was no chill on the stomach. She couldn't keep my good soup down and she was retching and soiling herself as though . . . as though she'd been poisoned.'

I remember gasping with disbelief. 'You think Betty poisoned her mother?'

'She always was a nasty spoiled child. And she's turned into a nasty spoiled woman. That's what I'll tell the police.'

'But you can't just accuse . . .'

'That woman was poisoned. I'm as sure of that as I am of my own name.'

Once Mother set her mind to something she could never be dissuaded. Therefore, when Mrs Bevan was lying in the big front bedroom next door, washed and laid out neatly in her best nightgown, it came as no surprise when Mother walked down to the police station and told the desk sergeant that she wished to report a murder.

The police searched the house next door, of course, and I heard later that they'd found a quantity of arsenic hidden in the wash house. At first Betty swore that she had no idea how it came to be there. Then later she changed her story and said that her mother was probably keeping it there to kill mice.

The story didn't convince Mother or myself. And it certainly didn't convince the police because a few days later two constables called next door to arrest Betty Bevan.

Rose and I watched from the window as the younger constable led her away, holding her arm gently like a bridegroom leading his bride from the altar. Betty's head was bowed and I knew she was crying. But I could feel no pity for her.

It was three days after Betty's arrest and even the most inquisitive of our neighbours had failed to discover what was happening. Mother talked little about the tragedy next door; Rose, however, chattered on about it with unseemly enthusiasm and I had to do my best to curtail her curiosity. Terrible murder is one of those things that should not be treated as entertainment for wagging tongues but I confess that I too wished to know what had become of Betty Bevan.

At number sixteen we tried our best to carry on as normal but on Thursday afternoon something occurred that made this impossible, for me at least.

I was peeling vegetables for the evening meal in our tiny scullery when I heard a scraping noise coming from next door. Our scullery was attached to the Bevans' and the walls were thin so we could often hear their voices, sometimes raised in dispute. However, I knew the Bevans' house was supposed to be empty so I stopped what I was doing and listened.

I could hear things being moved around next door; a furtive sound as though somebody was shifting the contents of the scullery shelves to conduct a clandestine search. I put down my knife and wiped my rough hands on my apron, telling myself that it was probably the police – but then the police have no need for secrecy. I had been no friend of the Bevans but if robbers were violating their empty house, I felt it was my duty as a neighbour to raise the alarm.

I crept out of the back door into our yard. The wall between the back yards was too high for me to see into next door so I let myself out into the back alley and pushed the Bevans' wooden gate open, trying not to make a sound. Once inside their yard, I crept past the privy and caught a whiff of something unpleasant. It had not been cleaned and scrubbed like our privy next door, but then I could hardly imagine Betty Bevan, or her mother for that matter, getting down on her hands and knees to wipe away the worst kind of filth.

When I reached the back door, I tried the latch and, to my surprise, it yielded and the door swung open. I do not know who was more surprised, myself or the young man standing there with a tea caddy in his hand. He was dressed in a dark, ill-fitting suit and his ginger hair was short and slicked back. With his sharp nose and small moustache, he reminded me a little of a rodent – a rat perhaps. As soon as he saw me his lips tilted upwards in an ingratiating smile and I saw that one of his front teeth was missing.

'You didn't half give me a shock,' he said with forced jocularity. His accent was local but I didn't think I had ever seen him before.

'Who are you?'

'Friend of Betty's. The name's Winslow . . . Albert Winslow. Here's my card.'

He produced a card from his pocket and handed it to me with a flourish. I studied it and learned that Albert Winslow was an insurance man. The local accent I'd detected in his unguarded greeting had vanished and now he spoke as if he was a person of the better sort, like the officers I'd over-heard talking when Jack's regiment had marched through town. I had no doubt he wished to impress me and I felt myself blush.

I handed the card back to him. 'You haven't said what you're doing here?'

'Neither have you, Miss.' There was impertinence in his statement but I knew he had a point.

'I live next door. I heard a noise and I knew the house was empty so . . .'

'You thought I was a burglar. I'm sorry to disappoint you. I've just come to retrieve something I left here on my last visit so you've nothing to worry your head over. And what a pretty head it is, if I may say so.'

I felt myself blushing again but I tried my best to ignore the remark. 'I take it you know that Betty's . . .'

He nodded, suddenly solemn. 'It's a bad business. She's innocent, of course. Devoted to her mama, she was.'

'Are you and Betty courting?'

He hesitated for a moment before nodding. 'We were hoping to get engaged this summer.'

'When did you meet?' I was curious for most young men – those who had survived – had recently returned from the war.

'I first met Betty when I called here regarding a life assurance policy.' He edged closer to me and I could smell some kind of cloying scent, his hair oil perhaps. It made me feel a little sick. 'They'll let Betty out soon, won't they? I mean she couldn't have done what they say.'

'I couldn't possibly say, Mr Winslow. The police think she is the only one who had the opportunity to poison her mama.'

Winslow looked worried as he shut the tea caddy he was holding and replaced it on the shelf.

'If they find her guilty she will hang.'

His body tensed and for the first time I felt I was witnessing true emotion. 'She can't. She's innocent.'

'How can you be so sure, Mr Winslow?'

When he didn't answer I experienced a sudden feeling of dread. I was alone with this man and I only had his word that the story of his association with Betty Bevan was true.

I decided to enquire further. 'You served in the war, Mr Winslow?'

'Naturally. I was at Wipers and Passchendaele. Why? You didn't think I was a conshy, did you? I wouldn't have got far with Betty if I had been. She could never stand cowards.'

'You were fortunate, then.'

'How do you mean?'

'To have got back alive. My brother, Jack, died in the last days of the war. He was, er . . . wounded in 1916 and he came home. But after a year he said he felt a little better and he insisted on going back. He didn't have to because he still wasn't right but . . . he felt . . . he felt obliged.' I could feel my hands shaking and my eyes were stinging with unshed tears. I knew that I had been foolish to bear my soul to this man. But feelings, long suppressed, can bubble to the surface when one least expects it.

I saw Winslow shuffle his feet as though my raw outburst had embarrassed him. 'I'm sorry,' he said quietly. 'I understand, I really do. I saw things over in France that . . .' His face clouded. Then he straightened his shoulders and gave a cheerless smile. 'But you have to keep your spirits up, don't you . . . think of the future. Pack up your troubles in your old kit bag and smile and all that.'

I took a deep breath. Some things were best dealt with by

stoicism and a cheerful attitude. Other ways might lead to madness. And there was a question I had to ask.

'The life assurance policy you mentioned . . . was it for Mrs Bevan?'

His pale-blue eyes widened in alarm for a second then he composed his features. 'That information's confidential, I'm afraid, Miss.'

'You might have to tell the police. If Betty stands to gain from her mother's death . . .'

'I know what you're hinting at and it's nonsense,' he said, taking another step towards me.

'Why did you really come here, Mr Winslow?' I felt I had to know the truth.

'If you must know I came to find something to prove Betty's innocent.'

'And have you found it?'

He paused and I knew he was making a decision. After a few moments he spoke. 'I might as well tell you. If she's charged it'll all come out anyway. Three weeks ago she insured her mother's life for a hundred pounds and I fear that she might have . . .'

'Poisoned her own mother?'

He nodded and, unexpectedly, I found myself feeling sorry for him.

It was a week after my encounter with Albert Winslow that we received the news that Betty Bevan was to stand trial for murder at the assizes. Little was said of the matter in our house. It was done and it was over and soon she'd be dead – just as my brother Jack was dead. I had never had any liking for her or her murdered mother and it would have been hypocritical in the extreme to start feigning grief now. I saved my tears for those who deserved them.

The following Monday Mother, Rose and I began our normal washday routine, setting the copper boiling in the wash house ready to receive our soiled linen. When I heard a loud knocking on our front door I wondered who would come calling on a Monday morning, a time when we never expected to receive visitors. I answered the door in my apron with my hair pinned untidily off my face and I was surprised to see Albert Winslow standing on the freshly scrubbed doorstep.

As he raised his hat I suddenly felt uncomfortable. I looked like a washer woman, hardly the sort an insurance clerk would take into his confidence, but he seemed not to notice the state of my apparel. In his right hand he held a small tin box as though it was something fragile and precious and his well-polished shoe hovered on the threshold.

'May I come in?' he said. The arrogance I had detected at our first meeting had vanished and he reminded me now not so much of a rat, but of a puzzled child.

I stood aside to admit him, then I led him into the parlour for I knew that this was a matter between ourselves. I had no wish for our conversation to be interrupted by my mother or my sister.

I invited him to sit and he placed the box on the small table beside the armchair. Suddenly self-conscious I took off my apron and sat up straight on the hard dining chair, my rough, reddened hands resting in my lap.

I waited for him to begin for I felt it was up to him to explain the purpose of his visit. Eventually he cleared his throat and spoke.

'When we parted the other day, I made a further search of the house next door.'

I tilted my head politely. 'And did you find anything of interest?'

'I'm not sure.'

'You told the police about the insurance policy?'

'Not yet. I wanted to see Betty before I . . .'

'Haven't you seen her?'

He shook his head. 'They won't let me speak to her but I feel I must. I need to ask her what it means.'

'What what means?'

He picked up the box as though it was hot to the touch. 'I found this.'

He handed the box to me and I opened it. Inside were five white feathers and a piece of paper.

'It's a list,' he said quietly. 'Your surname is Burton, is it not?'

I nodded, fearing what was coming next.

'The list includes the name Jack Burton. You mentioned your brother, Jack, died in the last days of the war.' He paused. 'This is a list of men Betty or her mother describe as cowards.'

'My brother was no coward,' I snapped. 'He fought for his King and country and he lost his life. My brother was a hero.'

'Yes, of course. But his name is on the list in this box.'

'Mrs Bevan and Betty were always too ready to judge others. Perhaps they put Jack's name on their nasty little list before he signed up for the army and omitted to remove it.'

A look of relief appeared on Albert Winslow's face. 'Of course.'

I looked him in the eye. 'There might be another reason. At one time Betty was rather sweet on Jack but another girl caught his eye. I think Betty was displeased with him and she might have included his name on her list out of spite.'

'You think that Betty is a spiteful girl?' He sounded as if his disappointment was deep and bitter. His goddess had feet of rough and dirty clay.

'She was spiteful and sinful and if I were you I'd forget all about her, Mr Winslow. It is likely she will hang, especially if you tell the police what you know about the insurance. I think you should go along to the police station and tell them now. Justice must be done.'

Albert Winslow nodded slowly and stood up. 'We must do our duty . . . do the right thing.'

I touched his hand. It was softer than mine. 'Chin up, Albert. Think how you'd feel if you said nothing and she went and did it again. Because they say when you've killed once it's easier next time.'

He knew I was right. I watched him disappear down the road, slowly with his head bowed like an old man.

Betty Bevan was hanged at the end of May. It was a beautiful day, cloudless and warm.

That morning I walked in the park and listened to the sound of the birds, glad it was over.

As I rested on the bench, enjoying the sun on my face, I held a conversation with Jack in my head. I often talked to him, told him things. If he'd been alive, I'm not sure how he would have taken the news but I felt I couldn't keep it from him. I was his loving sister after all. And everything I'd done had been for him. I'm sure sin isn't really sin when it's in a good cause.

Sitting there in the warmth of the May sun, I spotted something on the ground and my heart skipped a beat. It was a feather, shed by some passing bird. A white feather. I bent to pick it up, then I held it for a while, turning it in my fingers before throwing it back on to the ground and grinding it into the grass with my heel. Such small things can have such catastrophic consequences.

Jack had been sent home from France, unfit to fight. Every loud sound had made his body shake and he had woken each night, crying out at the unseen horrors that tormented his brain. He'd wander, half crazed from room to room, staring with frightened, unseeing eyes until one of us would guide him gently back to his own bed. How Mother cried in that year to see her only son, a boy who had always been so cheerful and good-natured, with his mind blasted into insanity by war. Sometimes I wished he could have been maimed some other way; even losing an arm or a leg wouldn't have been as bad as the way he suffered. But his body had been intact – then.

It was when Jack had been home almost a year that Betty Bevan and her stupid mother began their campaign. All men not at the front, they said in their loud, braying voices, were cowards. They collected white feathers and distributed them to the men they accused, haranguing them with insults as they did so. Their tongues were spiteful and wicked. How I wished I could have had them sent to the front to see how they liked crawling through mud and corpses to certain death.

Jack had always been a proud man and the accusation of cowardice caused him such shame. Mother, Rose and I tried to tell him that he was sick but he didn't understand. He saw only his strong body and his intact limbs and he swore that he was fit to return to France to fight. Nothing we said would dissuade him from contacting his regiment to say that he was recovered and ready. But his regiment had not heard his screams of terror as he dodged those phantom shells and bullets each night and they hadn't seen the empty fear and bewilderment in his eyes.

The Bevans must have known how he was. His cries through those thin walls must have kept them awake as they did us. But those two women ignored my mother's pleas and explanations and a month after Jack left for France, we received the telegram to tell us that he had died a hero.

The Bevans showed our family no mercy. And I showed them no mercy in return. It was a simple matter to soak fly papers and add the arsenic they produced to the soup Mother took to Mrs Bevan each day. It had suited my purpose well for Betty to get the blame when the police found the powder I had placed in their scullery. And now the law had punished her – albeit for the wrong crime for she killed my dearest brother as surely as if she had rammed a knife into his heart.

I suppose the death of Betty Bevan had been my second murder and it had been so easy, just as second murders are reputed to be. A third, I suppose, would be easier still. All sins, I imagine, improve with practice.

I examined the little watch pinned to the front of my dress. It was nearly time for my appointment with Albert Winslow. He said that on our marriage, he will insure his life for a large sum of money so that, should the worst happen, I would be very well provided for.

How I look forward to our wedding day.

THE ART OF NEGOTIATION
Chris Ewan

Chris Ewan was born in 1976, and his first novel, *The Good Thief's Guide to Amsterdam*, was published in 2007 to widespread acclaim. The Good Thief has subsequently provided guides to Paris and Vegas, and Ewan is currently working on a fourth book in the series. A qualified lawyer, he lives on the Isle of Man.

S ometimes when I meet a new man they like to guess what I do for a living. There are certain things they always begin with, such as model or actress or air hostess. Air hostess annoys the hell out of me. Once, I asked a guy to explain his thinking and he pulled a face like he'd just snagged his ankle on a tripwire. It could have been worse. I could have told him the truth.

It's the same with my clients. My clients are all men. The ones I turn down are the types who can't handle the idea that I'm a woman. It's not a feminist crusade. Fact is, if my client can't trust me, I can't trust them. And in my line of work, trust is everything.

I had no need to ask the American in the white linen suit his business. He arranged for me to meet him in Cannes, the week of the film festival, and everything about him said he worked in the movie industry. Not just the linen suit, but the cream espadrilles and the white cotton shirt, the tan and the capped teeth and the hair plugs. He looked like money, but not the old kind. I had him pegged as a studio executive or a producer. His first words placed him a little lower down the evolutionary scale.

He said, 'They didn't tell me you had ovaries.'

I left my carry-on suitcase in the doorway. The apartment was empty of furniture. No curtains. Bare concrete floors. A pair of sliding glass doors led on to a balcony. Beyond

the balcony was the ocean, nearer still La Croisette. Super
yachts. Red carpets. Movie stars. Hangers-on.

He said, 'Your fee is kinda high.'

'I prefer it that way.'

'They told me you'd negotiate.'

'I never negotiate.'

'They told me you'd consider it this time.'

I returned to my suitcase, lifted it from the floor and shaped
as if to leave.

'Jesus Christ.' The client ran his hand through his hair. He
favoured a style that had been popular during my teenage
years. Centre parting, long at the front, curling in over his
eyes. 'This is crazy.'

I checked the time on my wristwatch. Hitched my shoulders by way of response.

'How far did you fly to get here?' he asked. 'Halfway
around the world, right? West coast, I heard. And you'd walk
out – just like that?'

'I never negotiate.'

'All right, I get it. Jeez. Can't we at least discuss what I
need?'

'Just so long as you understand that the fee is non-
negotiable.'

'I said I got it already.'

I studied him for a moment, feeling tempted to leave
anyway. But he was right, I had flown long haul. Not from
the States. From Rio. But the principle was the same.

'Tell me about the job,' I said, and managed to sound
pleasant with it.

He licked his lips and glanced at the sliding glass doors,
as if he was afraid we were under surveillance. He had no
reason to be concerned. I wouldn't have been there if that
was the case.

'If you're planning on wetting yourself, I'll be off,' I told
him.

'Just wait, OK? Lemme think a minute.'

'One minute.'

I tapped my toe on the floor, keeping time with his thoughts.
Interrupting them, even. I didn't care. He had no need to
think. He needed to act. To give me the green light.

'The gear you use is untraceable, right?' he asked.

'Completely.'

'And this thing'll be contained?'

I tipped my head to one side. 'Explain "contained".'

'Just his yacht. The people on it. Jesus. Can you do that?'

'If you want something clean, you should hire a sniper. If you require a statement, hire me.'

The guy ran his hand through his hair again. 'I guess I need a statement.'

I nodded. 'The blast radius will be minimal, but they tend to cram these yachts in pretty tight at this time of year. I can't control that. And you'll need to have the fee in my account by tomorrow.'

'Tomorrow? That's not what I agreed.'

I cocked a hip and contemplated my nails. They were an immaculate fuchsia-pink. Perhaps it was time for something different. 'Things change based on my assessment of the variables. You're a variable.'

'Hey, come on. Be reasonable here.'

'I'm being reasonable. Your fee hasn't increased.'

The American threw his hands into the air, then clutched them to his head. He ran splayed fingers down over his face. 'I guess we're really doing this thing, huh?'

'Looks that way.'

Two days later, I arranged for my contact to route a call to the client. The call was safe for four minutes.

'My money,' I began.

'I paid half.'

'That's not what we discussed.'

'Hey, it's like you said, things change. Finish the job and you'll get the rest.'

'I told you – this isn't a negotiation.'

'Then you don't get paid.'

I heard the tinkle of female laughter. The roar of a car engine. The drone of wheels on asphalt.

'Wait,' I said. 'Do you have me on speakerphone? Are there people with you?'

'Hey, take it easy.'

'Christ's sake.'

'These are my people. You can trust them.'

'Hang up the phone.'

'Hang up the phone? Listen, lady, you're working for me now, OK, and I'll finish the call when I'm good and ready.'

I pressed a button on my laptop and killed the satellite link-up. I bet myself the twerp would call back in less than a day.

The twerp surprised me and waited thirty-six hours. I could hear the shuffle of waves on a beach. No laughter. No engine noise.

'We need to talk,' he said, once my contact had re-routed his call.

'Fine,' I told him. 'You have four minutes.'

'What, you have a hair appointment?'

My burgundy nail hovered over my mouse pad. Count to ten, I told myself. Give him an opportunity to redeem himself.

'So the truth is I don't have all the money,' he said.

'Then it's a shame my organisation doesn't offer refunds.'

'What? No, hey, no, that's not what I'm saying. You'll get the other half. You'll have it when I do.'

'You mean somebody is paying you?'

'My business partner.'

This just got better. 'Ask him for the money now.'

'He won't pay until the fireworks are through.'

'In that case, there won't *be* any fireworks.'

A new window popped up on my laptop. Seemed a former colleague from Thames House was trying to private-message me. I tapped out a coded reply, my fingernails clacking across the keys.

'I'm afraid you'll have to forfeit the cash you've already paid,' I told him.

'Hey, come on. Let's talk.'

'*You* talk.'

Four hours later, he called back.

'So I spoke to my business partner. We'll pay another twenty-five per cent of your fee.'

I stayed silent.

'And I know what you're thinking. But hear me out, OK?

I have a place along the coast. Antibes. It has a pool, a terrace, the works.'

'Give me the address. Perhaps I'll kill you in your sleep.'

He chuckled, nervously. 'Here's how it works, OK? When you're done, and this whole thing is through, come visit and we'll pay the rest of your fee, plus an extra ten per cent.'

'You're offering me a bonus?'

'See? That's what comes from negotiating.'

I turned it over in my mind. It wasn't a bad compromise.

'You'll be watching?' I asked.

'Huh?'

'The *fireworks*.'

'Oh. Sure thing. We'll both be watching – me and my business partner. You've been to our apartment, right? It has a view over the marina.'

'Then take my advice. Wear earplugs.'

On the given night, at the given time, I eased into the oily water in my diving suit. The suit was a snug fit, designed for flexibility, not warmth. I could live with the cold. Hell, considering the fee I was being paid, I could live with most things.

The swim didn't trouble me. Keeping fit was a requirement of the job, and I swam several hundred lengths whenever I visited my local pool. Tonight, the distance I needed to cover was less than half that far. The harbour tides were negligible, and I was wearing flippers. True, I was towing a floating bag of equipment tied off from my ankle, but it was the least of my concerns.

My primary hazard was being spotted. In most locations, approaching a super-yacht just after midnight (even a heavily guarded one), wouldn't involve a high degree of risk. Here, by virtue of the film festival, the situation was different. Floodlights bathed the geometric walls of the Palais des Festivals and the gleaming white hulls of the yachts moored beneath it, casting green halos of light into the murky waters along the quay. Partygoers were everywhere: strolling the Jetée Albert Edouard; toasting one another with chilled wine on hotel patios; gazing down from the vaulted decks and bubbling hot tubs of the yachts themselves.

The craft I was swimming towards went by the name *Lazy*

Jane. She was a sleek, 100-foot Italian vessel with five cabins, eight crew and, for this week in particular, a rental cost in excess of eighty thousand euros. She boasted three decks, a salon that doubled as a screening room, an aft lounge, a Jacuzzi sun deck, a shaded flying bridge and one highly recognisable target.

The target was a former action hero, from a franchise that had been big in the Eighties. His accommodation sounded impressive, but the reality was that no bankable movie star would stay anywhere close. The big names were hiding out in secluded villas up in the hills, where their privacy and security could be guaranteed. Yachts were reserved for middling organisations – start-out production companies, European sales distributors, a cable porn channel. Oh, and the former star of the *Vengeance* series of espionage thrillers.

He had begun his career as a kick-boxing champion with a fondness for steroid injections, a north European accent and a memorable name, and advanced until he was married to the daughter of minor Hollywood royalty, with a mansion in Beverley Hills, a three-way share in a chain of celebrity nightclubs and a shot at cementing his fame as a crossover star in a line of family comedies. It didn't work. His box office plummeted, younger stars nudged him out of the limelight, his wife divorced him and his popularity began to sag along with his pecs.

Unable to quit, he still made movies, but these days they went straight to video. Now, his star has faded so badly that he was worth more to the makers of his latest film dead than alive. Cannes was scheduled during a hiatus in shooting, but his insurance cover was ongoing. He was a cheque waiting to be cashed.

He was also standing on the aft deck of the *Lazy Jane*, bunched arms resting on the wood-and-aluminium rails, a mobile phone clasped to his ear. I was close enough by now to count the buttons on the open-neck Hawaiian shirt he was wearing, and to hear his side of the conversation. He didn't sound happy. The yacht was too noisy to sleep, he complained. There were too many tourists trying to sneak pictures of him. Some jerk from the cable porn channel hadn't let him board their ship. Didn't anyone know who he was any more?

I had a reasonable idea who he was talking to, and I could hazard a fair guess at what he was being told. The yacht was ideal. It was central. It was perfect for all the business meetings they had lined up.

And it was also vulnerable to attacks like my own.

Clutching my equipment bag to my chest, I ducked silently beneath the rippling surface and kicked for the cooler waters below the slick of diesel snaking away from the engine outlet and the wash of light from the submerged bulbs under the hull. I have the ability to hold my breath in excess of two minutes when the situation demands it, but I had no need for party tricks this time around. I came up to the side of the mini-deck at the rear of the vessel, where a pair of jet skis were moored. Tossing my bag up before me, I gripped the smooth timber with my fingertips and heaved myself aboard in one fluid movement.

First, I dried myself with the towel I'd packed inside my waterproof bag, since I didn't want to leave a giveaway trail of water running through the inner corridors of the yacht. Then I slipped my backpack over my shoulders, removed my flippers and climbed barefoot up the metal ladder to the deck above.

It didn't take long to locate the burnished wooden door to the master cabin, and it occupied but a moment's thought for me to kneel before the flimsy lock and coax the tumblers into tumbling with my picking gun. I slipped my hand inside and flipped a light switch, then entered a sumptuous world of highly polished teak, fine cotton sheets and thick woollen carpet. I scanned the lighted interior until my eyes settled on a small drawer in the fitted cabinet beside the bed. Perfect.

I was back in my compact hire car, towel coiled around my damp hair and a pair of field binoculars raised to my eyes, when I clicked the appropriate icon on my laptop to place the call. Minutes before, I'd watched the target flick a cigarette over the side of the yacht, check his watch and disappear below deck. Once the lights in his cabin had been extinguished, I'd made the connection. The American answered on the first ring.

'Yeah?'

'Are you watching?' I asked.

'Hell, yes. What kept you? We've been waiting hours already.'

'You wanted a thorough job.'

'You didn't tell us it'd be this late. Christ.'

I scanned the quay. 'Less people means less casualties. Less witnesses, too.'

'Yeah, maybe.'

'You're sure you still want to go ahead?'

'Sure I'm sure. Asshole's been griping on the phone, yanking my chain about his damn issues. Thinks he's still somebody. Nothing's good enough for him. Go ahead. Toast the schmuck.'

'I'll leave that to you, if I may.'

'Huh?'

'Write down this number.'

I delivered the sequence. He interrupted me halfway through.

'Wait. What is this?'

'Are you writing it down?'

'I don't have a pen.'

'Then get one.'

'OK. Jeez. Keep your panties on.'

I counted to ten. Made it to twelve. I was still shaking my head when he came back on the line.

'Give it to me again,' he said.

I did. Slowly. I had no desire to repeat myself.

'It's a telephone number,' I explained. 'For a mobile. I hid it in his cabin. You call the number and when he picks up it completes the circuit.'

'Ka-boom time?'

'Indeed.'

'No shit. And say, do you have some kind of master-control over all this?'

Funny. I had a feeling he might ask me that. 'Not any more,' I told him. 'It's all down to you.'

He paused. 'Wait. If I use my cell, it can be traced, right?'

'It could be.'

'Don't you think maybe you should have considered that?'

'Go to the kitchen in your apartment,' I told him. 'Open the bottom left cupboard beside the gas cooker.'

'Huh?'

'Just do it.'

I heard the cluck of his tongue, followed by the sound of his footsteps and the rasp of his breath. Then I heard the squeak of the cupboard hinge.

'Hey, there's a handset in here.'

'It's prepaid,' I told him, trying not to sound vexed. 'No trace.'

'Shit. You've been here?'

This time I failed to control my irritation. 'You invited me in, remember?'

I waited for the cogs to mesh. It took longer than it should have done.

'Lady, you're good.'

'I'm pleased that you're pleased. And I assume that I will be paid the rest of my money.'

There was a moment's hesitation. 'Oh, sure thing. The bonus too. Absolutely. No question. You're coming to Antibes, right?'

I let go of a weary breath and lowered the binoculars from my eyes. 'There's nobody on the Jetée just now. You should make the call.'

I closed the lid of my laptop, gripped hold of my steering wheel and craned my neck until my line of sight was clear. I turned the radio on low and was midway through a morsel of Euro-pop when I saw the bright pulse of blue-white light. The windows gave out in a flaming burst and a cloud of blackened smoke idled upwards on the faint night breeze. I muted the radio and awaited the boom.

Less than three minutes later, I was fitting my key in the ignition of my rental Citröen and getting ready to drive to the airport when I happened to glance across to the *Lazy Jane*. Standing on deck was a man in an Hawaiian shirt. He had a mobile phone clutched uselessly in his hand and his tanned face was lifted towards the fire raging through the exclusive apartment overlooking the harbour.

My name is Rachel Delaney and there are three things you'd do well to remember about me. I never negotiate. I always do my research, so I know if a client is lying about a place in Antibes, or anything else for that matter. Oh, and I'm a huge fan of cheesy action movies, especially the ones starring Rick van Hammer.

BRYANT AND MAY IN THE SOUP

Christopher Fowler

Christopher Fowler is a versatile author whose crime fiction series featuring Bryant and May has proved extremely successful, blending wit with imaginative plots; it now extends to eight books, the most recent of which is *Bryant and May off the Rails*. He has published no fewer than ten collections of his short stories.

I t was the thickest fog London had ever seen.

Acrid and jaundiced, it rolled across London on the 5th of December, 1952, and lasted for four days. It was impossible to keep at bay; yellow tendrils unfurled through windows, crept under doors and down chimneys until it was difficult to tell if you were inside or out. The fog stopped traffic and asphyxiated the cattle at Smithfield Market. At Sadler's Wells, performances were halted because it invaded the auditorium, choking the dancers and the audience. Down near the Thames, visibility dropped to nil. Cars crashed into pillar boxes, cats fell out of trees and pedestrians became lost in their own front gardens. On the low-slung Isle of Dogs, it was said that people could not even see their own feet. Only the highest point of Hampstead Heath rose above the dense yellow smoke. From there, all you could see were the hills of Kent and Surrey.

This bizarre phenomenon had been caused by an unfortunate confluence of factors. The month had started with bitterly low temperatures and heavy snowfalls, so the residents of London piled cheap coal into their grates. The sulphurous smoke from their chimneys mixed with pollutants from the capital's factories, and became trapped beneath an inverse anticyclone. The resulting miasma caused over 12,000 fatalities and stained London's buildings black for fifty years. The young and the elderly died from respiratory problems. Their lungs filled with pus and they choked to death.

The thought of suffering in so horrible a fashion clouded Harry Whitworth's thoughts. In the last few minutes he had found it difficult to catch his breath. Cramps were knotting his stomach, and he had to keep stopping beside the gutter to spit. When he reached his place of employment, the coach-works in Brewer Street, he was surprised to find the place almost deserted.

'Where is everybody?' he asked Stan, the skinny young apprentice who helped the mechanics tune the engines.

'Ain't you heard, Harry? The place has been closed until the fog lifts. We can't take anything out in this, not without someone walking in front of the vehicle, and we ain't got the staff. Charlie was supposed to phone you and tell you not to come in.'

'We're not on the phone,' Harry explained. 'Why are the engines running?'

'Maintenance. A couple of them are dicky. I thought if we couldn't take the coaches out, I'd at least be able to get some soot off the pistons.'

'I think my ticker could do with a decoke,' said Harry, patting his chest. 'I feel proper queer. I was sick a few minutes ago, and I've got a chronic pain in my guts. I've been coughing like a good 'un. Can't catch me breath. Let me get the weight off my feet, at least.'

'You know you're not supposed—'

Too late. Harry had climbed up into the driver's seat of the nearest coach, sat down and placed his hands on the wheel. With a weary sigh, he closed his eyes.

Two minutes later, he was dead.

Arthur Bryant realised how bad the fog had become when he tried to post a letter in a pensioner. Earlier that day he had asked a lamp post for a light.

He was on his way to meet John May, his fellow detective at Bow Street police station, but had somehow lost his way in the few short streets from Aldwych. Luckily, knowing that his partner was capable of getting lost inside a corset, May had come looking for him. Bryant had a distinctive silhouette, like a disinterred mole in a raincoat, and was easy to spot. When a hand fell upon his shoulder, he jumped.

'Ah, there you are,' said Bryant, as if it were he who had found the other. 'You left a message at my club?'

'You don't have a club, Arthur. It's a pub, and not a very nice one either.' May linked his arm in Bryant's and steered him out of the road.

'Perhaps not, but at least they've managed to keep out this blasted muck.' Bryant was lately in the habit of frequenting a basement dive bar underneath Piccadilly Circus that served high-quality oysters to low-quality clientele. 'Your note said something about a coach garage.'

'That's right, it's nearby.' May wiped his forehead and found it wet with sooty black droplets. 'I'd keep your scarf fastened tightly over your mouth, there's a lot of dirt in the air. You know you've always had trouble with your lungs.'

It took them ages to feel their way to Brewer Street. 'I got a call from my sister,' May explained. 'Her neighbour's boy, Stan, told her he had a dead body on his hands and didn't know what to do.'

The main gate to the coachworks was shut, but there was an unlocked side door. The interior of the building was wreathed in mist, but at least it was thinner than the air outside. A gawky boy with a face of crowded freckles ran towards them. He waved behind him, distraught. 'He's over here, sir. Come with me.'

They found Harry Whitworth behind the wheel of the green and cream coach. His skin was blanched to a peculiar shade of khaki. 'Did you find him like this?' asked May.

'No sir, he came in for work late this morning, about nine o'clock. He normally starts at eight but I think he had trouble finding his way because of this fog.'

'Did he complain of any health problems?'

'Yes sir, he told me he was having trouble breathing. He'd been sick, and had a sore tummy. And he was coughing a lot.'

Bryant climbed into the seat next to Harry Whitworth, reached over and opened his mouth. 'He's got a tongue like a razor strop.'

'Flat, you mean?' asked May.

'No, dry. Anybody else here?'

'No sir,' said Stan, 'they've all been given the day off.'

'So none of the coaches were running their engines?'

'Two of them were running. I was making some repairs, so the day wasn't wasted.'

'Any fog get in here?'

'Some, sir. It's difficult to keep out.' Stan looked distraught.

'But the doors and windows were all shut?'

'Yes. On the radio this morning they were telling everyone to stay indoors and keep everything sealed.'

'But you're in an enclosed space, lad. Did you not think about the exhaust fumes?'

'No sir. Couldn't be any worse than the fog.'

'Actually it could.' Bryant eased himself out of the coach cabin. 'I think this chap died of carbon monoxide poisoning.'

Stan's thin hands flew to his mouth. 'You're not saying I killed him?'

'Not exactly,' said May, anxious to placate the boy. 'It would have been an accident.'

'Surely you knew the danger of running the engines in an enclosed space?' asked Bryant sternly. 'You could have asphyxiated yourself. The engines are off now, though.'

'Yes sir, I turned them off to attend to Harry.'

'How old are you?'

'Seventeen, sir.'

'In good health?'

'As far as I know. I've always been good at PE.'

'And Mr Whitworth?'

'He had a bout of pneumonia last year.'

'He's a driver, yes?'

'No sir, not any more, not since his illness. He does the drivers' rosters.'

'So Harry Whitworth had a chest weakness, which is why the lad survived and he didn't,' May told Bryant. 'Open and shut case.'

'Do you know how we can contact Mr Whitworth's family?' Bryant asked.

'That's easy enough,' the boy told them. 'His son Clive works over at the ABC cafe on Wardour Street.'

'Come on.' May tugged at his partner's sleeve. 'Let's get it over with.'

'I won't go to prison, will I?' Stan was wringing his cap in his hands.

'No. But you're not to go anywhere until our men get here, do you understand? You're on your honour. They'll only be a few minutes.'

Bryant was still hanging around the coach as May made to leave. 'What's the matter?' he asked.

'Nothing,' Bryant decided finally. 'Only it's funny.'

'What's funny?'

'If Harry Whitworth has a desk job, why did he get behind the wheel?'

The two detectives left the coachworks and made slow progress through the thickening fog. Their hearing became almost as muffled as their sight. May was forced to yank his partner out of the path of a recklessly driven taxi. 'Do you mind?' Bryant complained indignantly. 'This is my best coat.'

'You were nearly buried in it,' May snapped back. 'There's the cafeteria. On your left. No, your other left.'

Ahead was a soft glowing rectangle of glass. Bryant felt around, located the door handle and pushed. The pair tumbled into the cafe, which smelled of boiled cabbage and roly-poly pudding. The radio was playing, its thin treble making Winifred Atwell's honky-tonk piano sound even tinnier than usual. Less than half a dozen customers sat at the tables; the fog was keeping everyone out of the West End. A pretty waitress stood listlessly examining her painted nails. Bryant went to the kitchen counter and rapped on it with his knuckles. 'Anyone at home back there?'

A tired-looking young man in a chef's hat appeared. One glance at his nose in alarming profile told the detectives that they had found Harry Whitworth's son. 'Are you Clive Whitworth?' May asked. When the young man cautiously nodded, he continued. 'I'm afraid we have some rather bad news for you.'

They seated him in the kitchen and gave him a tot of brandy from Bryant's hip flask. 'When did you last see your dad?' May probed gently.

'This morning.' Clive looked down at his hands. 'He often comes in for breakfast. Mum died a couple of years ago. He doesn't cook for himself.'

'You live in the same house?'

'I'd like to get my own place, of course. We normally come

in together from East Finchley. Not today, though. I had to start early.'

'How did he seem to you?'

'He was coughing a lot. I think the fog was getting to him. I told him he shouldn't have come in.'

'How did he get here from the station?'

'He'd have walked, I'm sure. In spite of the fog. He was stubborn like that.'

'Well,' said May, waiting for a suitable break in the conversation, 'we should be getting along. We'll make all the necessary arrangements for your father, you needn't worry yourself about that side of things.' He gave Clive Whitworth a comforting pat on the back and led the way from the kitchen.

Bryant was unusually quiet as they returned to Bow Street through the sickly yellow fumes. May knew better than to assume it was simply because he was heavily muffled.

'All right,' he said as they unwrapped themselves back at the police station, 'what's the matter?'

Bryant regarded him with innocent blue eyes. 'What do you mean?'

'I always know when there's something on your mind. Out with it.'

'Well, it's really unimportant.' Bryant dropped behind his desk and began to doodle aimlessly on a blotter.

'Really, getting information out of you is like pulling teeth some days. Are you going to tell me or not?'

'I've been thinking. Harry Whitworth had weak lungs, and had been out in the fog. The bloodless dry tongue is a classic sign of oxygen starvation, consistent with carbon monoxide poisoning. In both cases it's a form of hypoxia leading to death, but which of the two causes of death was it?'

'Does it really matter?' asked May. 'Most likely it was a little of both.'

'He told the boy he had an upset stomach when he arrived. Perhaps we should wait until Oswald Finch has had a chance to conduct a post-mortem.' Finch was the coroner used by the Bow Street police.

'Well, it's terribly sad, but I'm sure there'll be similar cases before the fog lifts.' May opened his report folder, happy to fill it in and move on.

They worked quietly until lunchtime. At ten to one, Bryant rose and knotted his scarf around his face once more, leaving only his eyes and the tops of his ears exposed. He looked like Wilfred from the Bash Street Kids. 'I thought I'd pop out and get something to eat,' he mumbled. 'I'll bring you something back.' And he was gone. This in itself was extraordinary, as May knew his partner always brought sandwiches in gruesome combinations that involved cheese, jam and sardines. Sure enough, today's greaseproof paper packet was still in the top drawer of his desk. What's he up to? he thought.

Half an hour later, he received a phone call. Bryant was ringing from the blue police box on Shaftesbury Avenue. 'I wonder if you'd be so kind as to meet me back at the coach-works?' he asked.

Harry Whitworth's body had been removed, but Stan the apprentice was still seated glumly in the manager's office, waiting to be released. He rose in anxiety as the detectives arrived. 'Will it be all right for me to go home soon, sir?' he asked. 'It's been a terrible morning.'

'Of course, Stanley, I just want you to repeat what you told me a few minutes ago.'

'About Harry and his son?'

'That's right.'

Stan turned to John May. 'I was telling Mr Bryant that they don't get on. Ever since Harry's wife died he's not allowed Clive out of his sight.'

'Not that part, the part about why Harry seated himself behind the wheel of the coach.'

Stan looked sheepish. 'He misses it, see. He's been banned from driving.'

'And why was he banned? Tell Mr May here.'

'After his wife died, Harry started drinking. He had an accident. He's been here all his working life, though, so Charlie put him in charge of the rosters. You don't need to drive for that position. He misses taking the coaches out.'

'And that little titbit of information was of interest to me because . . .?' asked May as he was virtually dragged back into the shrouded street by Bryant.

'Next stop, the ABC cafe,' said Bryant, ignoring him. When they reached the restaurant, Bryant prevented his partner

from going in. To May's astonishment, Bryant knocked on
the window and the pretty little waitress slipped out. She
sucked her crimson bottom lip and widened her eyes at May
in a way that reminded him of Betty Boop.

'Our prearranged signal,' Bryant explained. 'Dolly, tell Mr
May what you told me.'

Dolly was clearly excited to be part of an investigation.
'Just that Clive and the old man had a terrible bust-up the
other day, right in the middle of the restaurant.' May
couldn't help noticing that she had upgraded the ABC from
a mere cafeteria. 'Clive and me went out to the dancehall
last Saturday and got back late, and the old man was
furious, told him he couldn't go out no more, and Clive
said "I'm twenty-one, I've got the key of the door and can
do what I like", and the old man said "Over my dead
body", and Clive said he wished the old man would hurry
up and die.'

Released, Dolly reluctantly returned to her station in the
cafe.

'What is the point of all this?' asked May tetchily.

'Harry Whitworth was already sick when he got to the
coachworks.'

'Yes, so you said.'

'He hopped on a bus from the tube. Dolly was arriving
for work, and saw him getting off at the bottom of Wardour
Street. So he wasn't out in the fog for very long at all.'

'What about at the other end, from his house?'

'He lives right next door to the station, and leaves a minute
before the train arrives. She's a mine of information, Clive's
little lady.'

'So you're telling me he didn't die of either cause?'

'No, but I think somebody would like us to think he did.'

'Not Stan.'

'No. Stan was at the coachworks an hour before Harry,
and had been running the engines all that time, so there
couldn't have been enough carbon monoxide in the air to
hurt either of them.'

'Then what made him sick?'

'Harry came to work separately from his son this morning.
I think they had another argument, either this morning or

last night. The only thing he did before reaching his place of employment was have a bite to eat.'

'You think Clive poisoned him?'

'I'm just saying that I think we should search the kitchen.'

Harold Whitworth had eaten some scrambled eggs and had drunk a bowl of Brown Windsor soup, his favourite. His son watched in dumbfounded amazement as the two detectives checked every canister of ingredients. Rationing meant that powdered eggs were still in use, but May tasted them and found nothing wrong. Bryant tried everything from the lard to a piece of mutton shin that had been used for the soup.

'This is ridiculous,' May complained. 'Dolly, how many eggs and Brown Windsors have you got through serving today?'

Dolly checked the larder and returned. 'About two dozen eggs and six soups,' she told them.

'And did Harry Whitworth's come from the same place as all the others?'

'Oh yes, sir.'

'There you have it.' May threw up his hands in despair, but he knew that once Bryant was convinced of something, nothing would disabuse him of the notion until every last particle of doubt had been combusted.

'Clive, did you have words with your father this morning?'

'No, he had one of his sulks on. Barely said a thing, just ordered from the menu, ate and left without even paying.'

Bryant turned to Dolly, the waitress. 'Where did Harry sit?'

'Over there,' she said, pointing to a small Formica-topped table in the corner.

'Does he always sit in the same place?'

'No, of course not. We do have other customers, you know. We're very popular.'

'I can't imagine why.' Bryant wandered over to the table, tasted the salt, pepper and tomato sauce, and returned more dissatisfied than ever.

'Well, I'm sorry to have taken up so much of your time,' he told Clive finally. 'I'll let you attend to your customers.'

The moment they stepped outside, Bryant slapped his

partner in the chest and brought him to a standstill. 'I need you to stay in the doorway opposite and not let that young man out of your sight until I get back,' he said.

'In this fog? You must be joking.'

'Then take my scarf.' Bryant unwrapped it from his own neck and began to mummify May before he could protest.

Helplessly, May was forced to install himself in the shadowed doorway of a tobacconist's shop, but found he could barely see across the narrow road. The city had entered a state of limbo. Trucks and taxis hove into his blurred line of vision like prehistoric beasts, only to vanish just as suddenly. He could see black particles floating in the air. He wondered how much poison the people of London were being forced to consume, and how it would affect them.

The bell on the door of the cafeteria tinkled with each arrival and departure. The customers appeared as little more than phantoms, and it was hard to keep track of them all. May stamped his feet and wiped the beads of black water from his brow. He readjusted the scarf, and was alarmed to note that the patch covering his mouth was thick with grime. He wanted to go home and climb into a hot bath.

Two hours and ten minutes after he had left, Bryant returned. His stumpy figure was as unmistakable as ever in the gloom. He was panting. 'Sorry to leave you so long,' he apologised, 'but I had to get a preliminary result from a friend of mine who runs the chemist's shop in Oxford Street. Has he come out?'

'Who, Clive Whitworth? A result on what?' asked May.

'I tipped some of the salt and pepper into my handkerchief before I left the cafe. Dolly told me the old man didn't like ketchup, so I thought it had to be in the condiments.'

'You mean poison?'

'What else would I mean? The pepper was fine. The salt has been cut with an industrial chemical that causes hypoxia. But it's a very low dosage, too low to do any damage, no more than one grain to every thirty of salt. Hang on, someone's coming out.'

They both peered across the road. 'I can't see a blinking thing,' Bryant complained.

'It's Clive.'

'Damn, he's leaving early. I've arranged to have him placed under arrest, but the others aren't here yet. This blasted fog. We'll have to follow him.'

Tracking their quarry through the chaotic backstreets of Soho would have been tricky enough without the obscuring murk. But at least if they could not see him, Clive Whitworth could not spot that he was being followed. At one point when he disappeared behind a stack of fish crates, the detectives feared they had lost him, but he emerged from the other side, crossing into Greek Street and then to Soho Square. The watery sun threw shafts of strange green light through the branches of the plane trees, as if London was in the throes of an apocalypse.

'He's heading for St Peter's,' Bryant pointed out. The red-brick tower of the Roman Catholic church rose in the east quadrant of the square. The detectives followed their suspect inside.

Even here, blossoms of yellow mist were unfolding beneath the doors of the church. Fog hung in the air like the manifestation of some unholy spirit. Clive seated himself at a pew and dropped forward on to his knees in fervid prayer. The detectives crept into the row behind him and quietly listened.

After a few minutes, Bryant stood. 'A confession of guilt, I think,' he told his partner. Clive turned to look at them and started.

'I am arresting you for the murder of Harold Whitworth,' Bryant began, placing a hand on his shoulder. He liked to do things the traditional way. 'Anything you say . . .'

Clive tried to bolt, but was restrained by May's rugby-strengthened arms.

'Come on,' said Bryant, 'hold him tight and let's get out of this fog. I've had enough poison for one day.'

Back at Bow Street, Clive Whitworth did not attempt to rescind his confession. He looked utterly defeated. The detectives retreated back to their cluttered first-floor office. It was so gloomy that they had to turn on the lights. May placed a kettle on the gas ring, and Bryant filled his pipe.

'You're not going to smoke your navy shag in here, are you?' May complained. 'The air's thick enough as it is.'

'I'm replacing the coal smoke with the healthy aroma of

high-grade tobacco.' Bryant tipped back in his chair and began to puff. 'Come on, then, I know you're dying to ask me how he did it.'

'All right then. I can't for the life of me see how.'

'Clive and Harry Whitworth had a fight last night. Harry told his son he would never have the house. Clive took a powerful poison from his garden shed and carried it to work. He added a tiny amount to the salt. Harry always came in for something to eat before the start of his shift, even when they had argued.'

'But surely he couldn't know where the old man would end up sitting.'

'Precisely. So he measured out the poison and added it to each of the salt cellars in the room. It didn't matter where Harry sat.'

'Then why didn't any of the other customers become ill?'

'Harry used more salt than anyone else. Clive knew he would.'

'I really don't see how he could know that.'

'After the argument, Harry went down the pub and got drunk. You heard what Stan said; since the death of his wife he had become an alcoholic and lost his license. Excessive drinking removes the salt from your system. Alcoholics always oversalt their food. Harry had no choice but to do so – it was a biological necessity. For every thirty grains of salt, he consumed a grain of poison.'

'Well I'm damned,' said May. 'I wonder what gave him that idea?'

'Look out of the window,' Bryant replied. 'The city poisons us all. It's just a matter of degree.'

He blew a satisfying cloud of smoke into the air, and watched in amusement as John May had a coughing fit.

THE ASKING PRICE
Sophie Hannah

Sophie Hannah is a well-regarded poet who moved into crime fiction with the internationally acclaimed novel of psychological suspense, *Little Face*. It has been followed by *Hurting Distance*, *The Point of Rescue*, *The Other Half Lives* and most recently, *A Room Swept White*.

I took a present with me when I went to Ryhill, to fool Lynn and myself: if I did the opposite of what I felt, I might succeed in changing my feelings. I stopped the car when I saw the gateposts in front of me, with 'Ryhill' carved into the one on the left. Perhaps I don't need to do this, I thought. Perhaps it doesn't matter if I never know. But Lynn was expecting me, and I had been expecting, since I made the arrangement, to come here. I'm not a spontaneous person; the reversal of a long-established plan has always felt to me like vandalism.

The turning circle had been reinvented as a giant plant pot since I was last here – white flowers spilled out of the flat part at the centre, where once there had been only soil. The driveway was different too: the new approach to Ryhill was smooth, pale grey.

I parked and inhaled deeply as I stepped out of the car. It was a shining June day but the heat had a crispness about it; not the sort of heavy hot weather that made it difficult to move. And the freshness of the air . . . I shook my head. This was one of the things I'd forbidden myself to think about: Ryhill's hilltop position, lifted above the valley's pollution.

I rang the bell and waited. Lynn opened the door with a defeated smile on her face. She'd known I was coming, but had clearly been hoping I'd cancel. I mumbled a few of the things I might have said if this were a normal situation, and thrust the present at her: a plant I'd bought at a garden centre

on the way here, with bell-shaped purple flowers. I could
see instantly that she wouldn't want it. Purple didn't feature
in Lynn's colour scheme. The house's interior had been
comprehensively beige-ified. Tan furniture, cream walls,
ruched fawn-coloured cushions. Bland abstract pictures, all
the same size – bought in bulk from Ikea, no doubt. In my
mind, I saw Ryhill as it had been this time last year, when
I first came to look round, when the owners had been a Mr
and Mrs Tuft: dark-red and blue Persian carpets, antique
wood furniture, gold patterned wallpaper. I'd particularly
liked a leather-topped writing desk with hand-carved legs
that had been in the hall. Lynn had ditched all that in favour
of the toffee-yoghurt look.

'Thanks,' she said, pretending to examine the pot plant in
great detail. 'Come in. I was surprised you called. Even more
surprised when you said you wanted to come round.'

'You sent me your change of address,' I reminded her.

'I know, but . . .'

She didn't need to complete the sentence: *but I sent it to
everyone in my address book – including the people I hoped
never to hear from again.*

'You're divorced?' I asked her. 'There was only your name
on the change-of-address flyer.'

'Divorced and soon to be married again,' she said. 'You?'

'Still together.'

'I did you a favour then,' she said wryly.

She offered to show me round the house, from which she'd
banished all charm and character. Upstairs, the four bedrooms
looked identical. 'You should have seen it before,' said Lynn.
'Clashing patterns everywhere.'

'I did see it before,' I said.

Our tour of Ryhill came to an abrupt halt on the landing.
'What?'

'I came for a viewing last year, when it was first for sale.'

'But . . . What a coincidence!' Anxiety tightened Lynn's
features. She must have been considering the implications
for her status: the buyer of a house her ex-best friend rejected.
'So . . . you decided not to buy it?'

'We wanted it,' I said truthfully. 'We put in an offer . . .'

'Oh, my God!' Lynn's hand flew to her mouth.

'It was turned down. We came for a second viewing – we loved it so much, we thought we might offer a bit more – but the second time we got Mrs Tuft instead of Mr.'

'Damaris,' said Lynn. I could tell she wanted me to speak faster.

'We never got as far as first names. She barely let us inside the house. We'd not met her the first time – her husband had shown us round, and he'd seemed perfectly normal and friendly . . .'

'Damaris wasn't friendly?'

'Far from it. She left us to look round on our own, then ambushed us on the stairs and blurted out, "I might as well tell you – my husband put the house up for sale without consulting me".'

Lynn had started to pick at the skin on her lips. 'That makes no sense. Damaris was as keen on moving as John was.'

'She said to us, and I quote, "My name's on the deeds too – my husband can't sell it without me agreeing, and there's no way that's going to happen".'

Lynn's eyes had filled with tears. 'Now I know why you were so keen to come round. Never could be straightforward, could you? I'm sorry I've got the house you wanted, but—'

'I didn't want it,' I said. 'Not after that. We got a message via the estate agent the next day, from John Tuft, apologising, telling us that Ryhill was very definitely for sale, and he'd be interested in hearing our best offer, but there was no way I was going to buy the house after meeting his wife. Too much negative energy.'

Lynn and I stared at one another. 'You probably caught her on a bad day,' she said eventually.

'You said she wanted to move as much as her husband – how do you know?'

Lynn looked caught out. 'She told me. She said she was fed up of being stuck out in the middle of nowhere, couldn't wait to move back to civilisation.'

'Were those her exact words?'

'Probably not.' Lynn's tone was defensive. 'I don't remember her exact words – I've had a life between now and then – but that was the gist.'

'Seems a bit strange,' I said. 'That she'd be unwilling to sell to us and so eager to sell to you. Are we talking about the same Mrs Tuft? What did she look like?'

'Don't be daft! Look, whatever issues she had, it was nothing to do with you. She didn't even know you. What's this really about? I told you – I'm getting divorced. If you want my soon-to-be-ex-husband, you're welcome to him. I promise you, any preference he had for me over you is well and truly in the past – these days he prefers almost anybody to me.'

'How old was she?' I repeated stubbornly. 'Damaris Tuft.'

'I don't know! Can't say I noticed, and obviously I didn't ask her.' Lynn looked at her watch. 'Look, since it's clear this visit has nothing to do with you wanting to catch up . . .'

'You must have had some impression of her age. What colour was her hair?' I waited.

Lynn groaned. 'Late fifties. Brown curly hair. OK?'

'So you did notice.'

'Well? Was the Mrs Tuft you met a brunette in her late fifties? With curly hair?'

I nodded.

'Well, then.'

'The woman I met had no intention of selling,' I said stubbornly.

'So what are you saying? That her husband . . . what? Bullied her?'

'All I know is, she wasn't going to sell her house. She'd have done everything she could to stop the sale. Evidently that didn't happen, because you bought it. So where was she, if she couldn't stop you? Where is she?' In my head I was getting carried away, thinking up all sorts of strange scenarios.

'People change their minds, Tanya.' Lynn's eyes were hard. 'They say things they don't mean in the heat of the moment.'

'She meant it,' I said with conviction. 'I could still hear her saying it.

Lynn rolled her eyes. 'Maybe John Tuft *killed* her,' she said in a mock-scary whisper.

'Maybe.'

'Oh, I've had enough of this. I can see there's no other way . . .' Lynn turned her back on me and stomped down the stairs.

By the time I caught up with her, in the kitchen, she had her diary open on the work-surface in front of her and a telephone in her hand. 'Damaris?' I heard her say. 'It's Lynn Nadin. Fine, fine. No, the house is great, everything's fine. Except . . . look, this is going to sound mad, but bear with me, all right?' I cringed in anticipation. Would Lynn make me speak to Mrs Tuft? I felt ashamed; clearly she wasn't dead if Lynn was having a conversation with her. *For goodness' sake, of course she's not dead. Get a grip.* Why was I here, really? For the gory details of Lynn's marriage break-up?

'There's a woman here called Tanya Marshall – sorry, Tanya Lloyd. She looked round Ryhill when it was first for sale, and . . . you remember her? Right. Well, she also happens to be an old friend of mine. She's here now. Apparently you told her you had no intention of selling, and she thinks John murdered you, so . . . you wouldn't just have a quick word with her, would you, to convince her you're alive?' Lynn laughed. 'Yes, I did say that. I'll let Tanya explain.'

Lynn waved the phone at me, nodding for me to take it.

I backed away, mute with embarrassment.

'Come on, don't be shy.' Every time I took a step back, she took a step towards me. When we were in the hall and the front door was behind me, only a few feet away, I gave up trying to escape, and took the phone.

'Hello?' I said. Nothing. 'The line's dead.'

Lynn smiled nastily. 'Ring her back. Go on.'

'How do I know you phoned her?' I said, hoping I didn't sound as desperate not to be wrong – not to be a hopeless idiot – as I was. 'You could have phoned any number.'

Apparently you told her you had no intention of selling, and she thinks John murdered you.

A shiver of dread crept up my back. Who would ring the person they bought their house from – a virtual stranger, surely – and come out with that?

'You don't think I dialled the Tufts' number? Press redial.'

I did. Digits appeared on the screen: 609418. Lynn thrust her address book in front of my face. 'John Tuft', she had written. '609418'.

I was about to say that perhaps the Tufts were out; Lynn might have spoken to a ringing tone, but I knew she hadn't;

I'd heard a woman's voice. Faintly, but I'd heard it. Now a recorded voice was saying something about accessing messages. I passed the phone back to Lynn.

She looked at her watch again. 'I'd like you to leave now. We're going out tonight and—'

'We?'

'My fiancé and I. He'll be back any minute, and . . . God, I can't believe I'm trying to be tactful! Just go, will you? Or stay – I don't care.' Lynn went upstairs, tossing her blonde hair over her shoulder. I heard her talking on the phone again. Probably to her new man. I leaned against the front door. What should I do? I'd made enough of a fool of myself already; perhaps it was best to leave without another word, but I hate loose ends. I decided to wait until Lynn came downstairs. Then I would apologise briskly and leave. Lynn was right. People changed their minds; of course they did.

A key turned in the lock behind me. A man was letting himself into the house. Into the hall. There was no time to hide. 'Lynn's fiancé,' I said under my breath. I should have taken her advice, left when she first told me to.

My stomach heaved as he walked in and I saw his face: John Tuft. 'Hello, Tanya,' he said, with a nasty smile on his face. He locked the front door. I ran to the kitchen, hearing his footsteps behind me. The phone Lynn had used was still on the counter. I picked it up, pressed redial. *609418*. A woman's voice said, 'Sorry. If you want to access your messaging service from home, you must dial 1571. Goodbye.' I began to sob; Lynn had dialled her own number, Ryhill's number.

I heard John Tuft's voice in my ear, felt his hands in my hair. 'I hear you've been asking questions about Ryhill,' he said. 'It isn't for sale any more. Change of plan.' His voice became a whisper. 'Do you still want it, Tanya? My wife wanted it. She wanted it to be her forever home, and she got what she wanted. Do you want it to be your forever home too? Are you willing to pay the asking price?'

BOGNOR AND BOLZANO
Tim Heald

Tim Heald has published books on a wide range of subjects, including cricket and the Royal Family. A successful freelance journalist, he diversified into crime fiction with a series of books featuring Simon Bognor which were adapted for television, starring David Horovitch. More recently, he has created a new detective, Dr Tudor Cornwall.

Bognor was concerned to get things straight.

This was, as so often, a mistake. He was reminded of the British general who had once said to the not-so-British proconsul on the make, 'Dicky – you're so bent that if you swallowed a nail you'd pass a screw.' This was how, on occasions such as this, Sir Simon felt, and life was full of occasions such as this.

'I'm sorry,' he said, regarding his sharp subordinate with a mixture of pride and confusion, 'start and go more slowly. You're telling me that the minister charged with eliminating corruption is, in fact, the most corrupt of the lot.'

Harvey Contractor nodded. Sometimes his boss was incredibly thick. Thick in the nicest, most agreeably old-fashioned way, but still thick: slow on the uptake. A recent degree in semiotics from the University of Wessex was better than an old one in 'modern' history from an ancient university. Fact of life. They said experience compensated. They would.

'The minister,' said Bognor, 'is, inter alia, Minister for Expenses. He makes the rules. What he says goes. So *ipso facto* he can do no wrong. At least in this department. When it comes to expenses.' Bognor smiled across his fingernails which were mildly grubby and slightly chewed: signs of habit and of stress.

'Not according to the Prime Minister,' said Contractor.

'Ah,' said Bognor, 'the Prime Minister. I see.'

He didn't, of course, but always took refuge in this cliché when he wished to appear cleverer and better informed than he actually was. Contractor recognised the stratagem but ignored it.

'The Prime Minister thinks that Bolzano is after his job and he wants to do him for fiddling his expenses. The PM thinks this will destroy Bolzano's career and therefore the threat to his own.'

'Hmmmm,' said Bognor. This was a variant on 'I see'.

'The Prime Minister takes the view that being in charge of expenses is the perfect cover for fiddling them yourself. He even goes so far as to suggest that Bolzano took the job so that he could make illicit money at it.'

'But the Prime Minister gave him the job himself.'

'Poisoned chalice,' said Contractor. In case he had not made himself clear he added, 'The PM thought that if he gave him enough rope he might hang himself. In a manner of speaking.'

'But they belong to the same party.'

Contractor looked long-suffering. 'Different wings. Different friends. They've always hated each other.'

'But Bolzano's in the House of Lords.' This was true. Lord Bolzano of Tring. He came from one place, his ancestors from the other. As Albert Bolzano he had been a Member of Parliament before his elevation to the other place. No matter where he sat, he was a threat to the status quo. Any status quo not involving Albert Bolzano was under permanent threat. The old-fashioned view of the world was that one went in to politics in order to benefit other people; Bolzano's more modern take on the same subject was that one went in to benefit Albert Bolzano. Where there was a conflict of interest, which seldom occurred, then there was only one winner. It was the same with the Prime Minister. Rick. Rick had put Bolzano into the Lords. Given him a shove and hoped to get rid of him. He hadn't expected the recent rebirth.

'They're pledged to abolish the Lords. At least they're going to get rid of the hereditary element. "Reform" is Bolzano's baby. So biting the hand that feeds him is second nature. Does it all the time.'

'Never seen the point of Bolzano,' said Bognor. This was pretty bad. Not seeing the point of someone was almost the worst verdict he could produce.

'He owns Goering's old Schwimmwagen,' said Contractor as if everyone did something similar.

'I thought,' said Bognor, making a fatal stab at knowledge, 'that our German friends didn't come up with amphibious cars until the sixties?'

'That was the Amphicar,' said Contractor, not missing a beat. 'They produced a few in Berlin between '62 and '67 but the marketing was all garbage. Good engineers but not much cop at anything else. Then there was the Searider which is still around. During the wars the Americans had DUKWs which were terrific. They used them as landing craft. The Krauts had the technology but not, apparently, the application. The Reichsmarschall's was some sort of prototype – the 128 – but they only made a handful. The Führer didn't like them. Said that if God had meant us to float he'd have given us fins. Something like that. He was an incredible ass, Adolf, but luckily he had the courage of his convictions, batty though they usually were. Volkswagen and Porsche produced about 15,000 of them even so. There are still over a thousand around but only a dozen or so unrestored. The 128 is probably unique. But basically they foundered on the Führer's dislike. Roosevelt, on the other hand, liked DUKWs. Adolf liked cars to be cars and boats boats.'

'Just as well,' said Bognor. 'If he hadn't been so silly, but so convincing, not to say convinced, we might never have won.'

'Probably not,' agreed Contractor. 'Bolzano keeps it on Gozo. Uses it for shopping in Malta. Sometimes he waterskis.'

'Paid for by us?'

'Looks like it.' Contractor appeared to agree again.

'How much?'

'God knows what he actually paid,' said Contractor. 'He claims two tranches of fifty thousand, one for the car and one for the boat. It's all done according to what passes for the book.'

'Which he drew up?'

'Yes.'

*   *   *

Lord Bolzano didn't come to most people, even knights such as Bognor who ran their departments. Bognor and his aide, Contractor, went to him. Bolzano's office was high in a Puginesque turret with a view of the Thames through a slit-like window. Bognor had always found his lordship oleaginous on TV and he found him much the same in the flesh. Flesh was the operative word for there was a lot of it. Bognor half expected a forked tongue to flick out of the lordly mouth hurrying back with some more or less edible insect attached to it.

'Bognor, Board of Trade,' said Simon, by way of introduction. 'And this is my assistant, Mr Contractor.'

'Enchanted,' said Lord Bolzano not looking the least enchanted. He motioned to the two uprightish armchairs in front of the desk and sat down behind it in his revolving chair, also upright and finished in shiny black leather. He smiled ingratiatingly. 'Now what can I do for you, gentlemen?' And he smiled again. Bognor had seldom encountered a less meaningful smile in a lifetime of meaningless ricti.

'It's about parliamentary expenses,' said Bognor.

'Ah,' said Lord Bolzano, 'parliamentary expenses.'

'The Prime Minister asked me to look into them.'

'Ah,' said Lord Bolzano tapping his propelling pencil against his fingertips, 'did he now?'

'Yes,' said Bognor.

'Ah,' said Lord Bolzano.

After a less than comfortable pause Lord Bolzano continued. 'Well, what can I tell you, gentlemen? Anything to help the Prime Minister, though I have to say that I find his intervention a little . . . unorthodox. A little unorthodox . . . however . . .' And he seemed to pull himself together and become more businesslike. 'Anything I can do to help the PM. What can I tell you?'

Bognor saw no point in beating about the bush.

'Hermann Goering's Schwimmwagen,' he said. 'You charged it to expenses.'

'I did indeed,' said the minister. He had no portfolio which made for ease of action. He was obviously right on top of the Schwimmwagen, portfolio or not. 'Saved you and yours

a lot of loot. Half for dry land; half for the water. Could
have charged for a car and for a boat separately but I think
we should all exercise caution and sound housekeeping. Don't
you agree? Time to tighten our belts.'
'But do you really need a Schwimmwagen?' This was
Contractor. Lord Bolzano ignored him though not his question. He addressed his reply to Bognor.
'Everybody should have one,' he said. 'They combine all
the attributes of the boat on the one hand and of the car on the
other.'
'Yes but—'
'The Schwimmwagen enables me to check out the average
moat, the common or garden duck house, without so much
as dropping anchor. One minute I'm on dry land, the next
I'm on water. And vice versa. It's the perfect vehicle for
someone in my position and it costs the taxpayer half as
much as having a separate land and sea job. And it's twice
as effective.'
Bognor and Contractor were both tempted to say 'yes,
but' again but a glance at the minister told them that even a
mild remonstrance such as this would be ineffective and
possibly counter-productive.
'We understand she's in Gozo,' ventured Contractor.
'Correct,' said Bolzano. 'Yes.'
'Not a lot of work to do in Gozo,' said Bognor. This was
foolish and he realised as much the moment he said it for
Bolzano had his reply rehearsed and ready.
'She's undergoing trials,' he said, 'but all being well we
should relocate directly.'
'Trials!' said Bognor. 'But she belonged to Goering. She
must be at least seventy years old if she's a day. That's an
awfully long time to decide whether she's working properly.'
Bolzano sighed as if his patience was being tried by a
small boy. Even so he obviously decided to humour his
interrogator.
'They built things to last in those days,' he said, 'so the
frame and finish is pretty much original. The veneer is
mahogany; the lamps and horn are brass. But the engine has
had to be replaced. And much of the mechanics. She looks
like an antique but inside she's state of the art.'

'Paid for by us?'

'She's been charged entirely legitimately with an absolutely scrupulous regard for what is appropriate,' said Bolzano.

'And now if you'll excuse me.' The minister rose. Interview over. Nasty little threat overcome. Civil servant swatted aside. Easy. Next please. He was a crook making a reputation out of the body public and on top of his game.

'Slug,' said Bognor, when they had left without making excuses.

'I wouldn't put it as strongly as that,' said Contractor, 'I'm fond of slugs.'

Back in the office they both indulged in thought. This was not always a good idea but sometimes yielded results. This time they were both lucky. And in much the same way.

'We need to get back to the Prime Minister's office,' said Bognor.

Contractor said the same, simultaneously.

They both had the grace to grin.

Contractor made the call which was much as expected. The aide was scrupulously non-committal, marginally helpful.

'I'll tell the PM,' was what he said and he meant it. The message would get through but no more and no less.

This was not satisfactory but at the same time it would be difficult to say that it was *un*satisfactory. It was what was to be expected. End of story.

A little later they shared their thoughts. This was what they did. Sometimes it yielded results, sometimes not. But it was what they were paid to do and on the whole they enjoyed it.

'Don't care for Bolzano,' said Bognor.

Contractor agreed.

Prime Ministers these egalitarian days were known not just by their Christian names but, where possible, by diminutives. Rick's first name was Eric; and his surname was Thompson. In the old days not so long ago he would have been known by this, with maybe a 'Mr' thrown in as a concession to rank. But then in the old days no one had thought much of Prime Ministers. The paradox was that the interest and grudging respect had increased in inverse proportion to the job's importance. So, by a further paradox, had the blokey familiarity.

'Bolzano is claiming his toy amphibious car on expenses. This is morally repugnant but technically legitimate,' said Contractor.

'Technically,' agreed Bognor, 'but technicalities are what this is all about. We need to wrong-foot Bolzano on a technicality.'

'I am going to ask you questions,' he said. 'I expect you to know the answers.'

Contractor stifled a yawn. Bognor was always asking questions; he always knew the answers. This was tiresome but true.

'Is a Member of Parliament entitled to claim for a car?'

'Yes,' said Contractor. It was like some weird sort of television quiz show, he reflected.

'Is a Member of Parliament entitled to claim for a boat?'

'Yes,' said Contractor, stifling the urge to invite his boss to ask him another and playing the urge like the putative yawn down to fine leg. He did however add the words 'That is correct' because that made it seem even more like a TV game.

'But,' said Bognor, 'is a Member of Parliament entitled to claim for a boat and a car together?'

'Well,' said Contractor, on the point of embarking on a semiotically-induced argument, but thinking better of it. 'Well,' he repeated, groping for a precedent. 'It's never arisen.'

'But it has,' said Bognor. 'Lord Bolzano has claimed for a car and a boat at one and the same time.'

'Thereby saving the taxpayer half what he could have claimed for a car and half what he claimed for a boat.'

'Oh, come on,' said Bognor, 'we've only got his word for that. He keeps the thing in the middle of the Mediterranean as far away as possible from any other fiddled MPs' expenses. And it's an expensive toy. He could have got a serviceable car and a serviceable boat for a fraction of what he – or we – actually paid. But that's not the point. Technically he's entitled to those things even though they're an obvious fiddle. The other deviation is not such an obvious fiddle. In fact you could argue that it's not a fiddle at all. But it's technically wrong. There's no precedent. We've got him.'

Contractor seemed perplexed.

'But,' he said, not unreasonably, 'cutting the claim in half – sort of – is the only thing approaching decency in the whole story. And yet you're saying that it's the decent thing which is going to destroy him.'

'Bolzano's not nice.'

'Oh,' said Harvey, 'talking of Bolzano, there is a letter from his office. He is the Lord Great Seal in Ordinary isn't he?'

'Nothing ordinary about Bolzano but otherwise that's him all right. Great Panjandrum with all sorts of stuff falling out of his breeches. Let's have a look.'

Bognor took the letter which was handwritten but sealed with real wax and stamped with a crest which looked Ruritanian and fake.

'My dear Simon,' it read, followed by '(If I may)'. Bognor made a mental note that he forbad such intimacy but realised that this would have no effect whatever. 'It was good to meet you the other day, particularly as I have heard so much more and at a time when you must be preoccupied with planning your retirement details. With this in mind I can, naturally, confirm that a peerage would accompany your retirement provided there are no unexpected glitches. I think I might be able to throw in a rather elegant retirement home for you and your wife which has suddenly become available, along with an enjoyable and not entirely burdensome sinecure. This involves nothing more arduous than an adherence to the rules that you have so magnificently followed throughout your career.

'The ducks by the way are rubber and the moat self-cleaning though I hope to be persuaded to call round from time to time in my amphibian. I shall much look forward.'

It was signed 'Bert Bolzano'.

Bognor flung the letter down irritably.

'Bribe,' he said to a surprised Contractor. 'He wants me to stick to the rules. Rules he invented himself. Not taking it.'

And he smirked. A rule, as always, unto himself.

WHERE ARE ALL THE NAUGHTY PEOPLE?

Reginald Hill

Reginald Hill is best known as the creator of Dalziel and Pascoe, the mid-Yorkshire cops whose cases have been adapted for television with much success. He has, however, also written a wide range of other novels, as well as award-winning short stories such as 'On the Psychiatrist's Couch'. His awards include both the CWA Gold Dagger, for *Bones and Silence*, and the CWA Cartier Diamond Dagger.

A lot of kids are scared of graveyards.

Not me. I grew up in one.

My dad, Harry Cresswell, was verger at St Cyprian's on the north-east edge of Bradford. Once it had been a country parish but that was ages back. By the sixties it was all built up, a mix of council houses and owner-occupied semis, plus some older properties from the village days. We lived in one of them, Rose Cottage right up against the churchyard wall. We didn't have a proper garden, just a small cobbled yard out back, and out front a two-foot strip of earth where Mam tried to grow a few stunted roses to make sense of the name. A low retaining wall separated this from a narrow pavement that tracked the busy main road where traffic never stopped day or night.

Nearest park was a mile away. But right next door to us there were four acres of open land, lots of grass and trees, no buildings, no roads, no traffic.

St Cyprian's graveyard.

The wall in our backyard had a small door in it to make it easy for Dad to get to the church to do his duties. In the graveyard the door was screened by a bit of shrubbery. My mam liked to tell anyone who cared to listen that she was a Longbottom out of Murton near York, a farming family whose kids had grown up breathing good fresh air and enjoying the sight and smell of trees and grass. She wasn't about to deprive her own child of the benefit just because of a few gravestones, so when I was a baby, she'd take me through the door in our yard and lay me on a rug to enjoy the sun while she got on with her knitting. She was a great knitter. If her hands didn't have some other essential task to occupy them, they were always occupied by her needles. I've even seen her knitting on the move! And I've never had to buy a scarf or a pullover in my life.

As I grew older and more mobile I began to explore a bit further. Mam and Dad were a bit worried at first, but Father Stamp said he'd rather see me enjoying myself there than running around the street in the traffic, and in Mam's ears, Father Stamp's voice was the voice of God.

I should say that though St Cyprian's was Church of England, it was what they called High, lots of incense and hyssop and such, and the vicar liked to be called Father. It used to confuse me a bit as a kid, what with God the Father, and Father Stamp, and Father Christmas, and my own dad, but I got used to it.

And folk got used to me using the graveyard as my playground. I think them as didn't like it were too scared of my mam to risk a confrontation. She could be really scary when she tried. For her part, she insisted I should always stay in the area between our bit of the wall and the side of the church, and not do anything naughty. 'Naughty' in Mam's vocabulary covered a wide range of misbehaviour. She used to read the *News of the World* and shake her head and say disapprovingly, 'There's a lot of naughty folk in this world. Well, they'll have to pay for it in the next!' I assumed she meant bank robbers and such. But in my own case, I didn't have to assume anything. I knew exactly what naughty meant – doing anything my mam told me not to do!

My designated playground area was the oldest section of the graveyard. All the headstones here dated back a hundred years or more, and no one ever came to tend the graves or lay flowers on them. There were quite a few trees here too and it was hard to get a mowing machine in, so the grass grew long and lush and on the rare occasions someone did come round this side, I could easily drop out of sight till they'd gone. Occasionally I'd see Father Stamp but I didn't hide from him because he'd always wave at me and smile, and sometimes he'd come and join me. Often he'd produce a bagful of mint humbugs and we'd sit next to each other on a tombstone, his arm round my shoulder, sucking away in companionable silence till suddenly he'd stand up, ruffle my hair and say he had to go and do something in the church.

Once I'd started at school, I soon realised the new activities I was enjoying, like playing football or cowboys and Indians, you couldn't do in a graveyard. Even Father Stamp wouldn't have cared to see a whole gang of kids rampaging round his church, cheering and yelling. So I spent less time there, but I still liked to wander round by myself sometimes, playing solitary make-believe games, or just lying in the grass looking up at the sky till Mam yelled my name and I had to go in for my tea.

Occasionally I'd have one or two of my special friends round at the house and to start with I took them through the door into my playground. I thought they'd be impressed I had all this space to roam around in, but instead they either said it was seriously weird, or they wanted to play daft games like pretending to be ghosts and jumping out on each other from behind the old gravestones. As well as being worried about the noise they were making, I found I was a bit put out that they weren't showing more respect. Father Stamp had told me that I should never forget there were dead people lying under the ground. No need to be scared of them, he said, but I should try and remember this was their place as well as mine. So after a while I stopped taking my friends there. I was still very young but already old enough to realise it mattered at school how your classmates regarded you. I didn't want to get known as daft Tommy Cresswell who likes to play with old bones in the graveyard.

I was what they called a slow learner, taking longer than a lot of the others to get into reading and writing, but suddenly one day when I was about seven it finally clicked and I took to it big. I read everything I could lay my hands on, so much so that Mam and Dad went from worrying about me not reading to worrying about me reading my brain into train oil, as Granny Longbottom used to say.

I don't know exactly when it was that I realised the grave-yard was full of stuff to read! I'd seen there were words carved on the headstones, of course, but I never paid them much attention. I was more interested in the variety of shapes.

Some of the headstones were rounded, some were pointed, and some were squared off. Quite a lot had crosses on top of them, some of the older ones leaned to one side like they were drunk, and a few lay flat out. The ones I liked best were the ones with statues and these I gave names to in my private games. My favourite was an angel with a shattered nose that I called Rocky after Rocky Marciano who was my dad's great hero. Never got beaten, he'd say. I think he'd have called me Rocky rather than Tommy if Mam had let him.

It was Rocky the angel that got me looking at the words. I was lying in the grass one evening staring up at him when the words carved at his feet came into focus.

Sacred to the memory of David Oscar Winstanley
taken in the 87th year of his life
loving husband devoted father
in virtue spotless in charity generous
and a loyal servant of the General Post Office for
forty-nine years

He was probably a pretty important GPO official, but I imagined him as an ordinary postman, trudging the streets with his sackful of letters well into his eighties, and I was really impressed that he'd been so highly regarded that they'd given him an angel to keep watch over his grave and a full-blown testimonial. This is what started me paying attention to the inscriptions on other headstones. A few were in a funny language I couldn't understand. Father Stamp told me it was Latin and sometimes he'd translate it for me. Mam was always telling me not to bother Father Stamp because he had so much to do in the parish. In the same breath she'd say I could learn a lot if I listened to him, he was such an educated man. When I wondered in my childish way how I could listen to him without bothering him, she told me not to be cheeky. Things have changed, but back then a wise kid quickly learned that in the adult world he was usually in the wrong!

I quite liked Father Stamp and I certainly liked his mint humbugs, but when it came to practical information about the graves, I turned to the men who dug them. There were two of them, Young Clem and Old Clem.

I don't know how old Old Clem was – certainly no older than my dad – but he 'had a back' and seemed to spend most of his time standing by the side of a new grave, smoking his pipe, while Young Clem laboured with his spade down below. Nowadays they have machines to do the hard work in less than half an hour. Back then it took Young Clem the best part of a morning to excavate and square off a grave to his dad's satisfaction. Occasionally Old Clem would seize the spade to demonstrate what ought to be done, but after he'd moved a couple of clods, he'd shake his head, rub his back, and return to his pipe. I heard Dad complaining to Mam more than once that Old Clem ought to be pensioned off, but he got no support from the vicar. Father Stamp just shook his head and said there was no question of getting rid of Old Clem. Mam said it showed what a true Christian gentleman Father Stamp was, and I should try to be less naughty and grow up like him. When I asked if that meant that Mam was naughty because she agreed with Dad that Old Clem should be sacked and Father Stamp didn't, she clipped my ear and said she didn't know where I got it from. I saw Dad grinning when she said that.

Young Clem was my special friend. Nine or ten years older than me, he was a big lad, more than twice my size, and he always had a fag in his mouth, though that was OK in them days. Dad smoked twenty a day and even Mam had the occasional puff.

Clem had been around all my life, helping his dad out when he were still a kid, then becoming his full-time assistant when he left school at sixteen. Like me he clearly thought of the graveyard as his own personal play park. Wandering around in the dusk one spring evening I heard a noise I didn't recognise and dropped down in the long grass. After a bit, with the noise still going on, I reckoned I hadn't been spotted so I crawled forward and peered round a headstone. Young Clem was lying there in the grass with a girl. At eight, I already had some vague notion there were things older lads

liked to do with girls but I'd no real idea what it was all
about except that simultaneously it had something to do with
courting, which was all right, and something to do with being
naughty, which wasn't. We didn't have sex education in
Yorkshire in them days. Whatever it was, Young Clem and
his girl were clearly enjoying it. I watched till I got bored
then I crawled away. I had enough sense to know that I ought
to keep out of the way when my friend was doing his naughty
courting so whenever I glimpsed Clem in the graveyard with
a girl I made myself scarce.

But when there weren't any girls around to divert him, the
years between us seemed to vanish. Young Clem just loved
larking around. In his snap break, he was always up for a
game of hide-and-seek, or tiggy-on-gravestones. Or if I had
my cricket ball with me, he'd show me how to set my fingers
round it so that I could bowl a googly. One day he was demon-
strating how to do this up against the church wall when Father
Stamp came round the corner and I thought we would be in
real trouble. But Clem didn't seem bothered. He just lit a fag
and blew smoke down at Father Stamp (Clem was a good
six inches taller) till the vicar turned round and went back
the way he'd come, like he'd forgotten something.

'He must like you too, Clem,' I said, impressed.

'You could say that,' said Clem. 'Doesn't mean I have to
like him, does it?'

That struck me as odd even then. Under Mam's influence,
I'd come to think everyone in the world must like and admire
Father Stamp, so it was a shock to find that my mate Clem
didn't agree.

I noticed after this that Clem often seemed to show up
when I was with the vicar. I recall one occasion when I was
round the back of the church where there was this funny old
cross, very tall and thin with the actual cross piece set in a
circle and not very big at all. Another odd thing was it didn't
seem to mark a grave and I couldn't see any writing on it,
just a lot of weird carvings.

Father Stamp came and stood beside me and started
explaining what they all meant. I didn't understand a lot of
what he said but I did take in that it had been there for
hundreds of years, dating back to long before the present St

Cyprian's had been built. He told me there'd always been some sort of church or chapel here right back to what he called the Dark Ages and this cross had been put up then and it was quite famous, and experts came from all over just to look at it. Then he lifted me right up on his shoulders so I could get a good look at the fancy carving on the topmost piece of the cross, and I was sitting there, clinging on to his hair, with his hands clasping the top of my legs really tight, when there was a cough behind us.

Father Stamp swung round so quick I almost fell off, and in fact I might as well have done, as when he saw it was Young Clem he dropped me to the ground so hard I was winded.

'Sorry to interrupt, vicar,' said Young Clem, 'but Dad were wondering if you'd a moment to talk about tomorrow's funeral.'

It didn't sound to me all that important, but Father Stamp hurried away as if it was, and Young Clem said, 'Giving you a ride, was he?'

'He was showing me the carvings up on the cross,' I said.

'Is that right? Tell you what, Tommy. The vicar's a busy man. You want to play, you play with me. Or if you want to know about the carvings or anything, ask my dad.'

Even at that age, I couldn't imagine that Old Clem would know anything the vicar didn't but I followed Young Clem round the church to where his dad was sitting on a tombstone, puffing his pipe in the sun. There was no sign of Father Stamp so they must have finished their business quickly.

Young Clem said, 'Tommy here wants to know about the carvings on that old cross.'

Old Clem blew some smoke into the air reflectively then pronounced, 'Heathen, that's what they are. Nasty pagan stuff. Don't know what summat like that is doing in a Christian churchyard.'

For all its shortness, I have to say I found this more intriguing than Father Stamp's more rambling account but when I mentioned it to Mam, she said, 'You don't want to listen to Old Clem. What's he know? No, you stick close to a clever man like Father Stamp and you never know what you'll learn. But don't you go bothering him!'

Mam didn't like Old Clem much. She wouldn't use the

same words as Dad who said he was an idle old sod, but that's
what she thought. And she really gave him a piece of her mind
once when she found me searching through the long grass in
the graveyard and I told her Old Clem had lost his rubber
spade and asked me to help him find it. But she liked Young
Clem. She said he had a nice smile and I noticed she used to
pat her hair and sound a bit different when she was talking
to him. She even knit him a scarf that he said was the best
scarf he'd ever had though I never saw him wear it.

So what with the Clems and Father Stamp, I had plenty
of company in the graveyard if I wanted it. But most of the
time all the company I wanted was my own and that of my
friends in the ground. I had no fear of them. Why should I?
They were all such good people; I could tell that by what I
read on their headstones. I found it a really comfortable idea
that after you were dead, folk would come and read what
had been carved about you, just like I was doing, and they'd
think what a great guy you must have been!

Sometimes I'd lie in the grass by Rocky, looking up at
the sky and inventing things they might one day put on my
own stone.

Here lies Tommy Cresswell, loving son,
and the best striker ever to play for Bradford City and England

The more I thought of it, though, the more I was forced to
admit that it wasn't all that likely as Bradford were holding
up the bottom division of the league back then, and anyway
I was crap at football. But anyone could be a hero, I reasoned.
It was just a question of opportunity. So in the end I settled
for this:

Sacred to the memory of Tommy Cresswell,
beloved by all who knew him, who lost his life while bravely
rescuing 56 children from their burning orphanage.
"He died that they might live."

I got that last bit from the stone of some soldier who'd been
wounded in the Great War and then come home to die.

The graveyard was full of such inspiring and upbeat

messages. Those who reached old age had enjoyed such useful and productive lives it was no wonder they were sadly missed by their loving friends and families, while those who died young were so precociously marvellous that the angels couldn't wait for them to get old before claiming them.

But eventually after I'd done a tour of the whole graveyard, a problem began to present itself. I went all the way round again just to be sure, and it was still there.

I thought of applying to Mam and Dad for help, but I didn't really want them to know how much time I was still spending in the graveyard.

Father Stamp would certainly be able to answer my question. After all he was in charge of everything at St Cyprian's. But he didn't seem quite so keen on talking to me as he'd once been. If we did meet and sit down for a chat, after a while he'd get restless and jump up and say he had to be off somewhere else, even if Young Clem didn't interrupt him.

Then one Monday in early October on my way home from school still pondering my problem, I spotted the Clems digging a grave and it came to me that if anyone would know the answer, they would.

It was the usual set-up, with Young Clem up to his knees in the grave, digging, and Old Clem leaning on his spade, proffering advice.

I said, 'Who's this for?'

'Old George Parkin,' said Old Clem. 'They'll not be putting him in the hole till Wednesday, but we thought we'd get a start while this good weather holds. Poor old George. He'll be sadly missed. He were a grand lad. One of the best.'

That was my cue.

I said, 'Clem,' – letting them decide which one I was addressing – 'I know you bury the good folk in the churchyard. But where do you put all the naughty ones?'

Old Clem stopped puffing, and Young Clem stopped digging, and they both said, 'Eh?'

I saw that I needed to make myself a bit clearer.

I said, 'You only bury the good people in the churchyard. I can tell that from reading what it says about them on the headstones. But the naughty ones must die as well. So where are all the naughty people? What do you do with *their* bodies?'

There was a long silence while they looked at each other.
Old Clem put his pipe back into his mouth and took it out
again twice.

And finally he said solemnly, 'Can you keep a secret,
Tommy?'

'Oh yes. Cross my heart and hope to die,' I said eagerly.

'Right then,' said Old Clem. 'We puts them in the crypt.'

Young Clem said, 'Dad!' like he was protesting because
his father was talking out of turn.

Old Clem said, 'The lad asked and he deserves to know.
The crypt, young Tommy. That's where we dump all the bad
'uns. Pack 'em in, twenty or thirty deep till their flesh rots
down to mulch. Then they grind the bones to bone meal and
it all gets spread on the fields. But you're not to tell anyone
else, OK? This is between you and me. Promise?'

I repeated, 'Cross my heart, Clem,' and went away, leaving
father and son having what sounded like a fierce discussion
behind me.

This explained a lot! I knew there was this sort of big
cellar under the church that they called the crypt. And I knew
that there'd been bones and stuff down there because a couple
of years earlier there'd been some worry about the church
floor sinking and I'd heard Dad talking about clearing out
the crypt and setting some props to support the ceiling which
was of course the church floor. So all the naughty people's
remains must have been cleared out to spread on the fields
then. That thought made me feel a bit queasy, but, after all,
I told myself, if you were too naughty to be buried in the
graveyard, what did it matter where you ended up?

I mean, who'd want a headstone saying: *Here lies John
Smith who was really naughty and nobody misses him?*

I'd never been in the crypt, of course, though I knew where
the door was in a hidden corner of the church porch. There
was a notice on it saying: *Danger. Steep and crumbling steps.
Do not enter.* Not that there was much chance of that as it
was always kept locked.

But it had to be opened some time so that more naughty
people could be put in there, that was obvious. And if, as Mam
said, there were a lot of naughty people in this world, it was
probably getting full up again after the last big clear-out.

Suddenly I was filled with a desperate need to see inside the crypt. I wasn't a particularly morbid child, but I recall one of my teachers writing on my report, 'It's never enough to tell Tommy anything; if possible he's got to see for himself.'

So now I'd got the answer to my question, all I needed was for someone to open the crypt door for me and shine a torch in so that I could glimpse all the naughty people piled up there! Then I'd be satisfied.

But I was bright enough to know that this wasn't the kind of favour adults were likely to do for a kid. I was going to have to sort this out for myself.

The answer was as obvious as asking the Clems about the naughty people had been.

Dad could go anywhere in and around the church. Obviously he wasn't going to open the crypt door for me. But he did have a key. At least, I assumed he had a key. He certainly had a bunch of keys that opened up every other door.

And as I thought of this, I also realised that tonight being a Monday night was the perfect time to put my plan into operation. Not that I realised I had a plan till I thought of it! The thing was, Dad always went down the pub to play darts on Mondays and Mam curled up on the sofa with her knitting to watch Sherlock Holmes, her favourite TV series, and nothing was allowed to interrupt her.

So tonight was the night! It seemed like fate, but for a while it looked like fate had changed its mind. It turned out that Dad had been feeling a bit hot and snuffly all day and Mam was worried it was the Hong Kong flu virus that was just taking a grip around the country. But after tea, Dad said not to be stupid, it was just a sniffle that a couple of pints of John Smith's and a whisky chaser would soon sort. So off he went down the pub, and not long after I went up to bed without any of my usual arguments and lay there till I heard the swelling introductory music of Mam's programme.

It was part two of *The Hound of the Baskervilles,* I recall, and I was confident there was no way she'd move till it was finished. I had at least an hour.

I slipped out of bed. I didn't bother to get dressed. I was wearing tracksuit pyjamas and it was a warm autumn night, so warm in fact I was perspiring slightly and the thought of putting on more clothes was unpleasant. I tiptoed downstairs, carrying the torch I kept for reading under the bedclothes. The TV was going full belt, and I moved into the kitchen, plucked Dad's church keys from the hook by the back door and headed out into the night.

Our door into the churchyard was locked but I knew by touch alone which key I needed here.

As I passed through, I paused for a moment. The grave-yard looked different in the dark, and the bulk of the church silhouetted against the stars seemed to have assumed cathedral-like proportions. But I switched on my torch and advanced till I spotted the comforting outline of Rocky, my broken-nosed angel keeping guard over David Oscar Winstanley, the virtuous old postman. The long grass beneath my bare feet was pleasantly cool, the balmy air caressed my skin, and I felt sure somehow that Rocky would be keeping an eye on me too.

The door to the crypt was in a corner of the church's broad entrance porch. I thought I might have to unlock the church door itself as, ever since the theft of some items of silver a couple of years earlier, the building had been firmly locked at dusk. Tonight, however, the door was open. I didn't consider the implications of this, just took it in my super-hero mode as a demonstration that things were running my way.

Now all I had to do was find the right key for the crypt door.

It proved surprisingly easy. Close up, I saw it wasn't the ancient worm-eaten oak door I'd expected but a new door, stained to fit in with the rest of the porch, and instead of a large old-fashioned keyhole, there was a modern mortice lock.

That made the selection of the right key very easy and the door swung open with well-oiled ease and not the slightest suspicion of a horror film screech.

Now, however, the thin beam of my torch revealed that the bit about the steep and decaying steps hadn't been exaggerated. They plunged down almost vertically into the darkness where the naughty people lay.

Suddenly I felt less like a superhero and more like an

eight-year-old boy who got scared watching *Doctor Who* with his mam!

It felt a lot colder in the church porch and there seemed to be a draught of still colder air coming up from the crypt that made my sweat-soaked pyjamas feel clammy. I could smell damp earth – that was an odour I was very familiar with from hanging around the Clems while they were digging a grave. But what wasn't there, which I'd half expected, was any of that decaying meat smell I'd once got a whiff of as Young Clem's spade drove into an unexpected coffin.

Far from reassuring me, this only roused a fear that maybe the naughty people didn't decay like the ordinary good people, but somehow got preserved like the salted hams that hung in Granny Longbottom's kitchen. Maybe they even retained a bit of life?

In fact to my young mind, already well acquainted through the school playground with notions of zombies and vampires, it seemed very likely that the new door and its mortice lock hadn't been put there to keep the inquisitive public out, but to keep the still active naughty people in!

I could have shut the door and retreated and gone home to bed, and no one would ever have known of my cowardice. Except me, of course.

Daft, wasn't it? Just to prove to myself I wasn't scared, I began to descend that crumbling sandstone staircase. And all the time my teeth were chattering so hard I could hardly breathe!

What did I expect to find? Bodies hanging upside down from the ceiling? Coffins stacked six or seven deep? Heaps of bones? I don't know.

And I didn't know whether to be disappointed or relieved when all that the beam of my torch picked out was . . . emptiness! Except that is for seven or eight pillars of steel rising from metal plates set on the packed earth floor to give them firm grounding, and with metal beams running between them at ceiling level to support the sagging church floor.

And that was it. It dawned on me that Old Clem had been having me on again, like he did with looking for the rubber spade! I should have known. Making a fool of people is what passes for a joke in Yorkshire. I felt really stupid! Also, despite the chilly air down here, I felt very hot. I pulled off my pyjama top to cool down and used it to wipe off the streams of perspiration running down my face and body.

Suddenly I was desperate to be back in my bed and I turned to go.

Then I heard a noise.

And all my fears came rushing back full pelt!

It was a relief to realise the noise was coming from outside the crypt not inside.

Someone was at the top of the stairs.

I clicked my torch off and stood in the dark.

A voice demanded harshly, 'Who's down there?'

I almost answered but the thought of the trouble I'd be in at home – sneaking out after I'd gone to bed and stealing Dad's keys to get into the crypt – kept me quiet. Also, as I say, all my old fears were boiling up again. Maybe this was one of the wicked zombies returning from a stroll round the graveyard! I found myself praying to Rocky who'd never been beaten to come and help me.

Then a bigger fear erupted to push out all the others. Suppose whoever it was pulled the door shut behind him as he went away and left me locked in the crypt all night!

So I stuttered, 'It's me,' and began to move forward.

Then I stopped, blinded as a powerful torch beam hit me right in the eyes.

I heard footsteps on the stairs and a voice I now recognised said, 'Tommy! What on earth are you doing here?'

It was Father Stamp! I was so relieved I rushed forward up the steep steps and flung myself around him and hugged him close with my arms and legs. His arms went around my back and I felt his large strong hands cool against my hot skin. My tracksuit bottom was always a bit loose, and I think it had slipped down but I didn't care, I was just so relieved to be safe! I wanted to explain what I'd been doing but when I tried to speak, it came out as sobs, and he lifted me up and held me so close, I could hardly get my breath, and I tried to push myself free.

My memory of what happened after that is vague and confused. It was like my head was full of colours all forming weird shapes, constantly flying apart and changing into something else. And my body didn't feel as if it belonged to me, it was like a girl's rag doll that can be twisted into any shape you want, and I knew I would have fallen away or maybe even flown away if Father Stamp's strong hands hadn't been grasping my weak and nerveless flesh.

And then . . . I don't think I heard anything and I certainly didn't see anything, but I knew there was someone – or something – else on the steps. I just had time to think that maybe Rocky had answered my earlier call when there was an explosion of noise and violent movement, and something crashed into Father Stamp and together we went tumbling down the steep steps.

That was pretty well the end for me. I must have hit the crypt floor with such a bang that all of the breath and most of the consciousness was knocked out of my body. I had a sense of being embraced again but not in the strong muscular way that Father Stamp had embraced me. Maybe, I thought, this was Rocky. Then I was raised by strong arms and carried up the steps, and my lolling head gave me a view down into the crypt lit by a moving light that I think must have come from Father Stamp's torch, rolling around where he'd dropped it as we went tumbling down together.

Finally I was outside in the balmy night air and the sky was full of stars and I didn't remember anything else for sure till the moment when I opened my eyes and found myself back in my own bedroom with sunlight streaming through the window.

Four days had passed, four days that I'd spent being very sick, and sweating buckets, and tossing and turning with such violence that Mam sometimes had to hold me down. The doctor said I'd had a particularly extreme dose of Hong Kong flu, not just me but Dad too. He'd come back from the pub in almost as bad a state as me. How I got back to my bed, I don't know. I had some vague notion that Rocky had carried me there. My waking mind was awash with fantastic images of my visit to the crypt and these turned into really terrible nightmares when I sank into sleep, so no wonder I was tossing and turning so violently. I were poorly for nearly a fortnight, much worse than Dad who was up and about again after a week. And it was another two weeks after I first got out of bed before I really started getting back to something like normal.

By this time my memories and my nightmares had become so confused I found it impossible to tell the difference between them. Looming large in all of them was Father Stamp. Remembering how Mam always sang his praises as a visitor of the sick, I lived in fear of seeing him by my bedside. Finally when Mam didn't mention him, I did.

'Father Stamp's gone,' she said shortly.

'Gone where?' I said.

'How should I know. Just gone. Not a trace,' she said. 'Now are you going to take that medicine or do I have to pour it down you?'

I couldn't blame her for being short. Luckily for me and Dad, she'd somehow managed to remain untouched by the flu bug, but she must have been worked off her feet for the past few weeks taking care of the pair of us.

Also she'd had time to get used to Father Stamp's disappearance. When I was up and about again, I found out he'd been gone a long time. Exactly when no one was certain. It wasn't till he didn't turn up for old Mr Parkin's funeral on the Wednesday after my adventure in the crypt that folk started to get worried. He wasn't married and he lived alone in the vicarage, looked after by a local woman who came in every morning to clean the house and take care of his meals. That week she'd been down with the flu too, so there was a lot of vagueness about who'd actually seen him last and when.

Should I say something? Best not, I decided. When you're a kid, you learn it's usually a mistake to volunteer information that might get you in bother! Also, once I started sharing my memory-nightmare of that night, it would be hard to stop till I got to the bit where I was carried home by a marble angel with a broken nose, and I knew that sounded really loopy!

Yet for some reason that was the bit of my memories that I clung on to hardest. Maybe by clinging to what had to be fantasy, I was shutting out what might be reality. Anyway, soon as I felt well enough, I went back into the graveyard to say thank you to Rocky.

Young Clem spotted me and came over for a chat.

'All right, Tommy?' he said, lighting the inevitable fag.

'Yes thanks,' I said.

'Me and Dad were dead worried about you,' he said. 'Hong Kong flu it was, right?'

I really didn't want to talk about it, but I didn't want to offend Young Clem, especially not after Mam told me he'd called round nearly every day to ask after me when I was ill.

'That's right,' I said. 'Hong Kong flu.'

'Aye, it can be right nasty that. My Auntie Mary had it, just about sent her doolally, thought she were the Queen Mother for a bit, we have a grand laugh with her about that now she's right again. Owt like that happen to you, Tommy?'

'Just some bad dreams,' I said.

'But you're all right now?'

'Yes, thank you.'

'Grand!' he said stubbing out his cigarette on Rocky's knee. 'Everyone has bad dreams. Thing is not to let them bother you when you wake up. See you around, Tommy.'

'Yes, Clem, see you around.'

Father Stamp's disappearance was old news now. It seemed one of the papers had dug up some stuff about him having trouble with his nerves when he was a curate down south, and his bishop moving him north for his health. So most folk reckoned he'd had what they called a nervous breakdown and he'd turn up some day. But he never did.

After a while St Cyprian's got a replacement. He was nowhere near as High as Father Stamp; he wanted everyone to call him Jimmy, and he had all kinds of newfangled ideas. Dad and him didn't get on, and pretty soon there was a big falling out that ended with us leaving Rose Cottage and going to live with Granny Longbottom in Murton till Dad got taken on at Rowntree's chocolate factory and we found a place right on the edge of York.

So Mam got her wish and I was brought up breathing good fresh air, and eating a lot of chocolate, and enjoying the sight and smell of trees and grass with never a gravestone in sight. In fact after leaving St Cyprian's, Mam seemed to lose all interest in religion, and as I grew up I don't think I saw the inside of a church again, unless you count a visit to the Minster on a school trip. I'd only been inside a few minutes when I

started to feel the whole place crowding in on me and I were
glad to get out into the air. After that I didn't bother.

That was forty-odd years ago. I still live with my mam.
Lot of folk think that's weird. Let them think. All I know is
I never felt the need to get close to anyone else. I never went
courting. I did try being naughty with a girl from time to
time, and it were all right, I suppose, but I could never get
really interested and I don't think they liked it that much,
so in the end I stopped bothering.

Maybe I should have moved out. I know Dad thought I
should. I brought it up one night after he'd gone out to the
pub. Mam was sitting in front of the TV, busily knitting away
as she always did. That click-click-clicking of the needles
is such a familiar accompaniment that it sounds strange if
ever I watch a programme without it! She smiled up at me
when I broached the subject of moving out and said, 'This
is your home, son. You'll always be welcome here.'

Next year, Dad got diagnosed with cancer. After that I
think he was glad I was still around to help take some of
the strain off Mam. She was the best nurse he could have
asked for and she kept him at home far longer than many
women would have done. But three years later he was dead,
and since then the thought of leaving has never crossed my
mind.

As for Father Stamp and St Cyprian's, they never got
mentioned at home, not even while Dad were still living. Was
that good or bad? There's a lot of folk say everything should
be brought out in the open. Well, each to his own. I know
what worked for me. That's not to say I never wondered how
different my life might have been if the events of that October
night hadn't occurred. We're all what our childhood makes
us, the kid is father to the man, isn't that what they say?

Though I doubt if many people looking at a picture of me
back then could see much connection between little Tommy
Cresswell at eight and this fifty-year-old, a bit shabby, a bit
broken down, unmarried, living at home with his widowed
mam.

There is, though, maybe one traceable link between that
kid in the graveyard and this middle-aged man.

I'm a postman.

How much that can be tracked back to David Oscar Winstanley and Rocky, the broken-nosed angel, I don't know. I certainly don't aspire to anything like his memorial, either in form or in words. In fact I've lowered my sights considerably from the fantasies of my boyhood. 'He looked after his mam, and bothered nobody' would do me. I suppose I could rate as a loyal servant to the Post Office, if loyalty means doing your job efficiently. But if it entails devoting yourself wholeheartedly to your employer, then I don't qualify. I never had any ambition to rise up the career ladder. Delivering the mail's been enough for me.

Then the other day, my first on a new round, I knocked on a door to deliver a parcel, and when the door opened I found myself looking at Old Clem.

Except of course it was Young Clem forty-odd years on.

'Bugger me,' he said when I introduced myself. 'Tommy Cresswell! Come on in and have a beer.'

'More than my job's worth, Clem,' I said. 'But I'll have a cup of tea.'

Sitting in his kitchen, he filled me in on his life. He'd worked most of his life for the Bradford Parks and Gardens Service (though they call it something fancier nowadays), he'd been a widower for five years, and he'd recently retired because of his health. No need for details here. Most of his sentences were punctuated with a racking cough which didn't stop him from getting through three or four fags as we talked.

'Me daughter and her two kiddies live here in York,' he said. 'She wanted me to move in with them but I knew that 'ud never do. But I wanted to be a bit handier so I got myself this place. How about you, Tommy? You married?'

'Who'd have me?' I said, making a joke out of it. Then I told him about Dad dying and me living with Mam. And all the time he was sort of studying me through a cloud of smoke in a way that made me feel uneasy. So in the end I looked at my watch and said I ought to be getting on before folk started wondering what had happened to their mail.

But as I started to rise from my chair, he reached over the table and grasped my wrist and said, 'Afore you go, Tommy . . .' – here he broke off to cough – '. . . or mebbe I mean, afore I go, there's something we need to talk . . .'

I should just have left. I knew what he was going to tell me, and it had been a long time since Rocky was a barrier against the truth. But I stopped and listened and let him give form and flesh to what for so long I'd been desperate to pretend was nowt but an echo of one of my Hong Kong flu nightmares.

That night as usual I cleared up after supper and washed the dishes. Mam says it's no job for a man but she's been having a lot of trouble with her knees lately. There's been some talk of a replacement but she says she can't be bothered with that. So I do all I can to make life easy for her. Most nights after we've eaten, we sit together in the front of the telly and I'll maybe watch a football match while she gets on with her knitting. Like I say, doesn't matter how noisy the crowd is at the game, if that click-click-clicking of her needles stops, I look round to see what she's doing.

Tonight when I came in from the kitchen with a mug of coffee for me and cup of tea for her, she was knitting as usual but I didn't switch the set on.

I said, 'Met an old friend today, Mam. Remember Young Clem? Him and his dad used to dig the graves at St Cyprian's? Well, he's living in York now. So he can be close to his daughter and grandkids.'

'Young Clem?' she said. 'So he has grandchildren? That's nice. Grandchildren are nice.'

'Aye,' I said. 'Sorry I never gave you any, Mam.'

'Maybe you didn't, but I never lost you, Tommy, and that's just as important,' she said, her needles clicking away. 'So what was the crack with Young Clem then?'

She looked at me brightly. Sometimes these days she could be a bit vague about things; others, like now, she was as bright as a button.

I sipped my coffee slowly while my mind tried to come to terms with what Young Clem had told me.

My problem had nothing to do with his powers of expression for he'd spoken in blunt Yorkshire terms.

He'd said, 'I'd taken this lass into graveyard, for a bang, tha knows, and we'd just done when I saw this figure moving between the headstones. I nigh on shit meself till I made out it were your mam. She didn't spot me, but something about the look of her weren't right, so I told my lass to shove off down the pub and I'd catch up with her there. Well, she weren't best pleased but I didn't wait to argue, I went after your mam, and I caught up with her by the church door. She jumped a mile when I spoke to her, then she asked if I'd seen you. Seems she'd been watching the telly and all of a sudden something made her get up and go upstairs. When she found you weren't in bed, she went out into the yard and saw the back gate into the graveyard standing open and she went through it to look for you.

'I could tell what a state she were in – she'd nowt on her feet but a pair of fluffy slippers and she were still carrying her knitting with her – so I tried to calm her down, saying that likely you were just larking about with some of your mates. But she'd spotted that the church door were ajar, and nowt would satisfy her but that we went inside to take a look.

'Well, we didn't get past the porch. There was a noise like someone sobbing and a bit of a light and it were coming up from the crypt. That was when I recalled what Dad had said to you when you asked where we put the naughty people. I'd told him he shouldn't joke about such things with you as you were only a lad, but I never thought you'd take it serious enough to do owt like this.

'I told your mam I'd go first as the steps were bad, and that's what I did, but she were right behind me and she saw clearly enough what I saw down below.

'That mucky bastard Stamp were all over you. He'd just about got you bollock naked. I knew straight off what were going on. I'd been there myself, except I was a couple of years older and a lot tougher and more streetwise than you. When he started his tricks on me, I belted him in the belly and I told him I were going to report him, and I would have done, only I weren't sure anyone would believe me. They'd already marked my card as a bit of a wild boy at school plus I'd been done for shoplifting by the cops. So I said nowt, but when they started talking about giving Dad the boot because of his back, I stood in front of Stamp and I let him know that the day Dad got his papers was the day he'd find himself *in* the papers. I'd been keeping an eye on him when I saw him getting interested in you, and I thought he'd got the message. But there's no changing them bastards!

'Now I were on him in a flash. He must have thought God
had hit him with a thunderbolt, and that were no more than he
deserved. The pair of you went tumbling down the steps.
His torch went flying but it were one of them rubber ones
and it didn't break. He was lying on his back, not moving.
You were just about out of it. Your mam gathered you up
and it was only then I reckon that it fully hit her what the
bastard had been at. She put you into my arms and told me
to take you up the steps.

'I said, "What about you missus?" but she didn't answer,
so I set off back up to the porch with you in my arms. Do
you not remember any of this, Tommy? Nay, I see you do.'

And he was right. I was remembering it now when Mam
brought me back to our living room by saying impatiently,
'Come on, Tommy. Cat got your tongue? I asked what you
and Young Clem found to talk about?'

'Oh, nothing much,' I said. 'I told him about Dad, and he
told me that Old Clem had passed on too, about ten years
back, heart, it was. And we chatted about the old days at
Cyprian's, that's all.'

'Well, I'm sorry to hear about Old Clem, though he was
a bit of a devil,' said Mam. 'Remember that time he had you
looking everywhere for his rubber spade? I gave him a piece
of my mind for that!'

A pity you hadn't been around to give him a piece of your
mind when he told me about the crypt, I thought. Maybe life
could have been very different for me. Maybe I'd be sitting by
my own fireside now with my own family around me. I thought
of Young Clem, moving house so he could be handier for his
grandchildren. He was clearly made of stronger stuff than me.
He dealt with the crises in life by looking them straight in the
face and getting on with the life not the crisis. He certainly
gave no indication he blamed Old Clem and his daft lie for
what happened to me in the crypt. It was just another Yorkshire
joke, like sending a kid to look for a rubber spade!

Any road, the way it turned out, it wasn't strictly speaking
a lie any more. Old Clem had told me that the crypt was where
they put the naughty people. And the crypt of St Cyprian's was
where Young Clem had buried Father Stamp's body.

It must have taken him a couple of hours or more to dig a grave in that hard-packed earth. I wonder how long the poor lass he'd sent off to the pub waited for him? Maybe she'd forgiven him, maybe she was even the one who'd become his wife. I should have asked.

But the question that bothered me was, just how naughty had Father Stamp really been? That he had problems was clear. That he'd been foolish enough to grope Young Clem I didn't doubt.

But it wasn't his fault that I'd flung myself almost naked into his arms. And it had been me who'd been desperate to cling on to him, at least to start with. For all I know his intention was simply to carry me out of the crypt and take me home. However it had looked to Young Clem and my mam, there'd been no time for him to actually *do* anything.

No, it wasn't a memory of childhood sexual abuse that had dictated the pattern of my life. It was quite another memory, one that I'd only been able to bear because I could pretend to myself that it might after all just be the product of a sick child's fevered imagination.

My half-hour listening to Young Clem had removed that fragile barrier forever.

I don't know how long Mam and me have before us living like this. Granny Longbottom lasted into her nineties so there could be a good few years yet.

There it is then. Night after night, month after month, year after year, I'm going to be sitting here in this room, still able to hear the click-click-clicking of her knitting no matter how loud the telly.

And every time I glance across at her to share a smile, I'm going to see her as I saw her from Clem's arms in the fitful light of the torch rolling around the crypt floor. I'm going to see her kneeling astride the recumbent body of Father Stamp with those same click-click-clicking needles raised high, one in either hand, before she drives them down with all the strength of a mother's love, a mother's hate, into his despairing, uncomprehending, and vainly pleading eyes.

GHOSTED
Peter Lovesey

Peter Lovesey began his crime-writing career with a series
featuring the Victorian detective Sergeant Cribb that was televised
with Alan Dobie in the lead role. His award-winning books include
The False Inspector Dew, a stand-alone mystery; more recently
he has focused principally on the Bath-based contemporary detective Peter Diamond. A prolific short story writer, he has published
five collections. Like Reginald Hill, he has received the CWA
Gold Dagger and the CWA Cartier Diamond Dagger.

This happened the year I won the Gold Heart for
Passionata, my romantic novel of the blighted love
between an Austrian composer and a troubled English
girl getting psychotherapy in Vienna. I have never had any
difficulty thinking up plots even though my own life has
been rather short of romantic experiences. You will understand that the award and the attention it brought me was a
high point, because up to then I had written forty-five books
in various genres that received no praise at all except a few
letters from readers. I hadn't even attended before one of the
romance writers' lunches at which the awards were presented.
I was a little light-headed by the end. I still believe it wasn't
the champagne that got to me and it wasn't the prize or the
cheque or shaking the hand of one of the royal family. It
was the envy in the eyes of all the other writers. Utterly
intoxicating.

Whatever the reason, I can't deny that my brain was in
such a whirl when I left the Café Royal that I couldn't think
which way to turn for Waterloo station. I believe I broke the
rule of a lifetime and took a taxi. Anyway, it was a relief
finally to find myself on the train to Guildford, an ordinary
middle-aged lady once again – ordinary except for the drop-
dead Armani gown under my padded overcoat. That little

number cost me more than the value of the prize cheque. Just to be sure my triumph had really happened I took out the presentation box containing the replica Gold Heart, closed my eyes and remembered the moment when everyone had stood and applauded.

'Is that it?' a voice interrupted my reverie.

I opened my eyes. The seat next to me had been taken by a man with cropped silver hair. He was in a pinstripe suit cut rather too sharply for my taste, but smart. He had a black shirt with a silver tie and he wore dark glasses that he probably called 'shades'.

'I beg your pardon,' I said.

'I said is that it? One day as a star and you shove off home with your gong and are never heard of again?'

I tried not to catch his eye, but I'd seen the glint of gold teeth when he spoke. I've never liked ostentation. Whoever he was, this person had caught me off guard. Quite how he knew so much I had no idea. I didn't care for his forwardness or the presumption behind his question. Besides, it was the coveted Gold Heart, not a gong. I decided to let him know his interest wasn't welcome. 'If you don't mind me saying so, it's none of your business.'

'Don't be like that, Dolly,' he said, giving me even more reason to object to him. My pen-name is Dolores and I insist that my friends call me that and nothing less. The man was bending his head towards me as if he didn't want the other passengers to overhear. It's unnerving at the best of times to be seated next to someone in a train who wants a conversation, but when they almost touch heads with you and call you Dolly, it's enough to make a lady reach for the emergency handle. He must have sensed what I was thinking because he tried to appease me. 'I was being friendly. You're right. It's none of my business.'

I gave a curt nod and looked away, out of the window.

Then he added, 'But it could be yours.'

I ignored him.

'Business I could put your way.'

'I don't wish to buy anything. Please leave me alone,' I said.

'I'm not selling anything. The business I mean is a runaway

best-seller. Think about it. What's this book called – *Passion* something?'

'*Passionata*.'

'It will sell a few hundred extra copies on the strength of this award. A thousand, if you're lucky, and how much does the author take? Chickenfeed. I'm talking worldwide sales running into millions.'

'Oh, yes?' I said with an ironic curl of the lip.

'You want to know more? Step into the limo that will be waiting at the end of your street at nine tomorrow morning. It's safe, I promise you, and it will change your life.'

I was about to ask how he knew where I lived, but he stood up, took a black fedora off the rack, held it in a kind of salute, winked, placed it on his head and moved away up the train.

I didn't enjoy the rest of my journey home. My thoughts were in ferment. *Worldwide sales running into millions?* Success on a scale such as that was undreamed of, even for the writer of the best romantic novel of the year. The man was obviously talking nonsense.

Who could he possibly have been? A literary agent? A publisher? A film tycoon? I couldn't imagine he was any of these.

I decided to forget about him and his limousine.

I think it was the anticlimax of returning to my cold suburban semi that made me reconsider. Some more of the paint on the front door had peeled off. There was a rate demand on the doormat along with the usual flyers advertising takeaways. Next door's TV was too loud again. At least it masked the maddening drip-drip of the leaky kitchen tap. I deserved better after writing all those books.

Perhaps the award had really changed my luck.

After a troubled night, I woke early, wondering if the man in the train had been a figment of my imagination. If the car materialised, I'd know he had been real. Generally I wear jeans and an old sweater around the house. Today I put on my grey suit and white blouse, just in case. I looked out of the window more than once. All I could see at the end of the street was the greengrocer's dirty white van.

At five to nine, I looked again and saw a gleaming black

Daimler. My heart pounded. I put on my shiny black shoes with the heels, tossed my red pashmina around my shoulders, and hurried in as dignified a fashion as possible to the end of the street. The chauffeur was a grey-haired man in a grey uniform. He saluted me in a friendly fashion and opened the car door.

'Where are we going?' I asked.

'I believe it's meant to be a surprise, ma'am.'

'You're not telling, then?'

'That would spoil it. Make yourself comfortable. If you don't want the TV, just press the power switch. There's a selection of magazines and papers.'

'Will it take long?'

'About an hour.'

London, I thought, and this was confirmed when we headed along the A3. I was too interested in where we were going to look at the in-car TV or the magazines. But once we had left the main road I lost track. Before the hour was up, we were into parts of West London I didn't know at all. Finally we stopped in front of a gate that was raised electronically, the entrance to a private estate called The Cedars with some wonderful old trees to justify the name. Even inside the estate there was a ten-minute drive past some huge redbrick mansions. I was beginning to feel intimidated.

Our destination proved to be a mock-Tudor mansion with a tiled forecourt big enough to take the Trooping of the Colour.

'Will you be driving me home after this?' I asked the chauffeur.

'It's all arranged, ma'am,' he said, touching his cap.

The front door opened before I started up the steps. A strikingly beautiful young woman greeted me by name, my pen-name, in full. She had a mass of red-gold hair in loose curls that looked almost natural. She was wearing a dark-green top, low-cut, and white designer jeans. Her face seemed familiar, but I couldn't recall meeting her. She was younger than any of the women I'd met at the awards lunch.

'I'm so chuffed you decided to come,' she said. 'Ash was dead sure he'd reeled you in, but he thinks he's God's gift and not everyone sees it.'

'Ash?' I said, not liking the idea that anyone had 'reeled me in'.

'My old man. The sweet-talking guy in the train.'

'He made it sound like a business proposition,' I said.

'Oh, it is, and we need you on board.'

She showed me through a red-carpeted hallway into a sitting room with several huge white leather sofas. A real log fire was blazing under a copper hood in the centre. A large dog with silky white hair was lying asleep nearby.

'Coffee, Dolores?'

'That would be nice,' I said to her. 'But you have the advantage of me.'

Her pretty face creased in mystification. 'Come again.'

'I don't know your name.'

She laughed. 'Most people do. I'm Raven. Excuse me.' She spoke into a mobile phone. 'It's coffee for three, and hot croissants.'

Even I, with my tendency to ignore the popular press, had heard of Raven. Model, singer, actress, TV celebrity, she made headlines in whatever she'd tried. 'I should have known,' I said, feeling my cheeks grow hot. 'I wasn't prepared. I was expecting someone from the publishing industry.'

'No problem,' she said. 'It's nice not to be recognised. People react to me in the dumbest ways. Did you tell anyone you were making this mystery trip?'

'No. I kept it to myself.'

'Great. You live alone – is that right?'

'Yes.'

'And you've written all those amazing romances?'

I glowed inwardly and responded with a modest, 'Some people seem to like them.'

'I've read every one, from *Love Unspoken* to *Passionata*,' Raven said with genuine admiration in her voice.

This came as a surprise. Her own life was high romance. She didn't need the sort of escapism my books offered. 'I'm flattered.'

'You're a star, a wonderful writer. You deserved that award. You ought to be a best-seller by now.'

I secretly agreed with her, but I'm not used to receiving praise and I found it difficult to take. 'I don't think I could handle fame. I'm rather a coward, actually. I sometimes get asked to give talks and I always turn them down.'

'Who looks after your PR?'

'No one.'

'You must have an agent.'

'I wouldn't want one. They take a slice of your income and I can't afford that.'

'So you do all the business stuff yourself?'

I nodded.

Raven seemed to approve. 'You're smart. If I could get shot of all my hangers-on, I would.'

At this moment a woman arrived with the coffee on a trolley.

'I wasn't talking about you, Annie,' Raven said. 'You're a treasure. We'll pour it ourselves.'

The woman gave a faint smile and left.

'How do you like your coffee, Dolores?'

'Black, please.'

'Same as me. Same as Ash. He's Ashley really, like that footballer.'

I don't follow football and I must have looked bemused, because Raven added, 'Or that guy in *Gone With The Wind*, but no one calls him that. He'll be with us any sec. His timing is always spot on. Ash is smart, or he wouldn't own a pad like this.'

Raven poured three coffees. The croissants were kept warm by a kind of cosy on the lower shelf of the trolley. Mine almost slipped off my plate at the sudden sound of husband Ashley's voice behind me.

'Sensible girl.'

I'm not used to being called a girl, but I was junior to him by at least ten years, so I suppose it was excusable. I got a better look at him than I had when he was seated beside me in the train. He was seventy if he was a day, as wrinkled as a Medjool date. Today he was in a combat jacket and trousers and expensive trainers.

He held out his hand and I felt his coarse skin against mine. The grip was strong. My hand felt numb after he'd squeezed it.

'Can't say I've read any of your stuff,' he said. 'I've never been much of a reader. She tells me you're the best at what you do.'

'She's too generous,' I said.

'How much do you make in an average year?'

This wasn't the kind of question I was used to answering. 'Enough to live on,' I said.

'Yeah, but how much?'

'A writer's income fluctuates,' I said, determined not to give a figure. 'I've earned a living at it for fifteen years.'

'What sort of living?' he asked. 'Don't get me wrong, Dolly, but a semi on the wrong side of Guildford ain't what I call living.'

Raven clicked her tongue. 'Ash, that isn't kind.'

He ignored her. His brown eyes fixed on me. 'You put in the hours. You do good work. You deserve better. I made my first million before I was twenty-three. It was dirty work nobody wanted, so I did it. Collecting scrap from house to house. Waste management. Landfill. I've covered every angle. Now I have the biggest fleet of refuse lorries in the country. Ash the Trash, they call me. Doesn't bother me. I'm proud of it. I've got houses in London, Bilbao, New York and San Francisco. I did skiing every year until my knees went. And I'm married to the bird half the men in the world are lusting over.'

'That's crude,' Raven said.

'It's a fact.' Now his eyes shifted to his young wife. 'And you're more than just a pretty face and a boob job. I rate you, sweetheart. You've got ideas in your head. Tell Dolly your story.' He turned to me again. 'This'll get you going.' He sat next to her on the sofa opposite mine. 'Come on, my lovely. Spill it out.'

'Well,' she said, 'I don't know what Dolores will think of it. She's a proper author.'

'She has to get ideas,' Ash said, 'and that's where you come in.'

'He never lets up,' Raven said, fluttering her false lashes at me. 'It needs a bit of work, but it goes like this. There's this little girl living in East Sheen.'

'We'll change that,' Ash said. 'Make it Richmond.'

'All right. Richmond. And when she gets to thirteen, she's

already got a figure and her mum puts her in for a beauty contest and she wins, but then one of the other girls points out that she's underage. You had to be at least sixteen under the rules, so I was disqualified.'

'She,' Ash corrected her. '*She* was disqualified.'

'She.'

'We're calling her Falcon,' Ash said.

'I was coming to that,' Raven said.

Ash turned to me. 'What do you think, Dolly? Is Falcon a good name?'

'Fine,' I said, not wishing to fuel the obvious tension between husband and wife.

'OK,' Raven said. 'So this girl – Falcon – has to wait until she's older, but she learns all she can about beauty and make-up and fashion and then she enters for another contest even though she's still only fifteen.'

'And she won a modelling contract,' Ash said.

'You're spoiling it,' Raven said.

'That's what happened.'

'Yes, but I'm telling it. I was building up to the modelling. You don't come straight out with the best bit of the story, do you, Dolores?'

'Suspense is a useful device, yes,' I said.

'See?' she said to Ash. 'Now shut it.'

'Before you go on,' I said to Raven. 'I'm not entirely sure why you're telling me all this.' In truth, I had a strong suspicion. 'If it's your life story and you want to get it published, surely you should write it.'

'It's not supposed to be about me. Well, it is really, but it's a romance. I'm leaving out the stuff I don't want people to know.'

'And beefing up the good bits,' Ash said.

'In that case it's autobiography dressed up as fiction. I still think you should write it yourself.'

'She can't write,' Ash said.

'He means I'm not a writer,' Raven said. 'I can spell and stuff.'

'Which is where you come in,' Ash said to me.

'We want you to do the writing,' Raven said. 'Give it a makeover, if you know what I mean.'

'We're not daft,' Ash said. 'Her fans will know it's her life story and buy a million copies.'

'But if it isn't in Raven's own style, no one will believe she wrote it.'

'So you rough it up a bit,' Ash said to me. 'Knock out the long words. Give it plenty of passion. You're good at that, I was told. All the celebs hire someone to do the writing. It's called ghosting.'

'I know what it's called,' I said. 'I'm sorry to disappoint you, but I'm not a ghostwriter. I write original fiction. I've never attempted anything like this. I wouldn't know how to start.'

'It's all on tape,' Ash said. 'You write it down, juice it up a bit and with her name on the cover we've got a best-seller.'

'I'm sorry,' I said. 'I can't do it.'

'Hold on. You haven't heard the deal,' Ash said. 'You walk out of here today with ten grand in fifty-pound notes. Another ninety grand on delivery, all in cash. No tax. How does that strike you?'

The figure was huge, far more than I earned usually. But what would a ghosted book do to the reputation I'd built with my forty-six novels?

Ash gave me instant reassurance. 'You won't take any flak for writing it. We're keeping you out of it. As far as Joe Public is concerned, Raven wrote every word herself. That's why it will be a best-seller. She's got fans all over the world and she'll get more when the book hits the shelves. They want the inside story of the nude modelling, the catwalks, the reality shows, the pop concerts, all the stars she's met—'

'And how I met you,' Raven said to him. 'They want to know what I see in a man forty-two years older than me.'

'True love, innit?' Ash said in all seriousness. 'I'm nuts about you. That's why I'm funding this bloody book.'

She kissed his cheek and ruffled his silver hair. 'My hero.'

All this was bizarre. I was actually thinking what I could do with a hundred thousand pounds. The task of writing Raven's life story might not be creatively fulfilling, but it was within my capability, especially if she had recorded it in her own words. 'Just now you said it's on tape.'

'God knows how many cassettes,' Ash said. 'Hours and hours. She's left nothing out.'

This disposed of one concern. Any writer prefers condensing a script to padding it.

'You take them home today, all of them,' Ash said.

'I'm not saying I'll do it.'

'What's the problem, Dolly? You've got the job.'

'But we haven't even talked about a contract.'

'There isn't one,' Ash said. 'There's only one thing you have to promise, apart from doing the book, and that's to keep your mouth shut. Like I said, we're passing this off as Raven's book. If anyone asks, there wasn't no ghost. She done the whole thing herself. I wasn't born yesterday and neither was you. We're paying well over the odds and buying your silence.'

'How soon do you expect this book to be written?'

'How long do you need? Six months?'

This seemed reasonable if it was all on tape already. I wouldn't wish to spend more than six months away from my real writing. Heaven help me, I was almost persuaded. 'And if I needed to meet Raven again to clarify anything, is that allowed for?'

'Sorry. Can't be done,' Raven said. 'I'm doing reality TV in Australia for the next few months and no one can reach me, not even Ash.'

'So you want the book written just from these tapes, without any more consultation?'

'It's the best way,' Ash said. 'Raven is so big that it's sure to leak out if you keep on meeting her. You won't be short of material. There's loads of stuff on the internet.'

'What happens if you aren't happy with my script?'

Raven answered that one. 'It won't happen. That's why I chose you.' She fixed her big blue eyes on me. Her confidence in me was total.

I warmed to her.

'But I'm sure to get some details wrong. Anyone would, working like this.'

'She'll straighten it out when it comes in,' Ash said. 'Let's agree a date.'

*   *   *

I must be honest. I'd been persuaded by the money. At home over the next six months I set about my task. The tapes were my source material. Raven had dictated more than enough for a substantial book, but she had a tendency to repeat herself. With skilful editing I could give it some shape. Such incidents as there were had little of the drama I put into my own books. I would have to rely on the reader identifying with 'Falcon' and her steady rise to fame and fortune.

The first objective was to find a narrative voice closer to Raven's than my own. I rewrote chapter one several times. The process was far more demanding than Ash had predicted. 'Knock out the long words,' he'd said, as if nothing else needed to be done. Eventually, through tuning my ear to Raven's speech rhythms, I found a way of telling it that satisfied me.

The absence of a strong plot was harder to get over. Her story was depressingly predictable. A romantic novel needs conflict, some trials and setbacks, before love triumphs. I had to make the most of every vestige of disappointment, and the disqualification from the beauty contest was about all she had provided. In the end I invented a car crash, a stalker and a death in the family just to 'beef it up', as Ash had suggested.

The biggest problem of all lay waiting like a storm cloud on the horizon while I worked through the early chapters: what to do about Ash. How could I make a romantic ending out of a relationship with an elderly scrap dealer, however rich he was? If I took thirty years off his age he'd probably be insulted. If I changed his job and made him a brain surgeon or a racing driver, he'd want to know why. He was justly proud of becoming a legend in refuse collection, but it wasn't the stuff of romantic fiction.

And I have to admit that he frightened me.

Deliberately I put off writing about him until the last possible opportunity. By then I had shaped and polished the rest of the book into a form I thought acceptable, though far from brilliant. Ash was the last big challenge.

In desperation I researched him on the Internet. Being so successful, he was sure to have been interviewed by the press. Perhaps I would find some helpful insights into his personality.

I was in for a shock.

In 1992 Ash had been put on trial for murder and acquitted. His first wife, a young actress, had gone missing after having an affair with the director of a play she was in. Her family suspected Ash had killed her, but her body had never been found. The word 'landfill' was bandied about among her anxious friends. Before she disappeared, she had written letters to her lover telling of mental and physical cruelty. A prosecution had been brought. Ash had walked free thanks to a brilliant defence team.

All of this would have greatly assisted the plot of the book. Of course, I dared not use it. I felt sure Ash didn't want his dirty washing aired in Raven's romantic novel. Nor was I certain how much Raven knew about it.

After reading several interviews online, I concluded that Ash was a dangerous man. He had defended his empire of landfill and dustcarts against a number of well-known barons of the underworld who had threatened to take over. 'You don't mess with Ash,' was one memorable quote.

For the book, I called him Aspen, made him a grieving widower of forty-nine, called his business recycling, gave him green credentials and charitable instincts. He fell in love with Falcon after meeting her at a fund-raising concert and they emigrated to East Africa and started an orphanage there. The book was finished with a week to spare. I was satisfied that it would pass as Raven's unaided work and please her readers.

At nine on the agreed day in March, I walked to the end of my street with a large bag containing the manuscript and Raven's tapes and stepped into the Daimler. Even after so many years of getting published I always feel nervous about submitting a script and this was magnified at least tenfold by the circumstances of this submission.

As before, the front door of the mansion was opened by Raven herself, and she looked tanned and gorgeous after her television show in Australia. 'Is that it?' she asked, pointing to my bag, echoing the words Ash had used when we first met in the train.

I handed over the manuscript.

'I can't tell you how much I've been waiting to read this,' she said, eyes shining.

I warned her that I'd made a number of changes to give it dramatic tension.

'Don't worry, Dolores,' she said. 'You're the professional here. I'm sure whatever you've done is right for the book. Coffee is on its way and so is Ash. I'm going to make sure he reads the book, too. I don't think he's read a novel in the whole of his life.'

'I wouldn't insist, if I were you,' I said quickly. 'It's not written for male readers.'

'But it's my life story and he's the hero.'

'I took some liberties,' I said. 'He may not recognise himself.'

'What's that?' Ash had come into the room behind me, pushing the coffee trolley. 'You talking about me?'

'Good morning,' I said, frantically trying to think how to put this. 'I was explaining that for the sake of the book I had you two meeting at an earlier point in life.'

'So?'

'So you're a younger man in the story,' Raven put it more plainly than I had dared.

He frowned. 'Are you saying I'm too old?'

'No way,' she said. 'I've always told you I like a man who's been around a bit.'

'So long as he's got something in the bank. Speaking of which,' he said, turning to me, 'we owe you ninety grand.'

'That was what we agreed,' I was bold enough to say.

His eyes slid sideways and then downwards. 'Will tomorrow do? The bloody bank wanted an extra day's notice. They're not used to large cash withdrawals.'

'But you promised to pay me when I delivered the manuscript,' I said.

He poured the coffee. 'I'll make sure it's delivered to you.'

'A cheque would be simpler.'

He shook his head. 'Cheques can be traced back. Like I told you before, this has to be a secret deal.'

I have to say I was suspicious. It had been in my mind that Ash could easily welsh on the agreement. True, I'd been paid ten thousand pounds already, but I wanted my full entitlement.

As if he was reading my mind, Ash said to Raven, 'Is the message from the bank still on the answerphone? I'd like Dolly to hear it, just to show good faith.'

'What message?' she said.

He got up and crossed the room to the phone by the window. 'The message from the bank saying they wouldn't supply the cash today.' He pressed the playback button.

Nothing was played back.

He swore. 'Must have deleted it myself. Well,' he said, turning back, 'you'll have to trust me, won't you?'

'But I don't even have the address of this house, or a phone number, or anything.'

'Better you don't.'

'But you know where I live.'

'Right, and so does my driver. He'll deliver the money tomorrow afternoon.'

At that moment I acted like a feeble female outgunned by an alpha male. I left soon after, without any confidence that I would ever receive the rest of the payment.

Three days later I read in the paper that Ashley Parker, the landfill tycoon and husband of Raven, was dead. He had apparently overdosed on sleeping pills and lapsed into a coma from which he never emerged. He was aged seventy-two.

Raven inherited his forty-million-pound estate, and went on record as saying that she would gladly pay twice that amount to get her husband back.

The inquest into Ash's death made interesting reading. There was some gossip in the papers that Raven had over-played the grieving widow to allay suspicion that she had somehow administered the overdose. This was never raised at the inquest. There, she melted the hearts of the coroner and the jury. She said Ashley had always been a poor sleeper and relied on a cocktail of medication that 'would have knocked out most men'. He had been happy to the last, a man with a clear conscience.

A clear conscience indeed. I never did receive the second payment for my work on the book. In fact, I have never heard from Raven since. However, she had enough sense not to publish. I believe she worked out the truth of what happened that morning I visited the house.

You see, when Ash told me I wouldn't get paid that day, I became suspicious. I'd delivered the book and they had no further use for me, but I remained a risk to Ash's scheme. While I was alive I could pop up any time and earn a fat fee from the papers by revealing that I had ghosted the masterpiece supposedly written by Raven. I had become disposable, ready for the landfill. Easier still, I might succumb to an overdose and no one would ever know how it happened, or connect me with Raven and Ash. I'd heard of doctored drinks known as Mickey Finns, and I could believe that some slow-acting drug might sedate me until I got home and finally kill me. And that was why after the coffee was poured I took the sensible precaution of switching my cup with Ash's. The opportunity came when he acted out his little charade with the answerphone.

What neither of them knew is that as well as romantic novels I write whodunnits.

THE LAST PURSUIT
Rick Mofina

Rick Mofina was born in Ontario, and currently lives in Ottawa, but *If Angels Fall*, his first novel, was set in San Francisco, and had a crime reporter, Tom Reed, sharing the lead role with a cop called Walt Sydowski. Jason Wade, again a crime reporter, featured in a later series, while Mofina diversified into global thrillers with *Six Seconds*, which became an international best-seller.

Chains clinked in the maximum security unit of Saskatchewan Penitentiary as six men approached a cell segregated from the rest of the population.

Inside on his cot, inmate Robert Lazarus Yacine, turned his attention from his worn paperback copy of Nietzsche's *Beyond Good and Evil* to consider the men who had arrived outside his door.

'Time to go,' Powers, the deputy warden, said.

Yacine stood and slid his hands through the portal. Cold steel snapped around his wrists.

'Step back, please,' Farrell, the youngest guard, said.

Keys jangled and Yacine's cell door opened. He cooperated as a waist chain and leg irons were applied. Taking stock of the men, he knew Powers and Farrell but not the strangers. One passed him a pen and held a clipboard thick with forms before him.

'Your signature is required by the Xs.' The stranger flipped crisp pages of official documents for Yacine.

Letterheads flashed by: the US State Department, FBI, US Marshals, Royal Canadian Mounted Police and several other agencies.

It was awkward to sign; Yacine's chains knocked against the clipboard. Chewing gum snapped as one of the men eyed him: six feet two inches, two hundred bench-pressed pounds, laced with tattoos, all packaged in prison-issued green coveralls and sneakers.

The strangers wore jeans, khakis, polo shirts and windbreakers. They were all business assessing him amid the clang of steel doors.

From Yacine's scan of names on the documents he figured that two were RCMP Corporals, John Garrett and Terry Cox, and the other two were Deputy US Marshals, Arlo Phife and Moss Johnston.

'Washington DOC will give you toiletries and the like, when they process you at intake,' Powers said after witnessing Yacine's signature.

'May I bring my book?'

'Personal or library property?'

'Personal.'

One of the strangers examined it, concluding that it was harmless. Powers threw Yacine's request to the four strangers. It bounced among them until one of them nodded; an indication of who was in charge. The one who'd nodded had dark, distant eyes, the aura of a haunted man.

Dark Eyes.

They escorted him to the rear of the prison where a CSC van and two marked Chev Impalas from the RCMP's Prince Albert Detachment, waited. The gum snapper faced Yacine and never removed his eyes from him.

'Tell me –' the gum-snapper leaned forward – 'when you shared a cell with the big Russian, were you his bitch?'

One of the others turned away, smiling covertly.

Yacine stared at the gum-snapper, his chains tingling softly as he rotated his book without speaking.

RCMP Corporal John Garrett, the one Yacine tagged Dark Eyes, was not part of the taunt. Garrett didn't go for that crap and looked out the window as they passed through the gate. Funny, Garrett thought, while he was free to leave the prison, he'd never escape the one he'd built for himself.

'Billy, wake up! Daisy, wake up!'

Saskatchewan Penitentiary sat at the edge of Prince Albert, a city of some fifty thousand people, in the near middle of Saskatchewan, a province big enough to swallow some European countries. It marked the passage between the vast prairie and the northern boreal forest leading to the Northwest Territories and the Arctic.

Twenty minutes after exiting, they'd reached the small airport east of town. The vehicles halted near a twin-engine turbo prop. Once all the men boarded, the two RCMP pilots started the engines and the plane roared down the runway and lifted off on its secret flight.

The ground dropped, the wheels came up with a hydraulic moan. Vast stretches of land flowed below like an eternal patchwork quilt. Yacine peered out the window. One of the men sat behind him, one beside him, while Garrett and the gum-snapper faced him. None of Yacine's escorts carried firearms.

It didn't take long to reach cruising altitude where Yacine passed his time reading. Garrett studied Yacine's file.

Robert Lazarus Yacine, FPS Number 050300D. NCIC Number: M-51428683J. A US citizen of Algerian descent, born in Ashland, Kentucky; ex-military, Special-Ops in Iraq, ex-mercenary in Africa, was serving time in Saskatchewan after shooting two armored car guards in a botched heist at Montreal-Mirabel International Airport about a year ago.

The guards survived.

Yacine had good lawyers and got ten years.

But six months before the armored car hit in Canada, twelve people were shot, nine of them died, during a four-million-dollar bank robbery in Seattle. The masked suspects used AKs and tear gas in the commando-style attack.

A shoe impression from a suspect, who'd stepped on a freshly mopped section of floor in the Seattle case, matched an impression collected five months earlier in a robbery-homicide of a restaurant in Washington DC.

In that case seven people were wounded, three died, one of them a CIA operative who oversaw the capture of key terror suspects, a fact that was never released.

Behind the scenes, the CIA and FBI suspected the DC homicides were a cover for the CIA agent's assassination; and that the Seattle heist was a fund-raising operation. No arrests had been made and it looked like the Seattle and DC incidents would become cold cases.

But in the Seattle homicides, evidence emerged from an

eyewitness who'd glimpsed a unique spider tattoo, peeking from the gloved hand of the principal shooter. Seattle detectives obtained a detailed sketch and working with the FBI, checked it with tattoo artists, tattoo databases, jails and prisons across the US.

All efforts dead ended. As time passed, the tattoo aspect was also pursued by police in Canada and Europe. Last month, it yielded a match in Saskatchewan.

The witness's sketch of a spider in flames on a web of lightning was identical to the spider Garrett now saw writhing on the back of Yacine's right hand, as he turned the pages of his book.

Garrett went back to the file.

Upon discovering Yacine in a Canadian prison, the investigation kicked into overdrive as US, federal and state attorneys prepared charges in the Seattle case.

Of paramount importance, they needed the witness to physically identify Yacine as the owner of the unique tattoo, to put him in the bank pulling the trigger.

It was the foundation of their case.

It took weeks of high-level legal wrangling in Canada and the US before an agreement was reached to share files and secretly fly Yacine to Seattle where the witness could identify him. But there was a problem. The witness's health was deteriorating. He was near death.

Without the identification the case would collapse. Moreover, Yacine had an appeal going on his Canadian conviction. He'd been succeeding at every stage and could win his freedom within months.

Then he'd vanish.

Garrett closed the file folder. As time ticked by, the drone of the plane's engines lulled Yacine to sleep.

Garrett could not rest. Too much was riding on this assignment. He turned to the window, struggling to understand why in recent weeks, his failings loomed as large as the clouds out there. No matter how hard he tried, he could never bury the images of the night his life changed.

He'd just made corporal after six years on the job in Alberta. He was working nights, alone, when the call came from

Trudy Dolan at Plumtree Ranch, near Medicine Hat. Hubby Keith's been drinking; says he won't let Trudy leave with the kids. Keith's facing debts, they're losing the ranch.

He's suicidal. He's got a rifle.

Garrett, the senior member, was posted to a small detachment. One of his constables was sick and it was Garrett's seventh straight night shift. He was exhausted and considered alerting an off-duty member for backup but dismissed it.

That was his first mistake.

The complaint history of the Dolan place showed two previous calls in the last six months. In the first, Keith Dolan had been drunk, and had shouted threats before passing out. Trudy cancelled the call. They'd checked on her welfare. Her eyes, red-rimmed; she said all was fine, Keith was venting.

It was the same with the second call.

This time, as Garrett approached the house, his strategy was to try to talk Keith down.

That was his second mistake.

Garrett arrived alone to an ominous scene. Keith's idling pickup was T-boned behind Trudy's Toyota. No one was in sight. Garrett got out and inspected the dent in the Toyota's left rear quarter. It was fresh, as was the fractured glass on the driver's side window.

Keith must've stopped Trudy from fleeing.

The first bullet whizzed by Garrett's ear before he heard the shot. The second bullet hit his mid-section like a sledge-hammer – they told him later his vest saved him. Garrett was exposed without cover as the third shot nicked his thigh before he drew his Smith & Wesson semi-automatic 9-mil and returned fire at Keith who'd stood in his porch aiming to shoot again.

Garrett got off several rounds and Keith went down. Adrenaline pumping, gun drawn, he approached Keith, spreadeagled on his side porch, in filthy unlaced work boots, jeans, grease-stained T-shirt and a frayed John Deere cap. Garrett neared his corpse, puzzled by the heap of colors under him, trying to determine what it might be, then – Oh Jesus oh Christ! – he saw a tiny hand and the awful truth screamed with such velocity he vomited.

*Billy Dolan, aged five, his sister, Daisy, aged four, were
also killed by Garrett's rounds.*

*Garrett never saw them standing behind their father,
blocked by the porch wall. Never saw them until now. Tiny
eyes, frozen open, stared at the stars in the vast prairie sky.
Their little bodies shook slightly, from the tugging by their
three-year-old sister, Lori.*

'Billy, wake up! Daisy, wake up!'

*Garrett fell to his knees, his body shaking as he reached
for his radio.*

It happened in a heartbeat.

Trudy Dolan was already dead in the bedroom. Keith had
shot her and was midway through his suicide note on the
back of the foreclosure letter when Garrett had arrived.
Keith's note stated he would not harm Billy, Daisy and Lori,
whom he wanted his sister to raise.

All the investigations, the inquiries, and analysis pointed
to a justified shooting; calling it a tragic act of self-defense.
Garrett was cleared.

Absolved.

But not from the guilt he would bear for the rest of his
life.

He drank to drown the nightmares. In the worst ones, the
Dolan children stood at the foot of his bed.

A few months after the shootings, Garrett faced another
tragedy. His wife Cathy miscarried with their first child and
Garrett searched for a reason to keep living. He quit drinking
and took up long-distance running, isolating himself for mile
after mile into the night.

Would he ever escape his guilt?

Ultimately, Cathy divorced him.

'You have to forgive yourself, John.'

They never had children. Cathy was a teacher and married
a school principal. They had two daughters. Sometimes
Garrett called her, just to talk. She always listened.

Cathy was the only one who understood.

Most nights, when Garrett thought of her, happy with her
beautiful daughters, he felt like a ghost haunting the life he

should've had; the one that died that night near Medicine Hat. With counselling and time, Garrett returned to work, but could never touch a gun again.

A sympathetic superintendent assigned him to escort duty and he lived a solitary life, tormented by second guesses and an aching to do one thing – anything – that would redeem him.

A few hours later, they landed in Montana.

Garrett and the marshals talked to US Customs and Border Protection, showing them documents for signing to clear entry.

Yacine was allowed to use the plane's cramped lavatory with the door open and one of the men watching him. The others returned to the plane with sandwiches wrapped in plastic, chips and drinks.

The pilots started the engines and the plane ascended the Bitteroot Range for the final leg of the trip.

Before departure, the pilot, RCMP Corporal Eric Banner and co-pilot, RCMP Corporal Ken Leclair, had checked the aviation forecast for any advisories for Idaho and Washington. Weather over mountains often changed without warning.

Conditions were good until the sky clouded over eastern Washington. Rain streaked the windshield.

They received an updated advisory. A new disturbance was riding over the Yakima Ridge towards the Wenatchee Mountains with thunderstorms, wind gusts and lightning.

'Let's take things a bit north. Climb over it,' Banner said. 'Advise the centers we're steering clear of the mess.'

The rain came down harder. As the plane banked, the pilots looked through the cloud breaks over the North Cascades, reaching up majestically nearly ten thousand feet. They saw a range of broiling storm clouds pierced by lightning over Sawtooth Ridge.

'I've never seen anything move so fast.' Leclair cursed under his breath as the plane bounced in rough air.

Banner scanned the port side, massive walls of churning black clouds were closing in on them from all points.

'Let's put her down,' Leclair said.

Banner agreed and switched on the cabin intercom to advise his passengers.

'We've got weather with an attitude so we're going to land and sit things out. Be sure you're buckled up back there. It could get bumpy.'

The plane heaved throwing Leclair's head against the console. Blood webbed down his temple.

'You OK, Ken?'

'I'm OK but I can't believe this.'

Banner requested Seattle Air Center get them to the nearest strip as the plane jolted with a deafening bang.

'Fire in the starboard engine!' Leclair said.

The plane began yawing. The stricken engine flamed out. Alarms sounded. Instrument needles freewheeled. The pilots struggled with the controls taking the plane into a rapid descent as the starboard wing ignited.

'We're losing it!'

The plane was vibrating and increasing speed as it plummeted. The men in the cabin began shouting. One had reached for his cell phone and was attempting to call his family. The gum-snapper's knuckles whitened as he gripped the armrests. Yacine glimpsed slopes and forests rushing towards them and embraced death.

Garrett's heart filled with regret.

Was this the way he was going to die? Falling from the sky without making things right.

Blinding wind-driven rain pounded the plane. It nosed downwards, increasing in speed. Cockpit alarms bleated. Banner strained to pull the plane out of its dive as the surviving engine screamed. The nose was lifting, little by little. Leclair released a cheer.

Relief was emerging on Banner's face in the instant before they slammed into a mountainside.

The first 911 call went to the IceCom Dispatch Center in Jade Falls, Washington. It came on a sat phone from a local mountain guide.

'It was a small plane!'

'Can you give me an approximate location?'

'Across the lake from us, near Ghost Ridge, but we can't get to it!'

The dispatcher's keyboard clicked as she burned through

her agency alert list to activate the region's search and rescue operation.

Miles away, at the crash site, Robert Lazarus Yacine, was cold and wet.

He blinked at daylight and the small fires licking everywhere in the soft rain. Aside from cuts and bruises, Yacine was unhurt. The plane was in pieces at the edge of a forest. While Yacine remained cuffed and shackled, the crash had freed him from his seat, which had broken from the floor. He undid his seat belt, stumbled through the wreckage, chains chinking as he counted the dead.

The nearest body was missing its head.

It was the man who'd sat behind him: RCMP Corporal Terry Cox, according to the ID Yacine fished from his pocket. No handcuff keys. The man who'd sat beside Yacine, Deputy US Marshal Moss Johnston, had no pulse or handcuff keys, but he did have a lot of cash.

Both pilots were impaled in the trees.

That's four dead, two to go.

What about Dark Eyes?

Yacine scanned the wreckage, glimpsing a hand under the twisted metal of a wing. Dark Eyes had a bloodied face. Yacine felt for a pulse, not sure he had one, then moaning sounded nearby.

Yacine left Dark Eyes.

The gum-snapper, his taunter, was near the tail. A long strip of metal fuselage was embedded in his legs, slicing deep into both above the knee in a near-amputation. A brilliant blood pool was growing under him.

'Help me,' he pleaded. 'Please.'

Chains jingled as Yacine probed his pockets, finding the ID of Marshal Arlo Phife. Yacine grinned when he found handcuff keys in Phife's pants and freed himself. Then he opened the luggage of his escorts and changed from his prison greens into jeans, a buttondown shirt and a leather jacket. He returned to Phife and took his boots, lacing them on to his feet. Snug, but they'd do for this terrain.

'Help me, please,' Phife pleaded.

'Hang on there, partner.'

'Thank you . . .'

Yacine took Phife's head in his hands, gritted his teeth and twisted hard, watching Phife's eyes balloon as vertebrae snapped.

All of them were dead now.

Yacine found binoculars in the cockpit. He climbed to the highest point and scanned an eternity of forests and mountains until he spotted a road and a town, miles off. He started in that direction.

At that moment, some seven to ten miles south of the crash site, in a small double-wide perched on a hill crowned by ponderosa pine on the shore of Ice Lake, Nancy Dawson answered her phone.

'It's Eileen,' her daughter-in-law's voice broke. 'I'm at the hospital with Craig.'

'The hospital, but he looked so well on Sunday?'

'He was good, but he woke up in the night, in pain, so we brought him here to Harborview. Then he got worse. They said to call you now because Craig doesn't have much time. They've moved him up the national list but they don't think he's going to make it.'

Nancy's hand flew to her mouth. Craig, her only child, the father of her grandchildren, had severe chronic kidney disease.

'I'm on my way. Eileen? Can you hear me?'

'Yes.'

'You tell Craig I'm coming now!'

Garrett floated to consciousness in the rain-misted gloom, recalling the earth rushing up to hammer the plane.

Now, as he lay in the wreckage, he could not sense his right leg, pinned under a wing. He shifted to see below his hip. His legs didn't look bad. His brain flashed with images of someone helping.

Where did they go?

'Everybody OK?' Garrett called, extracting himself from the debris. No one answered and no one aided him as he stood massaging his leg until circulation returned.

He was sore but could move. Brushing blood and dirt from

his eyes he took careful stock of the aftermath. As he checked on the others, the toll emerged: Cox, Leclair, Banner, Phife and Johnston.

They were all dead.

Garrett pulsated with shock.

Steadying himself against a tree – where's his prisoner? – Garrett seized on the metallic glint of cuffs, chains, leg irons and tracks in damp earth, leading into the forest, until it became clear.

Yacine had escaped.

Reaching deep inside, clawing for whatever he had left, Garrett did what he was trained to do.

He pursued his prisoner.

For Yacine, the mountain air was as sweet as freedom. Moving fast over the rugged high country, he embraced the needled branches against his skin.

Anything was better than his cage in Saskatchewan.

But he had to stop. Disciplined bodybuilding did not make him a long-distance runner.

He doubled over. His sources on the outside had tipped him to what the US justice system had planned for him in Seattle, with their special witness.

Yacine laughed at his luck.

In just a few days, there would be nothing connecting him to any of his contract work in Seattle, DC, London, Madrid, or anywhere else.

They thought they had this old boy nailed.

They thought wrong.

Yacine caught his breath at a clearing that offered a sweeping view. He scanned it, calculating that all he needed was to get to that road, get into a vehicle, and he was gone.

He saw patches of highway beyond the next ridge.

He was almost there.

Nancy Dawson set her suitcase in her SUV, closed the door and got behind the wheel. She went through a mental check-list as she rolled along Timber Road to the highway and Seattle where her son was dying.

No he's not! Don't say that. Focus on the checklist.

She'd already taken Tipper to AJ's kennel, locked the house, and asked Leo, her neighbor, a retired firefighter, to watch over her place.

'I'll say a prayer for Craig, Nance.'

On the highway, she saw that she needed gas and wheeled into Grizzly's. As she filled her tank, she looked up at a helicopter thumping by, wishing she could use it to fly to Seattle.

Garrett drew on all he'd learned from survival and tracking courses he'd taken near Yellowknife. He pushed himself, came to a clearing and studied the view, fixing on slivers of a highway in the distance. A few hundred yards off, he noticed a tiny burst of black near the sway of bush.

A bear?

Garrett locked on to the spot and saw another streak of black then a tiny flash of pale white. *A face. That's him.*

Garrett was close.

For Nancy Dawson, Seattle was some three hours away.

As her SUV threaded through the mountains, she bargained with God.

'Please don't take him. Eileen and the kids need him. I need him.'

Hadn't Nancy's small family endured their share of hardship?

Chet, her husband, was killed ten years ago while changing a flat on his pickup near Coulee City. A Freightliner hauling logs hit a deer and lost its load. Chet never had a chance.

Craig took it so hard.

Then five years ago, nine people were shot dead during a robbery of the Seattle bank where Craig was a junior manager. He saw the whole thing. They never caught the killers.

For over a year afterwards, Craig struggled with the post-traumatic stress and during that time he was diagnosed with chronic kidney disease. Gradually, the severity of the disease increased and now it was reaching the final stage.

Then, just last month, the FBI said they needed to show Craig some sort of new evidence.

Lord, wasn't he under enough strain?

Nancy continued reasoning with God.

'If you have to take my son, please keep him alive long enough for me to get to his side; to tell him how much I love him. To say goodbye.'

Nancy was a brave woman but her fears were crushing. She broke down as she approached a two-mile stretch that curved around dense bush.

Stepping from the forest, Yacine exhaled and walked to the edge of the highway.

Bending over, breathing hard, he shook his head. Nearly home free. Gasping, Yacine kept his eyes on the lonely road and waited for a vehicle, ready to hitch a ride.

He'd be long gone before anybody got to the wreck. He'd get to LA where he had support; cash, passports and contacts. He'd fly to Frankfurt, then Lisbon, then Algiers and back to work.

He had to be the luckiest sonofa—

Crack!

Stars exploded and Yacine thought a rock had fallen on him just as he recognized Dark Eyes, whose swing of a club-sized tree branch had landed on Yacine's jaw.

Garrett took the murderer to the ground, manhandling him to his stomach, driving his knee into the back of his lower neck, drilling his face into the pavement, reaching for plastic handcuffs in his jacket, turning to the flash of a massive grill.

Tears blurred Nancy Dawson's vision when her SUV, traveling at seventy-one miles an hour, came upon Garrett and Yacine.

Before Nancy could react, before her brain issued the command to take her foot from the gas to the brake, before her mouth opened and her hands spasmed on the wheel, Nancy felt the heart-sickening thud.

Something – a man? – streaked over her windshield as something grazed under her!

Nancy shrieked, her stomach clenched, ice shot up her spine, her skin tingled.

She stopped the SUV but it was too late.

Rooted in shock, her memory of what followed came in rapid, staccato bursts. Two men, twenty–thirty yards apart bleeding on the road; other cars stopping, concerned faces, cell phone calls, blankets; the wail of sirens, ambulances, sheriff's deputies, Washington State Patrol.

Garrett was on his back, alive, but frozen in moments scored by sirens and emergency radios.

A distraught older woman was sobbing near a police car. 'I'm so sorry I didn't see them! What were they doing on the road? I have to see my son in Seattle. I have to go! Please I'm so sorry!'

Garrett felt nothing, saw faces, paramedics tending to him, getting a board under him, lifting him to a gurney.

'Sir, your friend is going to be fine. He went under the car, just some scrapes. But we want to get you to a hospital fast.'

Garrett searched hovering faces, saw the Stetson of a trooper or deputy and grabbed her wrist hard. She had a kind face, smooth skin. Warm. His eyes bore into hers for a connection. He squeezed harder and she met him in the moment.

Garrett heard words – it could've been him – but someone said, 'I am RCMP Corporal Garrett.' And recited his regimental number. Paramedics tried to quiet him but the trooper was making notes, her thumb holding Garrett's badge and ID to her pad as she wrote.

The words continued.

'We were on a plane . . . prisoner to Seattle . . . crashed . . . prisoner escaped that's him . . . Yacine . . . dangerous . . . custody . . . FBI Seattle.'

Garrett repeated his regimental number.

Again, the paramedics tried to quieten him. The trooper's eyes were green, intelligent. Absorbing his words, she reached for her radio.

Garrett lost consciousness during the ambulance trip to the county hospital. When he came to a woman in a white coat was with him. Now she had his wallet; was studying it and flipping pages on a clipboard.

'John, you're in Ice Lake Memorial Hospital. I'm Dr Niki Burton. Nod if you understand.'

Garrett nodded and Dr Burton moved her clipboard closer. His ID, driving license, medical card, business card and a card with numbers he'd penned on the back: records of his life.

'You're hurt too badly for us to fix everything here. We're going to airlift you to Seattle, is there someone back home we should call?'

Garrett touched his detachment number and the card with his ex-wife's numbers. Then he brushed his license and medical card until the doctor understood, then she glanced to someone; a nurse, holding another clipboard, who nodded and left.

The air pounded. The helicopter had arrived.

As they wheeled Garrett out, he glimpsed Yacine, on a gurney in the hall, complaining about tight handcuffs on his wrist and ankles to the half-dozen deputies and troopers guarding him.

One of them looked back at Garrett with a sudden glance that telegraphed a mix of respect and sadness.

The helicopter landed on the front lawn and a medical crew wearing helmets and headsets loaded Garrett through the clam-shell door.

Inside the hospital, Dr Niki Burton was in the quiet of her office, studying a computer screen displaying Garrett's vital information, accessed with the help of officials in Canada. Then she called a twenty-four hour hotline for a national organ donor network, discussed Garrett's situation, blood type, tissue type, age and consent. The network in turn, searched its databases and alerted a local transplant organization in Seattle, who assessed their waiting lists for a match.

Then Dr Burton, thirty-five-year-old mother of three children, and local soccer mom, steeled herself to make another call.

As the helicopter ascended, Garrett saw buildings shrink into oceans of green forest, then the majestic slopes of the Cascade Range.

The sky cleared and he saw snatches of stunning blue sky, then felt the warmest sensation of flying and falling through his life.

He smelled fresh baked bread, like when he was a boy

and his mother took him to the bakery in his hometown and bought him jelly donuts, so fresh they were still warm.

Then the sky turned azure like Ocho Rios in Jamaica, where he and Cathy spent their honeymoon.

Somewhere over the edge of metro Seattle within side of the Olympic Mountains in the east, Garrett's heart stopped beating.

At an elementary school, in suburban Calgary, the vice-principal left her office and phone off the hook so Garrett's ex-wife could take an emergency call in private.

'Yes, this is Cathy Pearson. Yes, John Garrett is my ex-husband.'

Cathy stared hard into the painting of the Rockies on the vice-pincipal's wall as Dr Niki Burton explained. The snow-capped peaks blurred through Cathy's tears, she squeezed the phone hard, wishing she could reach John Garrett's hand, she swallowed air and she found her voice.

'Yes, I can confirm he would have wanted that. We discussed it when we were marr . . . yes, you have my consent.'

In the adjoining office, the principal and vice-principal heard the thunk of the phone hitting the desk top, and a loud sob and rushed to comfort Cathy.

In Seattle, as the helicopter approached Harborview Medical Center and the specialists with the rapid organ recovery team prepared Craig Dawson for a kidney transplant, Garrett's life slipped from him.

He'd found peace and the joy that comes at the end of a heart's pursuit. His open eyes were staring, but at nothing of this world.

Billy Dolan and his little sister, Daisy, had been waiting for him. Smiling, they each took Garrett by the hand.

TWO STARS
Barbara Nadel

Barbara Nadel trained as an actress prior to becoming a writer.
A regular visitor to Turkey for many years, she utilised a Turkish
setting for her first series, featuring an Istanbul cop, which opened
with *Belshazzar's Daughter*. Her second series is based in the East
End of London, from where she hails, and the central character
is undertaker Francis Hancock.

'We'll start with Campari Aperativos and truffles.'
A huge smile spread across his fat face as well
as the anorexic visage of his companion. 'I think
your signature dish for the primo, Benito.'

Benito Berigliano said politely in his best English,
'Naturally Signor Adler-Smythe.'

Until Julian Adler-Smythe, the famous English food critic,
had started coming to his restaurant, Benito hadn't known
what a signature dish was. He certainly hadn't known that
he'd had one. Everyone in the village of Santa Caterina loved
his spinach ravioli stuffed with chestnuts and pigeon. But
until Mr Adler-Smythe had arrived, no one had suggested
that there was anything spectacular about it.

Julian Adler-Smythe smiled at the gaunt woman who was
sharing his table. Then he beckoned Benito closer. 'Chef . . .'

No one had called him 'chef' until the Englishman either.

'For the secondo, I do trust that we have managed to
secure . . .?'

'Ah.' Benito smiled. 'The *Gattu Serivaggiu*, signor. Yes.'

Any tension that Julian Adler-Smythe may have exhibited,
went. 'Marvellous!' Then he said to his companion. 'We
have the *gattu*, Nina!'

'Wonderful.' She said it with such disinterest, Benito
wanted to slap her. It had taken him six months to secure a
Calabrian wildcat. He'd had to bribe some people not a

million kilometres away from the Cosa Nostra. In truth some
of them *in* the Cosa Nostra although Benito hardly dared to
think about that. And for what? He'd tasted wildcat once and
he hadn't thought it was special. But then Mr Adler-Smythe
and his friends always wanted to eat strange things that only
peasants or mad people consumed. They called it 'fine
dining'. Like that cheese from Sardinia he had to get in for
him, *Formaggio Murcio*, covered with maggots. It was
because of that stuff that no one else but Benito would agree
to serve the Englishman.

'I will get your wine,' Benito said and then he left. Benito's
was filling up for the evening and, as well as Mr Adler-
Smythe's order, Benito also had to feed his regulars and a
party of wealthy people from Rome. That the Romans were
in his restaurant at all was down to the Englishman. Adler-
Smythe wrote for a famous English newspaper but his books
about cuisine were translated into many languages, including
Italian. Benito's had, so far, featured in two such books which
had attracted people from as far away as Venice. Not bad
for an ex-cafe in a village ten kilometres inland from the
Bay of Naples. Santa Caterina della Morte was hardly
Sorrento. It did possess a certain degree of fame but not for
anything culinary.

In the kitchen, Benito's brother-in-law Sergio was looking
at a small dish inside the oven. When Benito saw it, he said,
'Is that all there was?'

Sergio, who at fifty-five was a little younger than Benito
said, 'How much do they need?'

Benito hurried over to the oven. 'He and the skinny woman
are paying 200 euros for this, each. That's just for the cat!
What's in there? Five cubes of meat, onion, some garlic?'

'Pretty much,' Sergio said. 'Benito, if they're paying that
much, so will other people from the cities. I've frozen the
rest of it.'

'Oh, God!' So now he had a large amount of illegally
obtained Calabrian wildcat in his freezer. What on earth was
Mr Adler-Smythe going to make of his microscopic portion?

'That was absolutely fabulous,' Mr Adler-Smythe said as
he handed Benito 800 euros later on that evening. 'Keep it
up and I'll be awarding you a Dégustation Guide star.'

Benito glowed. The Dégustation organisation, which also employed Julian Adler-Smythe as an inspector, was almost as prestigious as Michelin. For a restaurant to be awarded one Dégustation star meant that the food in that establishment was first class. To be awarded two stars was not only an honour it also meant that the restaurant in question was exceptional. In order to attract two stars everything had to be amazing and unique. Benito had dreamed of getting one star and then progressing to two ever since he'd met Adler-Smythe.

'There's a restaurant in Serbia where they cook beef Wellington wrapped in gold leaf,' he said to Anna, his wife, as they climbed into bed later that night. 'Maybe next time Mr Adler-Smythe comes *I* could choose something for *him*. I've heard that there are Golden Eagles around Lake Como.'

Anna heaved her heavy body round and looked at her husband. 'Killing eagles is illegal,' she said angrily.

'I've heard that Don—'

'If you're going to tell me about some Mafiosi eating eagle then don't!' Anna said. 'Benito, stop thinking about mad food!'

It was a grey April morning when Julian Adler-Smythe called to say that he would like to make a reservation for the following evening. Benito, who had been trying to find a Golden Eagle for the Englishman's usual visit in July, was thrown into confusion.

'Mr Adler-Smythe,' he said as his hands shook around the telephone receiver, 'you do not usually come now.'

'I decided to do the festival,' the Englishman said.

The festival of Santa Caterina della Morte happened every April and involved the embalmed body of Santa Caterina being carried from the village church to the fountain where her miracle had taken place. Santa Caterina, who had lived in the tenth century, had apparently cured lepers at the fountain called La Magnifica. In addition, touching the surface of her embalmed skin was supposed to confer the gift of second sight. However, the body, which had been for centuries almost completely enclosed in a wood and gold casket, was virtually impossible to reach. Only the saint's tiny, wizened face peeped out from behind a gold hood and that was covered by a layer of toughened glass. But in the scrum of devotees

who came to the festival, at least one person always claimed
to have managed to touch the saint. Benito, who as a Knight
of Santa Caterina was responsible, with others, for carrying
the saint to and from the church, knew that was impossible.
But then if people wanted to fool themselves . . .

'Because my trip is on spec,' the Englishman continued,
'I'll leave it to you, Benito, to tickle my palate with something gorgeous, original and fantastically Italian.'

It was too late to organise an eagle. But Benito said, 'I'm
on it.'

'Good,' Adler-Smythe replied. 'I can see that Dégustation
star hovering over your establishment even as I speak.'

Benito put the phone down and panicked. Something
Italian, local and different – but what? In the past he'd given
Adler-Smythe wild boar, stag, he regularly procured bottles
of Centerbe, the liqueur made with 100 different herbs. What
now?

Benito, very reluctantly, picked up his telephone and dialled
the number he had used to get hold of the wildcat. When a
male voice answered he said, 'It's me, Benito Berigliano. I
am sorry to take your time with my insignificant problem.'

'The Italian origin is tenuous but the cooking and presentation . . . Marvellous!' Julian Adler-Smythe clapped his hands
together while Benito silently experienced palpitations. He
was now in debt to Don Craxi to the tune of one dead
Lipizzaner horse.

The original Lipizzaners had come from Spain. However,
the Austrian developers of the breed had crossed this Spanish
horse with an Italian Neapolitan. Now that the Neapolitan
horse was extinct, the Lipizzaner was its only surviving rela-
tion. So, as Mr Adler-Smythe had so rightly said, the Italian
connection was slight. But it was unique and the Englishman
was talking about stars again.

'This definitely takes you into one star country,' he said
to Benito. 'Keep it up.'

He was in moral and financial debt to Don Craxi and so
the idea of not getting a star after all this was impossible for
Benito to consider. Luckily he was still high on the adrenaline his body had produced to get him through procuring

the horse and then carrying the body of Santa Caterina through the streets of the village. The crowd, which this year had included Mr Adler-Smythe, had surged towards the heavy litter the eight knights carried and nearly knocked them down. But Benito flew around his restaurant that night, attending to everybody. Later, when everyone else had gone, Benito and the restaurant critic shared a bottle of Centerbe.

'Mr Adler-Smythe,' Benito said, 'what is the strangest thing you have eaten?'

'In Africa I ate baboon, giraffe and crocodile. Not particularly nice. You can't do fine dining baboon. Rat was vile.'

Benito felt a little queasy.

Anna and Sergio left them to it. Adler-Smythe, Benito realised, was on an alcohol roll. Benito was drunk but Mr Adler-Smythe was steaming when, at four o'clock in the morning, the Englishman said, 'Of course the strangest thing I have *ever* eaten is baby elephant. In South Africa.' He put his fingers up to his lips and said, 'Ssh!'

Benito's queasiness increased. Baby elephant! Holy Mary, they were cute, everybody loved them. They cried, it was said, like people.

'I went out with a gang of ivory poachers,' Mr Adler-Smythe said. 'Illegal. Poachers killed the adults for tusks, I cooked baby elephant steaks. Match or surpass elephant in terms of sheer outré value and I'll give you two Dégustation stars immediately.'

He passed out then with his head on the table. He left behind him a horrified Benito. Two Dégustation stars to match or surpass the meat of a lovely, baby elephant! He would have been willing to wager that Dégustation knew nothing of that! But Mr Adler-Smythe, as he knew, judged a restaurant very much upon how hard the owner was willing to work to amuse his palate. When he finally got to his bedroom he made such a noise taking his clothes off, that he woke Anna up.

Furious, she said to him, 'Flattering that Englishman again, Benito? You know sometimes I think the only reason you pander to people is because you feel inadequate. Named for Mussolini! Your stupid father did that, not you! You should get over it!'

*   *   *

Julian Adler-Smythe told Benito he was going to return in July. 'Do me proud,' he said as he left.

Benito knew that this meant he had to excel himself. Mr Adler-Smythe had promised *two* Dégustation stars straight away in return for something spectacular. But what? By his own admission he'd reached the zenith of culinary experience by eating baby elephant. Still, Benito had almost three months to come up with an answer.

A week before the critic was due back, he was still clueless. Three days prior to his arrival he was seen by Anna, crying. He'd lost weight and his eyes were bloodshot. He even went off to the church to pray later on that morning. In itself that wasn't unusual. Benito, as a knight of Santa Caterina, spent quite a lot of time in church, attending to the saint at festivals. But he rarely went to pray alone.

Anna was cleaning when Benito returned to the restaurant. As soon as he walked through the door she could see that something had changed. He looked calmer.

'Did Santa Caterina answer your prayers?' she asked.

Benito left to go outside. Anna saw him take his mobile phone out of his pocket and heard him say, 'Signor Adler-Smythe, I have something . . .'

Benito's hand shook as he placed the bowl of dark-brown risotto, its surface scattered with mushrooms, down in front of Julian Adler-Smythe.

'Is this . . .?'

'It's what we discussed,' Benito said, sweating heavily.

The Englishman sniffed the bowl. 'Mmm, earthy,' he said, 'but . . .'

'Signor Adler-Smythe, please don't talk!' Benito pleaded. Aware that Anna was watching him, he wanted no slip-ups. Alone, he had prepared and served the dish. It was entirely his own.

Adler-Smythe smiled as he ate the risotto. Then he looked up and said, 'Magical.'

Not knowing what to say, Benito muttered, 'Enjoy your meal,' and returned to the kitchen.

Sometimes in summer, Benito employed casual restaurant workers. This year in order to cover part of his debt to Don

Craxi, he had taken on the Mafia boss's daughter, Donatella. A weird mixture of American education and Sicilian super- stition, nineteen-year-old Donatella was telling Sergio about her attempt to contact a local witch.

'Dad wants me to marry this, like, *peasant* and so I went to see Strega Giovanna, the one who wears a cool mummified bat around her neck, to see if she could put a spell on him.'

'Put a spell on *your* father!' Sergio laughed. 'Giovanna wouldn't dare!'

'But the old woman was out or whatever,' Donatella said. 'Her door was shut.'

'Donatella, wine, table four!' a heavily sweating Benito barked. He didn't usually speak to her like that, her being who she was. But they were busy.

When the girl had gone, Sergio, who had noticed how jumpy Benito had been all day, said, 'The kid was just talking about visiting the *strega*.'

'To have her father enchanted, yes!' Benito responded angrily. 'Sergio, we cannot get involved in Don Craxi's affairs!'

'I'm not,' Sergio said. 'Benito, she went to see the *strega* and the old woman didn't answer the door. Maybe she saw the girl through the window and decided that she didn't need the bother of a Craxi. Anyway Donatella didn't get in.' Then he paused for a moment and said, 'But it's odd.'

'What is?'

'You know Giovanna,' Sergio said. 'Her door's always open. Her legs are bad and so having the door open means she doesn't have to get up. She only shifts to go to church and she only does that to annoy Father Alessandro.' He frowned. 'Maybe someone should make sure she's OK.'

Benito picked up a bottle from the table and then waved a dismissive hand. 'As you think . . .'

Once he'd gone, Sergio scowled. Like Anna he had begun to lose patience with Benito since he'd started 'fine dining'. Some of the food that he was using was very expensive and odd. And all for the right to put a red star and the word 'Dégustation' above the door. Who cared?

But Benito cared and so when, at the end of the evening, Adler-Smythe shook his hand and said, 'Congratulations on your *two* stars,' he cried.

'My father may have been a stupid, disregarded peasant,' he said to Anna later that night. 'A hated Fascist who named me for Mussolini, but I have a successful business. I have two Dégustation stars! Me!'

As soon as the stars appeared above his door, Benito began to get more customers. The tourist season was almost at an end but people still came from the cities and also, now, from abroad. To give thanks for his good fortune, Benito began spending even more time in church. He even joined the black-clad widows who cleaned the place three times a week. He was busy and getting wealthier by the day, but strangely he wasn't happy.

One day in December when they were alone in the kitchen, Sergio said to Anna, 'Benito looks ill.'

'I worry with all the work he will have a heart attack,' she said. 'I've told him. But he won't go to the doctor. If Strega Giovanna were still here, that would be different. But she's gone.'

Strega Giovanna, the witch of Santa Caterina, hadn't been seen since July. People had various theories about her disappearance. Some said that she had gone straight to hell. The more pragmatic believed that her daughter had probably had her put into a home. Whatever had happened, her disappearance remained a mystery.

'Maybe he'll feel better after the festival,' Sergio said.

'He could be dead from exhaustion by April!' Anna replied.

But come the Festival of Santa Caterina, Benito was not dead. He was thinner and greyer, but he lived. And rare colour did flood his cheeks when Mr Adler-Smythe asked Benito if he could serve his special risotto to a group of five other food critics he had brought with him for the festival. Benito said that was fine and he went out to one of the store-rooms to retrieve the ingredients.

Alone, Benito had prepared six portions by the time he went, together with the other seven knights of Santa Caterina, to the church. Crowds of people had gathered along the route to the fountain. Inside the church, the priest, Father Alessandro, exhorted the Knights of Santa Caterina to lift the litter upon which her body rested, carefully.

The eight men, including their leader, Sergeant Carlo Bracci of the carabinieri, hefted the saint on to their shoulders. She was heavy. But no one, least of all Benito, said anything as they began to move off, following Father Alessandro, towards the sunlit church door.

Benito shut his eyes and held his breath. Everyone watching, cheered. Only Benito's wife, Anna, frowned as he passed her. He hoped that she was just cross with him, as usual. But then her eyes widened and she said, 'There's water coming out of the litter! Stop!'

At first Father Alessandro ignored Anna. The procession needed to keep moving or the knights would tire. But when other people began to see water dripping from the litter, he asked the knights to lower her down on to the ground. While Benito Berigliano's heart pounded, the priest and the policeman Carlo Bracci walked around to the back of the litter to investigate. The crowd that surrounded them moved in closer.

'There's water,' Benito heard Father Alessandro say. 'But where's it coming from?'

Benito didn't look. Behind him he could hear the priest and the policeman shuffling. Then suddenly Carlo Bracci said, 'Ugh! God, what is that?'

Benito turned around in time to see Father Alessandro dip his fingers into some of the liquid behind the saint's casket and hold it up to his nose. 'It's foul!'

How the rumour started, no one would ever know. But within seconds the notion that Santa Caterina herself was melting had spread to such an extent that even the squad of armed carabinieri engaged to police the event were power-less to stop the stampede. If Santa Caterina was melting then intervention was needed.

Both the priest and Carlo Bracci were knocked to the ground. Other Knights tried to protect Santa Caterina, but in vain. Hands grabbed, eager faces pushed and everyone literally wanted a piece of the saint. Later, a young local boy admitted to opening up the casket. It was not, however, this boy, but actually Father Alessandro who was heard to cry,

'My God, it's Giovanna Ponti, the *strega*! There's the dead bat around her neck! Where is Santa Caterina?'

In the panic that ensued, Benito Berigliano saw the carabinieri draw their weapons. He couldn't have that. Even at the expense of himself, to put so many innocents in harm's way wasn't right. And so it was at that point that he heaved himself up on to what remained of the litter and shouted, 'I know! Me, Benito Berigliano. I know everything.'

Carlo Bracci told Benito to start at the beginning. Mr Adler-Smythe and his guests had left the village quickly after the ruckus outside the church and so there was no one to either confirm or deny his story.

'I didn't know fine dining,' Benito said sadly. 'I made my ravioli. Then along came Mr Adler-Smythe and the possibility of becoming one of the top restaurants.'

'The Dégustation stars.'

'Yes. At first it was normal. I got Mr Adler-Smythe nice, legal things. I should have said no when he asked me to get him a Calabrian wildcat.'

'But you continued.'

'He became more demanding!' Benito laid his handcuffed wrists on the policeman's desk. This was where Mr Adler-Smythe had, inadvertently, got him involved with Don Craxi. But he couldn't say anything about that to the carabinieri. 'I got him all sorts! I wanted that star! Then one night, back in July last year, we got drunk together. He told me something.'

'What?'

'I asked him what was the most amazing thing he had eaten,' he said. 'It was baby elephant.'

Carlo Bracci frowned. 'That Englishman has eaten baby elephant? That's disgusting!'

'In Africa,' Benito said. 'He told me that if I could find something more unusual than baby elephant, I could have two Degustion stars immediately. Two is Dégustation's highest accolade!'

Carlo Bracci looked down at the six bowls of risotto on his desk and said, 'Tell me, Benito, how you got yours.'

'I knew that Adler-Smythe would be back this July. This gave me almost three months to come up with something.

But a week before he was due, I still had nothing. Three days before, I went to the church to pray for inspiration. Nothing! It was only as I was leaving the church, as I passed by Santa Caterina, that it hit me.'

They looked down at the bowls of risotto and then very quickly they both looked away.

'What if I could give Mr Adler-Smythe an experience that combined gastronomy with something priceless,' Benito said. 'He'd eaten rat, crocodile and elephant! Where could I go?'

Carlo swallowed hard.

'I returned to the church that night,' Benito said. 'I was only going to shave a few grams from the saint's limbs! Just to sprinkle on the rice . . .'

'Oh, so that's—'

'Listen!' Benito pleaded. 'For an hour I wrestled with that casket! Tight as a nun! Then suddenly it gave . . . As I pulled the two halves apart the little that remained of her crumbled to dust. Even her face! I just sat there with my hands in dust, her dust . . .' He shrugged. 'And then there is the witch, Giovanna Ponti.'

'She saw you open the casket?'

'She saw me sitting amongst its ruins,' Benito said. 'She laughed. You know what a demon she was?'

'Benito, this is the twenty-first century, we don't kill witches.'

'I know, but she had *seen*!' Benito whined. 'What I'd done, how Santa Caterina was ruined! For my plan to work I needed the mystery of Santa Caterina to be intact. My food had to be spiritual, magic.'

'So you killed her?'

'I panicked! I hit her with the hammer I'd used to open the casket.'

'Which you put her into.'

'What was I supposed to do? Someone might have seen me,' Benito said. 'I took Santa Caterina out . . .'

'You took dust out,' the policeman corrected.

'Yes, I . . . In a plastic carrier bag. I had to squeeze Giovanna's face to make her resemble Santa Caterina.'

'Oh, poor you! Not only have you killed someone you've also destroyed a miracle-working saint!'

'I was going to take Giovanna out and bury her, but I never seemed to be in church alone after that,' Benito said. 'Even when she began to smell, I couldn't move her. I just had to go in with the widows whenever I could and do my best to deodorise her.'

'But you had two stars.'

'Yes.' Benito lowered his head.

'You sprinkled Santa Caterina's sacred dust into a risotto which you served to Mr Adler-Smythe,' Carlo Bracci said.

'He was bewitched!'

'Obviously. He gave you two stars,' the policeman said. He shook his head sorrowfully. 'Benito, the man is a culinary vampire! He'll eat anything! Why couldn't you see that?'

'Because he had Dégustation stars!' Benito wailed. 'Because he made me feel respected.' And then like a petulant child he spat out, 'How would you like to live with the name of a small, failed dictator? Eh?'

Carlo Bracci, who knew that the detectives who had been dispatched from Naples to take control were arriving soon, stood up. 'I wouldn't have liked it,' he said. 'But you didn't kill for Mussolini did you? You killed for two stars.'

And then, with one last look at the six plates of Santa Caterina risotto that sat before Benito Berigliano on the desk, he left his office and locked the door behind him.

FISHY STORY
Christine Poulson

Christine Poulson, an academic and art historian who lives in Derbyshire, turned to crime with her first book featuring Cassandra James, *Dead Letters*. It has been followed by *Footfall* and *Stage Fright*.

Rarely does it fall to a fish to be an instrument of justice. In fact rarely does anything at all happen here in the aquarium. It's not a bad life: decent food, no predators, water kept at a constant temperature. Would it be ungrateful of me to admit that it was just the tiniest bit dull?

Until a few months ago, that is.

What you've heard about fish having a seven-second memory? A gross calumny. I can recall every detail of the evening when it all began.

Kevin's been working here for, oh, five years it must be. He feeds us and cleans out our tanks now and then, but mainly he's a nightwatchman. It's thanks to him that I've learned most of what I know about the human race. You see, his office is opposite my tank and he spends a lot of his shift with his feet up watching TV. I watch it too. Of course I can't hear what they say, but I'm a pretty good lip-reader. Kevin enjoys crime and so do I – Inspector Morse is my favourite.

On that particular evening everything seemed normal enough at first. Kevin finished his jobs and switched on the telly. But he was restless, I could see that. He kept turning his head as if he was listening for something and he kept looking at his watch. Then he sprang up and began to walk up and down. Just as suddenly he stopped. He took the photo of his wife and son off his desk and gazed at it. He gave a start and looked round, as if he'd heard something. He stuffed the photo in a drawer and went off towards the entrance. My curiosity was aroused, I can tell you. Nobody, but nobody, visits the aquarium after closing time.

A minute later he came back and there was a young woman with him. I'm not qualified to say whether she was attractive or not, but Kevin certainly seemed to like her. She said how nice it was of him to show her round after hours. He said, not at all, it got a bit lonely here in the evenings. They went strolling out of sight, much to my disappointment. When they came back they were laughing and talking. They went into the office and he got a bottle of whisky out. They had a drink, and then another drink, and there was a lot more laughing and then he leaned over and kissed her. She kissed him back and then . . . well, as you can imagine, I was all agog. All that effort just to produce one baby, or two if you're lucky. Spawning is much more efficient. I lost count long ago of the children I've fathered. (Did I mention that there is a whole shoal of us in here?) Still, Kevin was enjoying himself – I could see that.

It was just the beginning. At first she came a couple of times a week. And then three or four times a week, and then every day except Saturday, which is Kevin's night off. They just got right down to it on the sofa in the office. Then they'd lie there talking and drinking whisky. She'd leave in the early hours. For two, maybe three months, things went on like that. I have to say I got a bit bored and I missed our evenings watching telly. Still I was pleased for Kevin. I may be cold-blooded, but I'm not cold-hearted.

We fish don't have much of a sense of sin, but I've gleaned a certain amount about the human viewpoint from my telly-watching. Once Kevin fell asleep, leaving the set on and I saw an Open University programme about Milton and *Paradise Lost*. So when things started to go wrong, I had an idea what the problem was. Kevin started neglecting his job. Just little things at first, but when he forgot to feed us two days on the trot, *and* neglected to clean our tank, well, it struck me that things were getting out of hand and I wasn't altogether surprised or sorry when earlier this evening things came to a head. I do wish though that things hadn't turned out quite the way they did.

The first thing that happened was that Kevin arrived late

and wet and in a very bad mood. I guessed what had happened, because it's happened before: his car had broken down and he'd had to walk the rest of the way in the rain. He got on the phone to his wife and asked her to come and collect him in the morning. Then he poured himself a whisky. He opened the drawer and got out the photo of his wife and son. He was still staring at it, when the doorbell must have rung. He got slowly to his feet and this time he didn't put the photo away.

He let the woman in and they went into the office. But when she put her arms round his neck, he pushed her away. I couldn't make out everything they said, but the gist was clear enough. He wanted out. She wasn't going to let him off the hook. She caught sight of the photo of Kevin's wife and son and swept it off the table. He slapped her. She hit him and he pushed her and she staggered and fell over on to the sofa.

Why, oh, why didn't she just get up and go? Instead she got out her mobile phone. Who was she going to ring? Kevin's wife? The police? I'll never know, because the next moment his hands were round her throat.

I couldn't bear to look. When at last I did, it was all over. Kevin was staring at her body as if he couldn't believe what he had done. He shook her, felt for a pulse, but even I could see that she was dead. He poured out a large whisky with a trembling hand and knocked it back in one. He sat down and put his head in his hands.

What on earth would he do now? I wondered. He'd have to dispose of the body somehow. Then I remembered: no car. He really was in a fix. He looked up and I swear he caught my eye. For a few moments we stared at each other and I knew what he was thinking.

As I said earlier it's rare for a fish to have the opportunity to be an instrument of justice, but that is the position that I find myself in now. Murder is wrong, I know that. I shouldn't let him get away with it, I really shouldn't. I have the power to bring Kevin to justice, simply by doing nothing.

But when it comes to it, I know I won't be able to help myself and the same goes for the rest of the shoal. Especially after two days without food. Once he tips that poor young woman in with us piranhas, it'll be problem solved, I fear.

RULES OF ENGAGEMENT
Zoë Sharp

Zoë Sharp published her first book featuring Charlie Fox, *Killer Instinct*, in 2001. The latest title in the series is *Fourth Day*. She combines writing with photography and journalism for an agency that she runs together with her husband Andy. The couple live in the Lake District.

A long time ago, when Angel was just starting out in the business, an old pro she met lurking in a doorway opposite the Russian embassy in Paris laid down the Rules of Engagement. 'Get in. Take the shot. Get out,' he'd said, with the careful solemnity of a man not quite sober at ten o'clock in the morning.

To this advice Angel had since added a bitter rider of her own.

Always get the money.

The fees for Angel's particular line of work were elastic, only sometimes connected to the difficulty of the shot. In this case, the money was nowhere near enough to justify attempting to evade capture across two hundred acres of jealously guarded parkland in Buckinghamshire. Not for an off-chance glimpse of her targets at the limit of her operational range.

There was only so much she could do for a decent covert photo – even with a 1000mm mirror lens.

'So, what exactly,' she'd demanded of George, when she'd buttonholed him in his office on the thirtieth floor and wheedled the assignment out of him, 'are you expecting from this?'

'Pictures of the happy couple holding hands, bit of snogging maybe,' said the rumpled little man who was her occasional employer, scratching his chin. 'Wouldn't hope for much else. The groom-to-be isn't so love-struck that he hasn't twisted a deal with Blackley's for piccies of the nuptials themselves. They'll have that chapel sewn up tighter than a fish's armpit.'

'How much?' Angel perched on the edge of George's desk, reaching for one of her Turkish cigarettes.

George, a forty-year nicotine addict, yelped, 'Don't!' jerking his eyes upwards. 'They've turned up the sensitivity on the sprinkler system again – bastards.' He nipped the unlit cigarette out of Angel's fingers and threw it into the filing cabinet behind him. He'd known her long enough to know she'd light up anyway, just to watch the indoor rain.

'How much is Blackley paying, George?' she asked now, voice husky.

George shivered. That voice went straight through him, plugged into his cerebral cortex and set his nerve endings quivering. She knew exactly what effect it had – even on men a whole lot younger and less susceptible. He was determined it wouldn't get to him – not this time.

'A mil,' he blurted, to his own dismay. 'Look, what's this to you, Angel? This is no bent judge or perverted politician. Just some pop star and some actress. I thought you hated celebrity fluff? You of all people.'

Angel raised an eyebrow, jiggling the little silver hoop through the corner, and snagged the job sheet off the pile.

'You remember when *those* pictures came out?' she said eventually, seemingly fascinated by the view behind the desk, out over Canary Wharf. 'Of me—'

'I remember,' George cut in softly.

'Blackley syndicated them,' she said, flat. She turned her gaze back on to him. Her eyes were startling violet today, with the slightest shimmer. 'That's what put him on the map. Anything I can do to wipe him off it again will be worth it.'

She slid off the desk and headed for the door with that long catwalk stride she'd never lost.

'Angel! Hey, kiddo, I—'

At the doorway she stopped, turned back with a wicked, dazzling smile.

'Trust me, George. Get a deal, and I'll get you pictures,' she promised. 'Besides, Johnny Franz is not just *some pop star*. He's got a certain . . . reputation. Maybe I just want to see for myself, up close and personal, if he deserves it.'

Now, lying under a rhododendron bush only 400 metres from the great west wing of the house, Angel began to question her breezy confidence.

The tabloids had whipped themselves to a frenzy for months over the 'Wedding of the Year'. Johnny Franz was a playboy rock star whose ego matched his prodigious talent with a Fender Stratocaster. Born on a council estate in Sheffield, he'd shrugged off his working-class beginnings further with every platinum disc.

Johnny's chosen bride was Caro Urquart, an English beauty whose tiny, perfect figure was made for crinoline and corsets, and she had the genuine cut-glass accent to match. Her diminutive stature – ensuring all her leading men seemed giants by comparison – was just one reason behind her international stardom.

They'd met at a Hollywood party and, oblivious to the eyes of the gossip press, struck instant sparks. By midnight they'd flown down to his villa in Mexico by private jet, ostensibly to watch the sunrise. Nobody had seen either of them for a solid week.

And now they were tying the knot at the bride's family estate, with all the pomp their fame and wealth could supply. Johnny's PR guru had issued a statement declaring he'd found his true love, was finally ready to settle down. Caro's studio press release claimed she'd never been happier and didn't care who knew it.

Blackley's picture agency paid seven figures for exclusive rights to the wedding photos, and hired an army of security to make sure nobody else got a look-in.

But that didn't mean Angel couldn't try.

Getting into the grounds hadn't been hard. Guile and flattery, for the most part, learned during the time Angel had spent taking her clothes off for a living. Even now, something of that former life exuded through her pores like raw sex.

The dogs hadn't caused her undue problems, either. Angel was good with dogs, often wondered if there'd been one in the family home of which she had no memory.

She'd found the kennels the first night and bribed the

motley collection of hounds. When they picked up her scent on their rounds they reacted as to a canine friend rather than an intruder. The handlers tugged the animals away, whining, from any proximity to her hiding place.

But Angel was bored. And boredom brought a restless recklessness that made those who knew her check nervously for the nearest emergency exit. She'd been here three nights without a sniff. Now, the sun had risen on the big day and she'd failed to snap a single frame. She was, she recognised, probably on the verge of doing something stupid.

And then somebody else did it for her.

She heard laughter. A girlie giggle, coquettish, pretending shock but hiding an edge of triumph. Angel recognised the giggle of a woman who's leading a man by the balls and both of them know it, and neither of them care.

She felt the slight tremble of footsteps through the earth beneath her. A pair of shapely female legs, clad in pale stockings, came within a metre of Angel's nose, picking carefully through the dewed grass, careful of telltale stains on the dainty satin shoes. The man's legs were in official pinstripe morning dress.

They passed close enough for her to smell their excitement.

The bride's mother was known as an uptight aristocrat who would never countenance the happy couple sharing a suite in anticipation. Maybe that was why they'd evaded their own babysitters for this last, unfettered quickie.

Angel kept her head down until the legs had gone by, squirmed round in time to see the couple weaving away across the billiard-table lawn. There was no mistaking the trademark wild black hair of Johnny Franz.

As soon as they were too far to hear the telltale whirr, Angel brought the camera up to her eye and kept the shutter pressed.

The Canon digital camera she was using was capable of ten frames a second and buffered just as fast. She took a long sequence of the couple's back view, their hands all over each other.

The garden had been laid out in the mid 1800s, a vast testament to formal good taste, manicured within an inch of its life. At the end of the impossibly vibrant lawn, invisible from the main residence, was a wooden summer house, built on a distant whim and rarely used. Angel knew entire families in Brixton who could have moved in and luxuriated in the extra space.

The couple headed for the summer house with clear intent, oblivious, almost grappling in their urgency. Johnny Franz had his hands up his intended's skirts and Angel wondered if they would even wait until they got inside.

George is going to want to have my children for this.

And then, just as he grabbed for the door, Johnny swung the girl around so that Angel's telephoto lens got a clear shot of her face for the first time, and she realised that wasn't all her boss was going to have. *A heart attack, most likely.*

Because the still-giggling girl Johnny pushed into the summer house was not who she was supposed to be. The long blonde hair was a similar shade and length, but the face was not the one that stared down from billboards and buses all over London. Angel checked the playback just to be sure, but there was no doubt.

So, Johnny Franz was cheating on his beautiful, famous bride on the morning of their wedding with, unless Angel was very much mistaken, one of the bridesmaids.

Even as the door closed behind them, Angel levered up, grabbing the padded backpack that held a second camera body, attached to a mid-length zoom lens. For this, she intended getting as close as she dared.

She sprinted across the grass. If the way Johnny had been tugging at the bridesmaid's dress was anything to go by, he wasn't planning a slow seduction.

The summer house had two windows and Angel edged closer to one where the light would fall without the need for flash, not if she bumped up the ISO speed just a touch. For what she was about to give him, George could put up with a little noise in the pictures. Too perfect and they looked fake.

There was nothing fake going on inside the summer house. By the time Angel silently set down her bag, raising the viewfinder to her eye, Johnny had the bridesmaid thrust face down over a stack of lounger cushions with her skirts thrown over her back.

With his trousers halfway down his skinny thighs, Angel could just make out yet another tattoo added to Johnny's collection since *Vanity Fair* shot him coyly naked for their best-selling summer issue. The name 'Caro' in gothic script across his left hip. Angel shot a decent close-up, just in case there were any later accusations of Photoshop.

Johnny reached forwards and wrapped his hand in the girl's hair like taking up the reins of a horse. He dragged her head back, his teeth bared in what might have been a snarl.

This isn't about the sex, Angel thought. This has never been about the sex.

She lowered the camera and stumbled back, knowing she'd got more than enough, seen more than enough. Knowing, too, that she wouldn't clear the foul taste from her mouth, even if she gargled with Stolichnaya for a fortnight.

She scooped up her pack and ran for the trees. By the time the couple re-emerged, less urgent but more furtive, adjusting their clothing, Angel had the memory card Bluetoothed to her Blackberry and uploading to her secure home server. Even if they caught her now, trashed her gear – as they had before – it would be too late.

She shifted back to the telephoto and took a series of them walking away. From this she surmised the bridesmaid had not altogether enjoyed the experience. Not enough to over-come an instant blossom of guilt. She hurried, flushed, awkward, not waiting when Johnny paused infuriatingly to dip his head and light a cigarette as if he'd all the time in the world.

Through the pin-sharp magnification of the lens, crosshaired by the focusing array, Angel watched him track the bridesmaid's hasty retreat as he blew out the first wreath of smoke. He didn't raise his head, but something about the predatory watchfulness of those legendary ice-blue eyes made her skin shimmy. Then he flicked the spent match into a nearby ornamental fountain, and he smiled.

That was what did it.

In her spacious bedroom suite at the top of the east wing, Caro Urquart fussed with her hair. When she and Johnny first met, the length and the colour and the weight of it had captivated him.

She'd been preparing for another wretched period drama – in Africa this time. Growing her own hair was less cumbersome, less hot, than using one of her selection of wigs.

Normally, the first thing she would have done after the final wrap party would have been a visit to her stylist in New York for a total makeover. Her screen agent warned her keeping static wasn't good for her career. 'You mustn't risk typecasting, darling,' he'd fretted at Cannes. 'You have to keep reinventing yourself.'

But when Johnny played her the hastily mixed demo for the new album, with 'The Girl With The Sun in Her Hair' as title track and debut single, how could she have it cut or dyed? The song had debuted at number one, the album following suit, and Johnny had given her the platinum disc as a keepsake.

Besides, once they were married she'd be cherry-picking roles anyway. On Jay Leno, Johnny declared he liked the idea of a working wife, but she knew that was just image talking. That secretly he'd be delighted to have her on the road with him, touring with the band – for part of the year, at least. Besides, she'd heard the rumours about those groupies . . .

Caro teased her fringe into artfully casual disarray. Nobody realised how much effort it took, looking this damned natural all the time. She twisted her head sideways. And maybe it was time for the little nip-and-tuck her beauty therapist suggested. She *was* nearly twenty-seven, after all.

A small stone flipped against the window pane behind her, making her start. Her rooms were right at the top of the house, five stories up. Who . . .?

Then a smile lit her face. *Johnny*!

The window led out on to a small balcony, level with the many-turreted rooftop. The suite had once been servants' quarters, but Caro loved the view and had long-since claimed it as her own.

She flung open the window and stepped out.

In the far corner of the balcony lounged a tall figure, just in the process of lighting a cigarette. She had the high-slanted cheekbones of a model, black and white spiked hair, and she wore urban-cam cargoes and a skinny sleeveless T-shirt that revealed a strange interwoven Celtic symbol tattooed on her shoulder.

Definitely not Johnny.

For a moment Caro froze. Then her eyes flicked to the bag at the girl's feet. To the very pro-looking camera balanced on the top of it.

'Get out!' she thundered, voice quivering with anger. 'How *dare* you!'

The girl exhaled, giving Caro a narrow-eyed stare through a lungful of smoke. 'I'm here to give, not take,' she said mildly. 'Call it an early wedding present, if you like. And it took some *dare* to climb that ivy, I can tell you.' For the first time Caro noticed that the girl's hands were shaking, her skin unnaturally pale and sheened with sweat.

'Are you *so* desperate to snatch some grubby shot of me in my wedding gown, you'd risk your neck for it?' Caro demanded, incredulous.

'I've got all the shots I want, and not of you,' the girl said. 'I was never here for that – not really.'

Cold fear trickled down the back of Caro's spine. She shivered in her elaborate dress, despite the balmy air.

'I know you,' she said, uncertain. 'You were that model. That one who—'

'Became a *paparazza*, yes,' the girl said flatly. 'I take pictures people don't want taken, of them doing things they don't want publicised.' She took a last long drag on her cigarette and looked up suddenly into Caro's face. The girl's eyes were a remarkable shade of amber, golden like a cat. *Coloured contacts?* 'And I've got something you really need to see.'

Caro recoiled instinctively. 'I don't want—'

'Didn't say you'd *want* to, babe,' the girl said, almost gently. 'But I've already cut a deal on these pictures. By tomorrow, you're not going to be able to avoid them. And then it'll be too late. Then you'll have married the slimeball.'

Caro swallowed. Common sense urged her to yell for help and have this insolent stranger thrown out. To watch as she was marched down the drive with Caro's largest minder twisting her arm up her back, and kicking the bag containing those expensive cameras alongside him as he went. But the image of those groupies still clung.

She stepped sideways, to the edge of the parapet, and glanced downwards. The creeper-clad stone walls stretched away towards the gravel below.

'You really climbed all the way up here,' she murmured, 'just to show me some pictures?'

'Yes,' the girl agreed gravely. 'And I don't fancy going back the same way. So, if you're going to have me chucked out, at least do it through the tradesman's entrance, would you?'

She picked up the camera. Caro stiffened, but the girl merely held it out to her. Cautiously, Caro took it from her. The action brought her near to the parapet again and her gaze returned to the seemingly impossible climb.

It was more years than she could count since someone offered a favour and expected nothing in return, and Caro had grown cynical. She held the camera out over the long drop. It was surprisingly heavy.

'What's to stop me simply letting go?'

The girl grinned. It transformed her face into that of a street urchin. 'Absolutely nothing,' she said cheerfully. 'But those Canons have a magnesium shell and are tough as old boots, so the lens would be knackered, but the memory card would survive. And that's the bit you should worry about.'

Caro considered for a moment, then slowly brought the camera back inside the parapet. 'You've already made a copy, haven't you?' she realised bitterly.

'Hell, yes,' the girl agreed, fervent. 'Made a copy and sold the rights, worldwide.'

'So, what do you want from me?' Caro asked with brittle dignity. 'Money?'

The girl laughed outright. 'Didn't I already say I wasn't selling? Johnny Franz deserves what's coming to him.' She put her head on one side. 'The only question is . . . do you?'

'He loves me.' But even an actress of Caro's skill heard the underlying uncertainty.

'Hm. I'm sure that's what all those star-struck teenagers thought, before he damn-near raped them,' the girl said deliberately. 'You know how many he's paid off?' When Caro didn't respond, she shrugged. 'Well, can't say I didn't warn you.'

She took the camera out of Caro's momentarily nerveless fingers, squatted to repack it into its padded bag, adding in conversational tones, 'Personally, I don't see what all the fuss is about with that boy. From what I saw, I'd rate him maybe a four out of ten – for energy if not for style. And that's only because sometimes I can go a little rough.' She rose easily, flashed Caro a doubtful smile from beneath that Cruella de Ville-style hair. 'Good luck, babe – you're going to need it.'

When Caro Urquart began her walk down the aisle, gasps from the assembled congregation greeted her appearance. The dress with its mile-long silk train carried by a single bridesmaid, that distinctive golden hair under the diaphanous veil, the perfect bunch of white orchids in her hands.

It took them a moment to wonder why she wasn't on the arm of her father, and another to realise she seemed in something of a hurry to meet the handsome rock star in his trademark swaggered pose alongside the waiting priest.

Caro reached the altar faster than rehearsals had predicted, paused while the organist tried to catch up and eventually floundered into silence. Her cheeks were faintly flushed, lips slightly parted, the bridesmaid fussing with her train.

Johnny Franz failed to notice any of this lapse in timing. He stepped forwards with that famous killer smile and gently lifted the veil away from his fiancée's face.

'You are the love of my life,' he murmured, just loud enough to carry to the guy ghostwriting his autobiography, seated two rows back.

'Really?' Caro said blandly, her own voice the one she'd perfected on the West End stage to be clearly audible in the gods. 'So, who was the little bitch-in-heat you were shagging in the summer house this morning, then?'

Johnny's guilty eyes flew to the bridesmaid, only then realising that she was taller than he remembered. She hadn't been wearing a blonde wig then, either, and he was pretty sure there'd been no tattoos.

And she definitely hadn't had a camera hidden somewhere that she was now using to fire off frame after frame of unflattering close-ups.

Bewildered by his own rush of guilt, his gaze jerked back to Caro.

'"The Girl With The Sun in Her Hair"?' she thundered,

temper finally breaking loose. 'How about "The Girl With Her Fist in Your Face", you cheating bastard!'

Johnny never saw the first punch coming.

The tabloid banner headlines quoted her verbatim headline the following day, above one of Angel's exclusive photographs from the church. It showed Caro's delicate clenched fist frozen at the very moment of contact, square on the side of Johnny Franz's jaw. A perfect shot, with his chin tucked back and his eyes shut and his cheeks bloated in shocked surprise, just a fleck of spittle spraying outwards to show the force of the blow.

Caro's own face had blazed with righteous fury, proving that she was one of the few women who truly *was* more beautiful when she was angry.

Immediately afterwards, Caro's agent started fielding calls from the major studios, offering her leading roles in big-budget action adventures. She chose that of an ice-cool assassin in a sci-fi epic, playing it with golden contacts, spiked black and white hair, and a number of curious tattoos.

She refused to be drawn by David Letterman on her source of inspiration. The movie became the blockbuster hit of the summer.

After Angel's pictures from the summer house hit the Internet, three girls came forward to lodge formal complaints about Johnny's often vicious sexual style in the back of the tour bus after gigs. One of them was only fifteen.

The resultant police investigation meant the second single from 'The Girl With The Sun in Her Hair' barely made it into the top twenty on release, and dropped rapidly down the charts. His next album tanked.

Blackley's agency attempted to recover their outlay, but since the pictures Angel took were, strictly speaking, not of the wedding, Johnny's lawyers were stalling. He had other things to worry about.

Caro sent Angel an open-ended offer to be her bridesmaid for real – as and when the actress made another trip down the aisle. Angel's texted refusal was more regretful than it sounded. She had no desire to become her own prey.

George, who perhaps knew her best of anyone, sent her a case of Stolichnaya.

With her commission, Angel went to Oklahoma for the start of the tornado season, capturing shots of an F4 touching down just outside Tulsa that she sold to *National Geographic*. 'Stunning,' George said, thoughtful, when she brought him a copy of the magazine. He peered at the invented byline. 'Bloody shame you couldn't use your real name on this, kiddo.'

Angel was lounging by the cracked-open office window, blowing experimental smoke rings out over Canary Wharf. Today, her hair was pink and her eyes were a vivid aquamarine. She shrugged. She hadn't forgotten the guy in the doorway opposite the embassy.

Always get the money.

'As long as they get my name right on the cheque,' she said, with a smile that didn't quite reach her eyes, 'what do I care?'

TICK-TOCK
Chris Simms

Chris Simms made his crime-writing debut in 2003 with *Outside the White Lines*, which was swiftly followed by *Pecking Order* before *Killing the Beasts* introduced DI Jon Spicer, who has now appeared in six books, most recently *Cut Adrift*. The Spicer novels are set in Manchester, Simms' home city.

The incessant sound finally forced his eyes open. There it was, sitting on the breeze-block beside the mattress. Tick-tock, tick-tock. Round-faced pain in the arse. He focused on its hands. Twenty to three. In the morning? he wondered. What time did we crash out? Surely later than that. He swivelled an eye.

The small rip in the bottom corner of the blanket nailed over the window frame was glowing white. Day, then. His stomach growled and he had the notion it was twisting in on itself, trying to wring out any fragment of food that might have been within it. Tick-tock, tick-tock. Letting out an exasperated sigh, he turned on to his back. 'Fucking starving.' From under the sheets beside him came a low groan. 'Elaine? I said—'

'Fuck off.'

He propped himself on one elbow, blinked a few times and looked down at his body. He still had his T-shirt and tracksuit bottoms on. His battered trainers poked out from the other end of the grimy sheets. Letting his head fall to the side, his eyes went to the little tray on the bare floorboards. A quick hit, just to dull the hunger. Among the paraphernalia next to the little perspex bag was a syringe, soiled teaspoon and lighter. Frowning, he collapsed forward on to both elbows, the movement taking his upper body off the mattress and his face to within inches of the tray. Empty. The fucking bag was empty. He was about to curse her when a memory fought its way through the cotton wool filling his head. I had the last hit. After she'd passed out. Bollocks.

He raised himself on to his knees, further disturbing the sheets in the process. She yanked them back over her head without a sound. His stomach rumbled again and he got to his feet. Walking a little unsteadily, he crossed the room and stepped out into the dim corridor.

The kitchen was opposite. Opening the door revealed a room with ruptured plaster where a cooker, dishwasher and radiator had once been. In the middle of the room was a table. On it was a bottle of ketchup and a crumpled plastic bag. He looked inside, removed the final slice of bread, squirted ketchup over it then smeared it about with his finger. After licking it clean, he folded the slice over and crammed the entire thing in his mouth. The jaw muscles of his gaunt face pulsed slowly as he chewed. The first swallow sent his guts churning, reverberations spreading straight to his lower stomach. He forced the last lumps down before stepping back out of the kitchen and into the bathroom next door. A single cardboard tube was lying on the cistern. 'Shit,' he murmured. 'I need to shit.'

The front door opened and his head poked out. Littering the floor of the shared hallway was the usual assortment of junk mail and flyers. Hanging from the letter box was someone's newspaper. Quick as a flash, he tugged it through and retreated into the little flat; a trapdoor spider with its prey. The headline on the front cover announcing that day's royal visit was torn in two as he scuttled back to the toilet.

She heard a door bang shut followed by the plastic clatter of the toilet seat. Immediately she grubbed across the bed, head emerging above the works spread out on the tray. Bastard. The last of the gear was gone. Bastard. 'Bastard!' she shouted.

No reply.

When she stepped off the mattress, the floor felt cold underfoot. She slid her feet into her trainers, fingers running through her lank brown hair as she did so. Out in the corridor, she thumped a fist against the bathroom door. 'Bastard.' But the word was delivered with less venom: last to sleep got last go with the gear. That was the unspoken rule.

Dropping the empty bread packet back on the table, she checked the bathroom door was still shut before crouching at the filthy cooker in the corner and opening the drawer in its base. Inside was a three-pack of Mars Bars. She ripped the wrapper off one and started to bite. The toilet flushed just as she swallowed the last of it down. 'You finished the end of the bread,' she announced as he stepped back into the room.

'Come on,' he replied, gently probing the sore below his left nostril.

'What?'

But the question didn't need asking. Their supply of heroin was gone and the clock was ticking on when the need for more started to really kick in.

'The station,' he said. 'We haven't done that for a bit.'

She hovered at the chiller section, one ear cocked towards the till. As soon as she heard him say, 'Green, not red,' she lifted the tube off the shelf and stuffed it up the elasticated sleeve of her faded red top. When she joined him at the counter, the cashier was turning back with a pack of green Rizlas in her hand.

She eyed the pair of them suspiciously. 'Anything else?'

He shook his head.

'Then that's twenty-five pence.'

Rummaging in the pocket of his tracksuit bottoms, he extracted a few coins and held his palm out.

Gingerly, she picked out the correct amount.

As they tottered along the pavement with stiff little steps, he spoke from the corner of his mouth. 'What did you get?'

She produced the tube of Dairy Lea.

He scowled. 'That it?'

'Yes.' She unscrewed the cap, tilted her head back and squirted a worm-cast of pale yellow into her mouth. Memories came flooding back. The farm out near Oldham, sitting in the kitchen as her mum placed a mound of triangular slices on the table, each one thick with creamy cheese.

'Give us it, then.' His hand was raised, fingers outstretched.

She held it out, tongue pressing the blob against the roof of her mouth, forcing it between the gaps in her teeth.

The gently curving concourse which led up to the entrance

of Piccadilly Station was heaving. His eyes darted about. Handbags were hanging off shoulders everywhere. They continued along the pavement, a row of shops on their left. Every ten metres, he noted with irritation, there seemed to be the Day-Glo tabard of a British Transport Police officer.

Behind the bus shelter to the side of the station's main entrance was an eight-metre high metal post. The CCTV camera on top of it whirred faintly as the lens angled down.

Inside the station's monitoring room a man in a white shirt marked Security spoke up. 'Darren Fletcher. You don't want him in here.'

Next to him was a man wearing a dark-blue suit, white shirt and turquoise tie. 'Who?' he asked with a crisp, Home Counties accent.

The camera operator pressed a couple of buttons, his other hand working a joystick mounted at the centre of the console before him. The main image on the bank of screens switched to the flow of people outside. 'Him,' the operator stated, zooming in. 'Utter scrote. He'll get in with the crowd, looking for handbags.'

The man in the suit checked the digital clock on the wall. Two minutes past three. 'The cavalcade is due in twelve minutes, the train departs at three twenty-five. Can you radio your colleagues at the entrance to pull him to one side?'

The operator nodded before speaking into his headset. 'Gavin? You've got a bag-snatcher at about ten o'clock, moving towards the doors. Male, mid-twenties, shaved head with a black shell suit and dirty white trainers. Tell him to hop it.'

Fletcher saw the British Transport Police officer standing by the far side of the doors raise a hand to his ear piece. Instinctively, he changed direction, putting a large man between him and the officer. The policeman gestured to his colleague and they started straight towards him, eyes sweeping the flow of people. Fletcher kept in close to the overweight man, head ducked down. The policeman went up on tiptoes as Fletcher passed through the doors. Some kind of crowd control barriers were up ahead and he cut into Superdrug.

Elaine trailed him in. 'What are you doing?'

'Can't believe the amount of pigs,' he replied, making his way to the rear of the shop. 'Wasn't sure if the two at the doors had spotted me.' Moving behind a shelving unit, he unzipped his top. 'Swop.'

'You what?'

The skin on his neck was beginning to itch and he felt sweat breaking under his arms. An hour, he thought. Even if things go well, we won't be scoring for another hour. He jiggled from foot to foot. 'Give us yours. Come on.'

She peeled off her hooded top, revealing a pale-green T-shirt beneath. Once they'd exchanged items, he licked his lips, thinking about the barriers. Must be a football match or something. The sleeves of her top were too short for his arms and he checked to make sure the track lines on both his forearms weren't showing. 'Right, we keep away from the main hall. That bit outside the coffee shop with all the chairs? Let's try there first.'

'OK.'

He moved back to the shop's entrance, aware he was about to become visible to the station's CCTV cameras once more. Lowering his head, he rejoined the mass of people, oblivious to the enormous plasma screen high up on the far side of the terminal.

The local news was beaming out; a live report about Prince William opening a new drug treatment centre in Salford. The footage showed the next-in-line-to-the-throne waving at a modest crowd before climbing into the rear of a black Daimler. The car took central position in a row of vehicles which were then led off down the street by two police motor-bikes. The camera swung back to the reporter who announced the prince was travelling by public train back to London.

Skirting round the base of an escalator leading up to the balcony terrace, the pair made their way past a Boots and Orange store. The shops ended at a seating area. Waist-high canvas screens bearing the coffee chain's logo had been erected around a cluster of metal tables and chairs. People were sipping at drinks and picking at muffins.

Fletcher sidled up to the perimeter, making a show of studying the departure screens above the entry points for the

platforms. Pointing at the screen for the three twenty-five to
London, he murmured, 'Four tables along. Woman with her
back to us. See?'

Elaine's eyes slid across. The lady was somewhere in her
fifties. An expensive-looking beige leather handbag was
hanging off the back of her chair which was within easy
reaching distance of the screens. Giving a nod, Elaine said,
'Ask to sit at her table?'

Fletcher's lips twitched. 'That should freak her out.' He
thought about the little pub tucked away in the maze of
streets making up the Northern Quarter nearby. 'Meet outside
The Crown and Anchor if I get it.'

The control room operator narrowed his eyes. 'Fletcher. Next
to Café Gino. He's scoping it out.'

The man in the suit sighed. 'Which screen?'

'Four. Changed his top somehow. Might be working with
that skinny lass. The one just entering the seating area now.'

The suited man looked at the screens displaying the view
of the station concourse. Officers were positioned at the
barriers at the end, preventing any vehicle from turning off
the main road. He raised a handset to his lips. 'Control Point
Piccadilly. Cavalcade status, please.'

'Mancunian Way, passing the University buildings. ETA,
five minutes.'

He lowered his handset. 'I don't need any commotion
when they enter the terminal. Get that little prick lifted.'

The camera operator flicked to another view. Four British
Transport Police officers were positioned at the top of the stairs
leading up from the taxi rank at the back of the station. 'Dave.
You and one other. Café Gino. There's a male, mid-twenties,
shaved head, red top. He's standing by the side of the parti-
tions of the seating area. Remove him from the terminal,
immediately.'

Elaine made her way between the tables, stopping before
their target. 'That chair taken?' she asked, wiping her nose
with the back of a hand.

The woman looked up, registering the dishevelled
appearance and unwashed hair. 'Erm – sorry.' She gestured

towards the cafe. 'My husband. He's in there getting served.'

Elaine pretended to be in two minds over whether to sit down anyway as Fletcher unhooked the handbag and stuffed it up the red top he now wore. He started making for the stairs which led down to the station's taxi rank. Two fluorescent jackets appeared directly in front. One officer raised a hand. 'You!'

Fletcher span on his heel and burrowed back through the crowd, risking a glance over his shoulder as he did so. The two officers were trying to wave people out of the way, one of them speaking rapidly into his radio. Fletcher moved past the Orange store and Boots, realising the net would now be closing. The bag had too much inside to give up yet.

Through the plate glass doors at the entrance, he saw more officers starting to turn their heads as a colleague waved a hand. Shit. That left the far side doors, the ones leading out into the car park. He broke into a half run, knocking some kid over. The crowd thickened closer to the barriers and he bent forward to force his way between the press of bodies. Past a Cornish Pasty place and then out into the fresh air.

He ran round the corner, lungs burning. Before him a deserted service road ran along the back of the shops that lined the station's concourse. Markings on the concrete denoted bays where delivery vehicles were permitted to unload. On the other side of the road was row upon row of vehicles.

Fletcher started towards the main road, but quickly realised he would never make it from sight before the pursuing officers appeared behind him. After fifty metres, he veered into the car park. Gasping for breath, he crouched down beside a vehicle and peeped through its windows. Three officers ran round the corner of the terminal, slowing to a stop and looking to each side.

On the roof of the renovated warehouse next to the railway terminal, a man lowered his binoculars. 'Something going on in the car park behind the station.'

'There?' his colleague asked, gazing downwards.

'Yup. A guy just ran out. See him squatting behind that

car? About a dozen rows in. I think those three officers are after him.'

His colleague spoke into the mouthpiece of his headset. 'Obs Point Five to Control Point Piccadilly.'

The suited man in the station's monitoring room lifted his handset. 'Go ahead Obs Point Five.'

'We've got an adult male concealing himself in the British Rail car park behind the station. Three Transport Police appear to be trying to locate him.'

'You have visual contact?'

'Yes. He's . . . hang on . . . fourteen rows down, next to a dark-blue people carrier. Renault, I think. It's six cars in.'

The suited man turned to the camera operator. 'Did you get that?'

'I did, but we've got no cameras there. Gavin? Surveillance unit on the roof of that apartment hotel overlooking you has him. Fourteenth row of vehicles down. Hiding by the side of a dark-blue people carrier, six cars in.'

The suited man spoke into his handset. 'Control Point Piccadilly. Cavalcade status?'

'Turning off the Mancunian Way. ETA three minutes.'

Fletcher could feel his heart hammering at the back of his throat. He looked down where the sleeves of Elaine's top had ridden up. Beneath the rivulets of black dots running down each forearm, his veins strained against the skin. They'll give up, he told himself. There must be hundreds of cars here.

The uniform in the middle seemed to look up at something then nod. He spoke quietly to his colleagues. One peeled off to the left, one to the right and all three started forward. Fletcher glanced in the other direction. A good hundred metres to the main road and the safety of the Northern Quarter beyond. The officers were now three rows in. They'll give up soon. They must do. But they continued to advance, one with his eyes firmly on the vehicle Fletcher was hiding behind.

A small white van appeared round the corner of the terminal, coming from the direction of the catering units used for supplying the intercity trains with food. The officers were now eight rows away. Fletcher watched as the van pulled up in the loading bay behind one of the shops and turned its hazards on. A man of about twenty got out, hurried round the vehicle and disappeared through the rear door of the premises. Fletcher realised he'd left the engine running.

'Obs Point Five to Central Control. A van has pulled up at the rear of one of the shops facing out on to the concourse.'

The suited man looked at the bank of screens, wishing he could see what was going on. 'From where?'

'Hang on . . .'

Keeping as low as possible, Fletcher ran along his aisle of cars and bounded across the narrow road. As he yanked the driver's door open, one of the officers behind him shouted. Keys were hanging from the ignition. He jumped in, slammed the gear-stick into first, popped the handbrake and shot forward. In the rear-view mirror, he watched the three sprinting officers rapidly falling behind. 'Come on!' he screamed triumphantly.

Peering down from the roof, the surveillance officer said, 'The male has just taken the vehicle! He's proceeding towards the main road, turning right . . . no, he's stopping . . .'

Fletcher pressed the button for the passenger side window. 'Elaine!'

The officer on the roof spoke again. 'He's picked up a female pedestrian. They've now turned right, heading away from the station along Store Street.'

In the monitoring room, the suited man's shoulders relaxed. 'Away from the station? That's fine by me. Cavalcade status?'

'We are nearing the junction of London Road. Train station is on our right.'

The camera operator pointed. 'Number two.' The screen showed the main road outside. Led by the two motorbikes, the state vehicles were slowly approaching.

Fletcher pulled the handbag out and tossed it on to Elaine's lap. 'Fuck me! Soon as I took it, every pig in that place was after me.'

Elaine was laughing with excitement. 'I was sure they had you.' She unzipped the bag, wondering what the smell was as she reached straight for the purse. 'Sound!' A fan of tens and twenties were in her hand.

Fletcher was now turning off Great Ancoats Street on to some waste ground behind a derelict mill.

As the suited man watched the motorbikes turning right, something needled him. The barriers at the end of the concourse were raised, an officer waving them through. 'Control Point to Obs Point Five. Had that van approached from the main road?'

'No – from the direction of the terminal. A service road – looks like it leads to some kind of commercial premises at the far end of the staff car park.'

Fletcher came to a halt in the shadow of the mill. 'What else is in there?'

The farm, Elaine thought. The smell reminds me of the farm. The mobile phone in the handbag's inner compartment started to ring. Elaine took the call. 'Yeah, yeah – you've lost your stuff, Mrs.' She pressed red and tossed the handset on to the white bags filling the rear of the van.

The suited man was frowning. 'All deliveries to those shops were suspended. Can you still see the vehicle?'

'Negative, visual contact lost when it turned off Store Street.'

Elaine looked over her shoulder at the sacks. That's the smell, she realised. Fertiliser. She reached over her seat and opened the uppermost sack. Wires running into the pale-blue granules. And a little digital clock. The display was ticking, a few seconds off twelve.

The cavalcade was halfway up the concourse when, just over a kilometre away, a dull whump reverberated across the city. The surveillance unit on the roof watched a massive old building collapse on its side as a huge cloud of smoke billowed up towards the sky.

LITTLE RUSSIA
Andrew Taylor

Andrew Taylor was awarded the CWA John Creasey Memorial Dagger for his first detective novel, *Caroline Minuscule*, which introduced William Dougal. His series set in the 1950s, in the fictional Borders town Lydmouth, has earned much critical praise; so too did the Roth Trilogy, televised as *Fallen Angel*. *The American Boy*, a novel set in the 19th century, became a best-seller. *Bleeding Heart Square* is another historical mystery, set in the 1930s. He was awarded the CWA Cartier Diamond Dagger in 2009.

'Little Russia?' Jill said. 'Where?'

Amy Gwyn-Thomas looked up from her shorthand pad. 'It's on the other side of the river. You can see it from the road to the forest.'

'That can't be its real name.'

'It's what everyone calls it. It's a little valley that doesn't get much sun even in summer. It's always cold. Anyway, it's where Stalin lives.'

'What *are* you talking about?'

'His real name's Mr Joseph, but people call him Stalin or Uncle Joe. He's a widower – and a frightful stick-in-the-mud. He's always writing to us about how awful everything is. You know the sort.'

Jill did. 'What's this about a crash?'

'It's the children I feel sorry for,' Amy continued, turning the pages of her notebook. 'The girl's a sweet little thing. I hear she's in the accounts department at Broadbent's. At least the boy's got away from home – there's something to be said for National Service.'

'But this crash?' Jill said.

'I made a note here.' Amy tapped the tip of her pencil on the page. 'They think the driver took the bend too fast – it's a hairpin – and the car went over the edge. It's a steep drop.'

Jill glanced at her watch. 'When did it happen?'

'Yesterday evening.'

'I think I'll go to the press briefing.' Jill avoided Amy's eyes and opened a drawer of her desk. 'The police must know more by now, and it would do as the lead. It's not as if we've got much else.'

'But Miss Francis – we haven't done the post yet, and I know Mr Marr wanted to see you about the advertising figures.'

'Later.' Jill found her notebook, slammed the drawer shut and stood up. 'Everyone else is out. You might as well type those letters now.'

Amy departed, tight-lipped with suppressed irritation. Jill put on her coat and adjusted her hat in front of the mirror. It was only a few hundred yards from the *Gazette* office to police headquarters. She walked quickly down the High Street. She had spent the last few days in London and by comparison Lydmouth looked grubby and under-sized, like a slum child who has never had much of a chance in life.

At the police station the desk sergeant gave her a nod of recognition and waved her into the conference room. The press briefing had already started. Jill's arrival caused heads to twitch around the big mahogany table; after several years in London she had only recently returned to Lydmouth to edit the *Gazette*. She took a seat near the door, unbuttoned her coat and let it fall behind her on the chair. A fog of smoke blurred the outlines of the uniformed officer at the head of the table, who was talking in a soft Welsh accent.

Sergeant Lumb was chairing the briefing. Not Richard Thornhill, Jill thought; not important enough for him or the deputy chief constable. Lumb was talking about a spate of shoplifting. She began to make notes. Not Richard. Her vision blurred. Her eyes were watering. The smoke was irritating them.

There was a sound behind her, and a sudden draught of cool air on her neck. Once again, the heads twitched around the table. She did not look round.

'And then there's last night's fatality,' Lumb said, and paused with a sense of occasion to relight his pipe. 'Nasty business.' The match went out and there was another pause. 'Car went off the forest road about eleven p.m. Misty night, as you know. He took the Little Russia bend too fast by the look of it. Nasty drop there. Poor chap was dead when we got there.'

'Who was he?' Fuggle of the *Post* asked. He glanced at Jill as he spoke – no, not at her, but past her.

'Timothy Wynoll – young chap,' Lumb replied, glancing down at his notes. 'He was at university in London. Parents are abroad. Singapore. They've been notified by now. His aunt lives up near Ashbridge. It was her car, as a matter of fact.'

'Isn't it term time?' Jill asked, wondering if there was someone behind her, and if so, who. 'What was he doing in Lydmouth?'

'The aunt's away – on a cruise, lucky for some, eh? – and he promised he'd come down and check the pipes hadn't frozen after that cold snap. There was a letter from her in his pocket.'

'These students. All paid for with our taxes. Marvellous.' Fuggle rearranged the phlegm in his throat, making a sound like shingle shifting beneath a retreating wave on the sea shore. 'Been drinking, had he?'

'I'm afraid I can't say, Mr Fuggle.' Lumb sat back in his chair. 'No doubt the details will come out at the inquest.'

Jill raised her hand. 'Anyone else involved? Another car?'

'Not that we know of, Miss Francis.'

She glanced over her shoulder. Richard Thornhill was in the doorway. He gave her a hint of a smile and retreated. The door closed behind him.

'Chicken,' she murmured to herself or perhaps to him. 'Chicken.'

Fuggle stared at her with hard, shiny eyes like a pair of boiled sweets.

'The thing is, sir,' PC Porter said, 'it was odd. That's all.'

'What was?' Thornhill asked.

'The car, sir. The one in Little Russia.' Porter had waylaid Thornhill on the stairs at police headquarters. He was a very large young man, and he loomed like a mountain of flesh over the detective chief inspector. 'Sergeant Lumb sent me out to fetch it with the truck from the garage,' he went on apologetically. 'There it was, little Ford Popular, terrible state, windscreen gone. Shame really, couldn't have been more than a year or two old but it's only good for scrap. Mind you, could have been worse – he was smoking, look, and the whole thing could have gone up in flames if the petrol had leaked, yes and him too, not that it—'

'But what was odd?'

'Sorry, sir. Well, for a start, the car was in first gear.'

'Damn it, Porter, what's so odd about that?'

The young constable flinched as if Thornhill had hit him. 'If he was coming up the hill from Lydmouth he'd be in third, maybe, and then change down to second for the bend. But not first. Not unless he'd stopped for some reason.'

'Why would he have done that?'

'Maybe he pulled over on to the lay-by. But then why would he have gone over the edge? So I still don't understand how it could have happened. And anyway, if he was coming up and missed the bend he wouldn't have gone over the edge there. It . . . it doesn't feel right. Even if he was plastered.'

Porter ran out of words and stared with dumb hope at Thornhill. He had a childish faith in the chief inspector. Thornhill tried to ignore the knowledge that the briefing would soon be over, and therefore Jill Francis might come out of the conference room at any moment. Most of his colleagues thought Porter was stupid, and with some justification. But, as Thornhill knew, sometimes Porter's stupidity was more effective than mere cleverness could ever be; and, besides, he had a strangely profound understanding of cars and their ways.

'This lay-by,' Thornhill said. 'It's actually on the outer edge of the bend, isn't it?'

'Yes, sir. Old line of the road, maybe. There's a fence over the drop, but that's mainly gone. He went over at the downhill end. But, sir, if he'd missed the bend, he'd have gone over higher up.'

'Witnesses? Anyone live around there?'

'Only the Josephs, sir, down the bottom of the valley. Sarge went to see them, said they'd heard nothing.'

'What was it like where the car was?'

Porter wrinkled his broad, pink forehead. 'Came down twelve or fifteen feet – slammed into a rock, that did a lot of damage, and then banged into an old cooker. Folks tip their rubbish down there . . . look, it's not right. Driver's door comes open and out he comes. Head's a real mess, they say – all cut and bloody. Not nice at all.'

A drunk in a car, Thornhill thought, a winter night, poor visibility, an unexpected bend with a dangerous drop beyond. What was so odd about the fact that the car was a wreck and the drunk was dead?

'I found the wallet down there,' Porter was saying, his mouth forming the words very slowly as if no one had ever said them before. 'Just by the cooker. Sarge wondered where that had got to. Must have been loose in the car and fell out when he did.'

Thornhill glanced at the conference room door. 'Any sign of theft?'

Porter shook his head. 'Six quid in the wallet.'

'Where is it?'

'Upstairs, sir. With the rest of his stuff. Sergeant Lumb's got it.'

'I'll take a look at it,' Thornhill said reluctantly. 'And the clothes.'

The relief on Porter's face glowed like a neon sign. Thornhill led the way upstairs. Lumb's desk was almost invisible beneath a mound of files and papers, lightly powdered with pipe ash. Porter pulled out one of the cardboard boxes on the floor beside it. Thornhill looked quickly through Wynoll's clothes: a khaki-coloured duffel coat, a college scarf, a tweed jacket, flannel trousers, an Aertex shirt, vest, pants and socks. No hat, no tie, no jersey. The shoes were black Derbys, stained with mud. One shoulder of the duffel coat was thickly encrusted with blood, still tacky to the touch.

He looked up. 'Where is he?'

'Up the RAF, sir,' Porter said, which meant in the mortuary of the town's RAF hospital on the Chepstow Road.

'Possessions?'

Porter held out an old shoe box. Thornhill looked at the wallet first. No surprises: a cheque book; a letter from the aunt, postmarked Southampton and addressed to a student hostel in Bloomsbury; a membership card for the Photography Club at University College; a driving licence with an address near Ashbridge, presumably the home of the aunt; a condom, carefully disguised in an outer wrapping torn from the corner of an envelope; a book of stamps with one used; a bus ticket from Lydmouth to Ashbridge; a return train ticket to London; and six pound notes.

Wynoll had kept a running total on his bank balance in his cheque book. He had had well over a hundred pounds in his current account, so lack of money hadn't been one of his problems. According to the letter, the aunt had expected her nephew to come down yesterday afternoon. The dates on the tickets confirmed it.

There was also a packet of Park Drive with two cigarettes left. Another cigarette, half-smoked but not stubbed out, had fallen inside the duffel coat, where it had caused a burn before going out. Wynoll's other possessions were car keys, a Chubb door key, and a handkerchief, once white and now almost the colour of the duffel coat. And a bottle of Teacher's, still with nearly an inch of whisky in the bottom and a smudge of blood on the label.

'What about in the car? Anything there?'

'It's in the yard, sir.'

'Let's have a look.'

They went down to the yard at the back of police headquarters. There was a separate shed reserved for cars under investigation and equipped with an inspection pit. The Ford Popular was still on the trailer that had brought it back to Lydmouth. The front offside of the car was like crumpled wrapping paper. One of the headlights had come adrift and was dangling by the side, attached only by wires. The windscreen and the driver's window were broken.

Thornhill pulled open the door, which was hanging drunkenly on its hinges. He looked along the row of instruments on the dashboard. He turned the handle that had wound the driver's window up and down. At the moment the glass had broken, the window had been closed. He crouched to peer at the floor.

'Put some gloves on,' he said, straightening up. 'I want everything out of the car.'

Porter stared open-mouthed. 'What?' There was a pause. 'Sir.'

'Everything that moves. Mats, whatever's in the glove compartment, contents of the ashtray, even the sweet wrappers. Put it all on the bench. I'll be back in ten minutes.'

The briefing had finished. Thornhill found Lumb skimming through a file in reception.

'The Little Russia crash,' Thornhill said. 'Keep me posted, will you?'

The sergeant frowned. 'Any reason, sir?'

'Just in case.'

Lumb tapped the file. 'We've traced Wynoll's movements yesterday. He was drinking in the Bathurst most of the evening with a young man about the same age as him. Barmaid didn't know who it was but she said they were having a bit of an argy-bargy about something at closing time. Couldn't say what about.'

'Description?'

'Little chap. But she said he wasn't bad looking, for what that's worth. Trouble is, kids all look the same these days. They left together.'

When Thornhill returned to the yard, Porter was waiting by the door of the shed. Thornhill picked his way through the contents of the car. Apart from a surprising quantity of small stones and pieces of dried mud, there were half a dozen cigarette ends, more Park Drive by the look of them, along with used matches, an AA handbook and ten or twelve vividly green and purple wrappers from Brasher's Mint Imperials. He put to one side a selection of less predictable items from a piece of string to a brown-paper bag containing two dried apple cores, from a travelling sewing kit to a half-used jar of Marmite.

Marmite, he thought, mints and matches. String. A sewing kit. Apple cores. His mind strained to combine them into something that made a pattern.

Matches?

When he had finished he went back outside. Porter stared expectantly at him. The constable's mouth was open as though he was hoping his superior officer might feed him with a titbit.

'Yes,' Thornhill said at last. 'Perhaps it is.'

'Yes, sir. But what, sir?'

'As you said, Porter: perhaps it's odd.'

'Chicken,' Jill said aloud.

She was alone in the lay-by, standing under an umbrella in the rain beside her green Morris Minor. Behind her was the road, snaking up to Ashbridge and the forest, divided from the lay-by by a ragged crescent of saplings, bramble and long grass. It was unexpectedly private. In front of her was the rusting remains of a barbed-wire fence, draped on rotting posts. Sections of it had fallen away.

The view was beautiful. The densely wooded Little Russia valley stretched downhill, narrow and steep-sided, funnelling outwards and curving to the north in the direction of the invisible river below. The lay-by itself was less attractive. A rotting mattress, disgorging its horsehair bowels, lay at one end, among rusting tins, empty bottles and the remains of a sack of plaster that had left dirty-white streaks in the mud.

She walked slowly across the cracked tarmac to the largest of the gaps in the fence, a stretch of about five yards towards the end closest to the road downhill. The drop was almost vertical. The underlying sandstone was exposed. At the bottom was a jagged rock about the size of a small caravan. Beside it was a rusting gas cooker on its side, a selection of empty tins and a couple of bald tyres. It would be possible to scramble down there, but it was not something to attempt in a decent coat, a snugly-fitting skirt and two-inch heels.

Farther down the slope a roof was visible through the branches, the clay tiles streaked with lichen. A little barn, perhaps, she thought, or a shepherd's hut. It must be invisible in summer. The forest was studded with these mysterious little buildings, usually ruinous, which must once have had necessary reasons for being where they were. Unlike her.

She stared at the rock. This was where the boy had died. Shards of glass glinted beside the rock. She wondered if she was imagining a smear of pale-grey paint on one side. What had she expected to find? An explanation? The confirmation of a hunch?

There was a rustling below her, somewhere in the bushes below the rock. Jill felt suddenly guilty, as though detected in a small, shabby crime. She glanced down into the ravine and at the same time took a step backwards.

Her movement was too little, too late. Not five yards from the rock, a face appeared among the branches. There was no possibility of a silent and dignified withdrawal now.

'Hello, Richard,' Jill said.

Formal as ever, he touched his hat. 'Good afternoon, Miss Francis.'

'When we're alone you might as well call me Jill, don't you think? I know things between us have . . . well, things have changed, but it's quite absurd to be so pompous.'

Colour rose in his face. 'Very well. What are you doing here?'

'I'm a journalist,' Jill said. 'Remember?'

'I can hardly forget.' He touched his hat again. 'I won't keep you.'

Jill turned on her heel, leaving Thornhill in undisputed possession of Little Russia. She climbed into the car, lit a cigarette and started the engine.

Her hands were shaking slightly. Chicken, she thought. That's the trouble with all of us – we're all bloody chicken.

When he was alone in Little Russia, Thornhill methodically quartered the scene of the crash, picking his way among the rubbish, the shattered branches and the fragments of rock. It was a shocking waste of time to be doing this himself, he told himself, particularly as his reason for doing was so tenuous – in fact not really a reason at all. And what had Jill been up to? Damn it, she was editing the *Gazette* now – if they wanted local colour for their piece on the crash, why not send a minion?

Shivering because of the cold, Thornhill set off towards the forestry road where he had left his car. He followed a winding track that pursued an eccentric four-footed logic, for Little Russia was more frequented by deer and rabbits, badgers and foxes than by humans. He stumbled into a puddle, spattering filthy water on the skirts of his navy-blue overcoat. It began to rain, and he had not brought his umbrella.

The track passed the corner of the small stone building with its sagging roof of double Roman pantiles, patched in places with corrugated iron. There was an unglazed opening high in the gable but no other windows. The door, held in place with a rusting, hand-forged Suffolk latch, was still sound.

An unexpected colour, a vivid mauve, caught Thornhill's eye on the ground immediately outside the door. He stooped. There were two ticket stubs a few inches from the door jamb. He picked them up and felt them between finger and thumb. They couldn't have been there long, for they were still dry. A tiny oddity? He slipped them between two leaves of his notebook.

Thornhill lifted the latch, pushed open the door and went into the barn. The air smelled damp but unexpectedly fresh. The roof was still weathertight. He stood in the doorway and watched the rain drifting over the treetops towards the valley below.

He turned his back on the weather and, as he moved, his foot snagged on a soft, yielding obstruction. He looked down. There was a filthy brown blanket on the earth floor.

His immediate thought was that at some point a tramp must have passed a chilly night here. He walked about the building, automatically looking for something that would confirm or refute the theory. He found nothing. In the doorway again, he bent down to the blanket and examined it more closely. There was a cluster of darker spots on the coarse wool, fresher-looking than the ancient dirt on the fabric. He angled the blanket towards the light from the doorway. The spots were rust-red and dry to the touch. Blood? If it was, then the colour suggested it was relatively recent in origin.

Thornhill straightened up. The rain was petering away, driving north-east up the river valley below with a freshening wind behind it. Suddenly he was in a hurry to get back to Lydmouth, to the warmth and familiarity of police headquarters.

The path between the barn and the forestry track was easier going than the path to the site of the crash. In less than ten minutes he reached the broad ride, surfaced with rubble. From there it was only a few yards to the junction of the track and the road, where he had left his car.

A brick house stood on the corner – a square, modern building in an unkempt garden overshadowed by gangling conifers. As Thornhill approached, an ambulance was pulling out of its concrete driveway. It swung on to the road, where it turned left towards Lydmouth.

Thornhill unlocked his car door. He glanced up at the house. He was just in time to catch sight of a face, little more than a pale blur, before it vanished from an upper window.

'He's not absolutely sure,' Amy Gwyn-Thomas said. 'The boy doesn't come to chapel very often now. Of course they change so quickly at that age, don't they? And he's been away in the army.'

'Who isn't sure?' said Jill, who had not been listening to her secretary.

'Ronald – Mr Prout.' Amy blushed. 'I happened to bump into him in the Gardenia, quite accidentally. The rush at lunchtime is getting worse and worse. We had to share a table.'

Jill didn't believe in that sort of accident. She suspected Amy of conducting a clandestine courtship with Mr Prout, who kept a toyshop and played the organ in the Baptist chapel.

'Whatever was Mr Prout doing in the Bathurst Arms?' Jill asked. 'I hadn't put him down as a drinking man.'

The blush intensified. 'Of course not. He was collecting for the Mission Society. Anyway, he said, there were two young men in there, obviously rather the worse for wear, if you know what I mean, at one of the tables in the saloon bar. They didn't give him anything – just waved him away; people can be so rude, can't they? Ronald was almost certain that one of them was Little Joe. He wasn't sure, or he would have said something.'

'Has he got a car?' Jill said. 'Little Joe, I mean. What's his real name, by the way?'

'Mark. Mark Joseph. And I don't think he's got a car. He can't be more than nineteen or twenty. He couldn't afford it. But he might have the use of his father's. I know Mr Joseph's got one, I've seen it at chapel. It's black. Why do you ask?'

'I just wondered.' Jill picked up her handbag, which was
beside the desk.

'Are you going out again?'

Before Jill could answer, Amy's telephone rang in the next
room. She went to answer it. As Jill was leaving her office
a moment later, Amy waylaid her. There was a pink, moist
spot on each of the secretary's powdered cheeks.

'Well I never,' she said. 'That was Ronald – Mr Prout.
He went to see his mother at the hospital after lunch. And
guess who he saw being carried out of an ambulance there?
Little Joe.'

Acute carbon monoxide poisoning turns your cheeks cherry
pink and gives them a misleadingly healthy appearance. By
that time, however, you may well be dead or comatose.

Mark Joseph was alive, but only just. The consultant
thought it likely that, if the boy recovered, his neurological
functions would be considerably impaired, perhaps in the
long term. Translated, that meant it might be a long time
before the police would be able to get any sense out of him
– assuming, of course, that he survived.

Sergeant Lumb and a policewoman had been to the
house in Little Russia. On his return he told Thornhill that
Little Joe had used strips of a dust sheet to attach the hose
of the vacuum cleaner to the exhaust of his father's
car, which was parked in a garage beside the house. He
had run the hose through the driver's window and sealed
up the cracks with Sellotape and brown paper. Then he
had climbed into the car, started the engine and waited to
die.

'It was the sister that saved him,' Lumb said. 'Sylvia –
she's ill, having a day or two off work. Came downstairs to
make herself a drink, and she heard the engine running. Doc
said he'd have been dead in another half-hour.'

'Why did he do it?' Thornhill asked.

'Don't know, sir. But it was suicide – he left a note: but
all he said was sorry. And he sent his love to his sister.'

Thornhill considered. Then: 'Not to his parents?'

'Mother's dead. He don't get on with his dad. To be fair,
not many people do – they call him Uncle Joe round here.

As in Stalin. He's a nasty old bugger, excuse my French, the holier-than-thou type.'

'Has he been told?'

Lumb shook his head. 'He's staying with friends in Scotland. No telephone. We've contacted the local boys, asked them to take a message over.'

'I'll go and take a look at the house. I'd like to talk to the sister, too.'

Thornhill took his own car, along with the uniformed WPC who had accompanied Lumb to Little Russia earlier in the day; it was all too likely, Thornhill thought, that Sylvia Joseph would be difficult to handle – emotional, possibly hysterical – and dealing with that sort of thing was woman's work.

The problem was, he realised when he drew up outside the Josephs' house in Little Russia, the wrong woman had already turned up to deal with it. A green Morris Minor was parked outside. He walked quickly up the concrete path, buttoning his overcoat for the air seemed much colder here. Jill Francis opened the door before he had time to ring the bell. For an instant they stared at each other, both of them conscious of the silent policewoman at Thornhill's side.

He raised his hat. 'Good afternoon, Miss Francis. We've come to see Miss Joseph.'

'She's downstairs now,' Jill said. 'In the sitting room.'

'How is she?'

'Shocked. Miserable. Just sits there eating sweets and hoping it will all go away. Would you like to come through?'

'Perhaps you and I might have a word beforehand.' He turned to the WPC. 'Go and see Miss Joseph. I won't be long.'

The young woman glanced at him, the confusion evident on her face. But she said nothing. Jill showed her into the room where Sylvia was sitting. Thornhill glimpsed a child-like figure in a dressing gown. She seemed scarcely older than his own daughter. She was sitting in a chair, her fingers delving into a green and purple box on her lap, and she did not raise her head to look at him. Lank brown hair curtained her face. The door closed.

Jill draped her coat over her shoulders like a cape and joined him on the doorstep.

'What are you doing here?' Thornhill whispered to Jill, conscious that once again she had put him in an absurd position.

'I told you this morning – my job.' She stared ahead, declining to look at him. 'It's a story. A boy tried to kill himself. You'll want to see the garage, won't you? Why don't we talk there?'

It was as good an idea as any. The garage was a brick building that leaned against one side of the house, with double doors now propped open. The car was a large black Austin at least twenty years old. The vacuum cleaner hose still ran from the end of the exhaust to the driver's window.

'You'd better not go inside,' he said. 'We'll need to look in here.'

'I already have been inside.' Her voice was flat. 'Sorry. Shall I tell you why he did it? Little Joe, I mean.'

He stared at her. 'I think you'd better.'

'In a way it's because Timothy Wynoll had seen a film up in London. *Rebel Without a Cause*. James Dean and Natalie Wood. It only opened a week or two ago. I saw it the other day when I was up in town.'

'For God's sake. Jill, I haven't time for this.'

'Bear with me. There's a scene in which James Dean and another boy have what they call a chickie run. Each of them has a car. They drive towards a precipice. And the first one to bale out is chicken. In the film, the other boy tries to but a strap on his jacket catches on the door handle. And he goes over the edge.'

'But there's nothing to—'

'Mr Prout saw Timothy Wynoll and Mark Joseph in the Bathurst Arms last night. Arguing about something. I think it ended with Wynoll challenging him to play chicken. But Wynoll didn't bail out in time.'

'You've no evidence for that.'

But as he spoke, Thornhill remembered the mauve tickets he had found near the barn this morning. Cinema tickets? Or was that too fanciful? Anyway, what had the tickets been doing outside the barn?

'Look at the nearside wheel,' Jill said.

Thornhill stared at it. There were spots of the pinkish-brown mud on the rim, just as there were on the rims of his own car, and also something white embedded in some of the tread and smeared on the side of the tyre.

'I think it's plaster,' Jill said. 'Someone dumped a sack of it in the lay-by above Little Russia. So that car was up there, and recently.'

Thornhill smiled, not at her but because, as he grasped what she was suggesting, a possible solution to a small puzzle slotted into his mind. 'I wondered how he lit the cigarette.'

'Who?'

'Wynoll,' he said. 'You see, he was smoking when he went over the edge. But he didn't have any matches or a lighter with him. And the car doesn't have a cigarette lighter, either. I thought it was odd from the start. Then Wynoll kills himself without meaning to, is that what you're suggesting?'

'Yes,' Jill said. 'And then Mark tries this stunt –' she glanced at the car – 'because he blamed himself for Wynoll's death. It's—'

'You don't have the ticket stub, by any chance?' he interrupted.

'What?'

'From when you went to see that film.' But perhaps she wouldn't have the stub, Thornhill thought, because a man had taken her, and of course the man would have paid.

'I don't know.' She looked up at him. 'Perhaps.' She opened her handbag, took out her purse and rummaged inside it. 'I'm not sure – so much rubbish accumulates – what about these? Yes, look, you can make out "ion" on that one. The film's on at the London Pavilion.'

He looked down at the palm of her hand at two mauve ticket stubs. *A man would have paid*. He felt a small and squalid relief, almost worse than the absurd jealousy that had preceded it.

The front door opened. They both turned towards the sound, pulling sharply away from each other as though jointly guilty of a nameless crime. The girl was walking stiffly towards them, an overcoat over her dressing gown. The policewoman hovered anxiously behind her.

'Sylvia,' Jill said, starting forward, 'you shouldn't—'

'It's my fault,' the girl said in a thin, dull voice. 'I can't wait.'

'Miss Joseph,' Thornhill said. 'Your brother's still alive. He's very ill but—'

'Not him,' she snapped, with a flash of temper. 'Tim.'

He stared at her. 'You'd better say what you mean by that.'

Sylvia nodded at Jill. 'She guessed some of it. Did she tell you? Tim was down at Christmas. We met at the Young Conservatives party in the Ruispidge Hall. I . . . I was a bit tiddly. And we . . . well, I was stupid and so was he. And I realised what had happened when I was late.' She ran out of words.

'Her period,' Jill said, and touched the girl's arm.

'You're pregnant?' Thornhill said to Sylvia.

She didn't speak.

'She was,' Jill said. 'She miscarried last night.'

'Dad would have killed me if he found out,' the girl whispered. 'Me first, then Tim.'

'So you got rid of it?' Thornhill said, thinking that the last thing he wanted was an illegal abortion on his plate as well.

'No!' she glared at him. 'It wasn't like that. I wanted Tim to marry me, to make it all right. But he laughed at me. Mark was home on leave so I told him, and he said he'd talk to Tim and make him see sense. They met in the Bathurst. All they did was quarrel and get drunk and do the chickie run in Little Russia.'

'Did your brother tell you?'

'Yes.' Sylvia gave a brittle laugh. 'When he came in last night. It was because of that James Dean film. Tim thought it was marvellous. He took me to see it when I went up to London . . . to tell him about . . . about the baby. I told him after we'd been to the cinema. I thought perhaps if we got married . . .' The thin, anguished voice sank to a murmur. 'He said I wasn't a patch on Natalie Wood. He didn't really like me at all. He only went with me that one time because he was drunk. And all he really wanted to talk about was that stupid, bloody film.'

The ticket stubs, Thornhill thought. The blood on the

blanket. The lighted cigarette. The wallet. Something was missing. Something that made it all add up. Then suddenly there it was – the connection: two colours glowing brightly and freshly in the forefront of his mind. Tenuous but undeniably there. *Freshly*, that was the point.

'Sylvia should be sitting down,' Jill said. 'She's lost a lot of blood because of the miscarriage. And a doctor should see her.'

Thornhill ignored Jill. 'Where were you last night?'

Sylvia's eyes widened. 'Here, of course.' She touched her stomach. 'I was already feeling – you know – funny down there.'

'Richard,' Jill said. 'Is this really necessary? Here?'

The policewoman took a step forward, looking to Thornhill for direction.

'But you weren't here at all,' Thornhill said to Sylvia. 'You were in Wynoll's car, weren't you? Waiting while he was in the pub, perhaps, maybe hoping for a reconciliation? You were with him when he drove up the hill to the lay-by. You lit the cigarette he was smoking when he went over the edge.'

Sylvia clung to Jill's arm for support.

'You survived,' he said harshly. 'Timothy Wynoll didn't. You took out his wallet after the crash. What were you looking for? A letter from you? A photograph?'

The girl's expression changed, cracking like ice on a frozen pond when someone throws a stone in the middle.

'The ticket stubs for that film were in his pockets,' he went on, 'probably in his wallet. I found them this morning near the barn in the woods between here and the car. Still dry, so they hadn't been there long – they wouldn't have lasted long like that in this weather. You must have dropped them last night.'

'You can't be sure of that,' Jill said. 'He might have dropped them there himself – before last night, I mean.'

Thornhill shook his head, his eyes still on Sylvia. 'Wynoll didn't reach Lydmouth until yesterday afternoon. The tickets in his pocket prove that. So who dropped the tickets in the woods over there? It can't have been Wynoll or your brother, Sylvia. It must have been you. How else could they have got there?'

'She . . . she might have paid for the tickets herself,' Jill said in a voice not much more than a whisper.

'I doubt it. Why should she, when she was with a man who wasn't exactly short of money?'

Jill glared at him. But he didn't notice. The tickets were by the barn, he thought, and there had been blood on the blanket.

Another link in the chain?

'You stopped in the barn on your way back here last night,' he said to Sylvia. 'You were already bleeding from the miscarriage.'

Sylvia let go of Jill's arm. She stared at the grubby concrete of the path, her face invisible behind the lank hair. 'I hate you,' she muttered. 'I hate you.'

Who was she talking to, Thornhill wondered – himself or Wynoll? The entire world? The unwanted baby? Or even herself? He turned to the policewoman. 'Take Miss Joseph inside. Stay with her until I tell you otherwise. Don't leave her alone for any reason.'

When they were alone, Jill turned on him. 'What in God's name are you doing? She's a victim, can't you see that? Anyway, there's nothing to show she was there, nothing to *prove* it.'

'She was there.' He stared at her. 'And I think she might have—'

He broke off. Sylvia had had the presence of mind to search Timothy Wynoll after he was dead. All along, there was something cold and calculating about her behaviour. Had she prevented Wynoll from braking? Or had she hit him afterwards, with a rock or even the whisky bottle with the blood on the label? He had nothing like hard proof, of course, he was far short of that. But he'd send the SOCOs into Little Russia immediately, and once they had the pathologist's report on Wynoll and his head injuries . . .

'Tell me what you think happened,' Jill said softly. 'What gave you the idea she was in the car in the first place? Trust me.'

He shook his head. Accepting the invitation would be like signing a blank cheque.

'Chicken,' she said.

Thornhill looked at her. A blank cheque? Who cared? He would bankrupt himself if she asked him. He opened his mouth to speak, to say, 'Brasher's Mint Imperials are wrapped in green and purple papers.'

The wrappers on the car floor hadn't been there long. Sylvia had been eating them this afternoon as if her life depended on them.

But the front door opened before he had time to say anything at all. The policewoman was running down the path towards them. He knew at once what had happened from her white face and her open mouth, from the red smear on her navy-blue skirt and the door hanging open behind her. He knew that it was too late for Sylvia, and also perhaps for himself and Jill.

YESTERDAY
Charles Todd

Charles Todd is an American mother and son crime-writing team comprising Caroline and Charles Todd. *A Test of Wills*, set in 1919, introduced Scotland Yard cop Ian Rutledge, and the latest of the duo's fifteen mystery novels is *An Impartial Witness*, featuring their other series character, Bess Crawford. Again, the Crawford books are set in the UK.

English Channel, early 1915

Newly minted Lieutenant Ian Rutledge stood at the rail of the transport carrying him to France. The hull cut through the winter grey water smoothly, and a little of the spray reached him now and again. He'd always been a good sailor, and this was an easy crossing for the time of year. Still, behind him he could hear men retching. Some of them had never seen the sea before, much less set sail on it.

Yesterday, he thought, he'd been an inspector at Scotland Yard. Well, not quite yesterday, but it seemed so. Now he was a soldier on his way to his first battle. He looked around at the men he'd be commanding. Highlanders for the most part. The Scots had a long history of fighting well, even when they lost. A quarrelsome race, someone had once called them.

The transport was a converted ferry, men crowded into the public rooms and lounges, officers given the few cabins available, and the hold crammed with their gear. Rutledge walked from the bow to the stern, looking back at England, at the still-sunlit white cliffs, though cloud banks were building in the west, and the wind had picked up considerably. More soldiers lined the ship's rail now, heads down, stomachs retching.

A man running for the rail caught his toe in a coil of rope

and sprawled headlong almost at Rutledge's feet, vomiting as he went down. He wiped his mouth, took note of the boots of an officer not inches from his nose, and looked up quickly, on the point of begging pardon.

They recognised each other in the same instant, and the soldier scrambled to his feet with the speed of fear and took off down the crowded deck, disappearing through the nearest companionway.

Rutledge gave chase, pushing through the clusters of men and officers and launching himself through the open companionway in his turn. But there was no sign of his quarry. A tall Highlander was coming up from below, and Rutledge asked, 'The man who just came through here – did you see where he went?'

'I didna' see anyone,' the Highlander replied, his voice bland, though Rutledge knew very well that he had most probably come close to colliding with the fleeing soldier. 'Sir.'

'You couldn't have avoided him,' Rutledge retorted. 'Which way, damn it?' He had almost added, 'I'm a policeman', for old habits die hard.

The young Highlander smiled. 'I didna' see anyone,' he repeated, and stood his ground.

Rutledge considered telling him that the fleeing soldier was one Thomas MacBride, wanted for three murders in London. There had been a city-wide and then a country-wide manhunt for him, and still MacBride had slipped through the net. It was suspected that he'd had help, possibly had been concealed by old friends who were not above giving the police as much trouble as they could without finding themselves in gaol. But no amount of persuasion or threats had brought answers. Or else he'd hidden himself away in some remote Highland village that had never heard of a warrant issued by Scotland Yard for MacBride's arrest. This had been nearly six weeks before war had been declared, and Rutledge could see that joining the army could appear to be a clever way out of the country, with an eye to desertion once in France. What he needed now was the name under which MacBride had enlisted. Surely not his own?

'If you didn't see where he went, what is his name? His company?'

The Highlander said, 'As I didna' see him ata', sir, I canna' tell ye his name.'

Rutledge was sorely tempted to put this man on report, but knew it would only spell trouble. The reputation of being a short-tempered Englishman wouldn't serve him once they landed in France and he had to command men like this.

He said only, 'Do you remember your own name?'

The Highlander hesitated, then replied, 'Sir. Private Hamish MacLeod. '

Rutledge nodded and turned back the way he'd come.

Swearing to himself, he debated whether to speak to one of the officers on board, then decided against it. MacBride was wanted by Scotland Yard, and not the army. Very likely Rutledge himself would be called to order for harking back to his civilian life.

MacBride's third victim, one Alec Cameron, had named his killer to the constable who had found him bleeding from stab wounds in a doorway near the British Museum. Cameron had died on the way to hospital. The other two murders had been linked to MacBride because it appeared that both the weapon – a thin, very sharp knife – and the skill with which it was used were the same, added to the fact that the dead were close associates of Cameron's in a doubtful export firm that was suspected of specialising in selling articles stolen in Britain to equally doubtful dealers on the continent. The war had put paid to that enterprise. Had MacBride foreseen that, and decided to rid himself of people who could point a finger at him? His dealings had most certainly brought in considerable sums, and no matter what the police suspected, they couldn't prove any of it. If MacBride chose to retire for the duration, colleagues who could tell tales would become dangerous friends. That, at least, had been the thinking of Superintendent Bowles. Rutledge suspected MacBride no longer trusted his former associates, and they had had a falling out.

The alternative to reporting MacBride's presence was to search the transport ship himself. Rutledge began at the bow, worked his way aft, and he took care to glance at each face he passed. There was no sign of MacBride on deck – he hadn't expected to find him there – and Rutledge went below, working through the common rooms full to capacity with soldiers and their kit. He saw Private MacLeod again, and felt the Scot's gaze following him as he strode by men sleeping, playing cards, writing letters, or simply staring into space as if they could see what was to come.

He was just leaving the converted lounge when Private MacLeod came up to him and saluted. 'Sir. Someone just told me ye were a policeman before the war.'

'Yes,' he answered reluctantly, wondering who had recognised him – and then he realised it must have been MacBride himself. 'Inspector, Scotland Yard.'

'And ye're no' an inspector now?'

'I've taken a leave of absence. For the duration of hostilities.'

MacLeod, as if that explained matters for him, said, 'Once a policeman . . .' He let his voice trail away. 'Aye, and what has yon soldier done that ye're after him still?'

'He murdered three men in cold blood. The last one named MacBride before he died.'

'Ye ken, he willna' see matters the same way.'

'No.' Rutledge had no illusions. If he asked for their help, the Scots would close ranks to protect one of their own, and there must be nearly as many places to hide aboard here as there were soldiers bent on thwarting him. And he knew that if he pushed them too far, his authority as an officer would be diminished before he had even given them their first order. 'I'm willing to hear his side. But I have a duty, and I can't turn my back on it.'

'Aye. But would he no' serve better in France killing Germans than he would mounting yon scaffold in London?'

'Assuming,' Rutledge said, 'that MacBride even arrives at the front. France is wide. As is Spain and Portugal. He could be in South America or China before we have a hope in hell of catching him up.'

MacLeod considered that. 'We?' he asked after a moment.

'Yes, all right, the Yard.' Yesterday he could have had this man taken into custody for obstructing the police in the performance of their duties. Today, he had to rely on the man's innate sense of justice. 'But if I take him now, I can radio England and have the Portsmouth police meet the ferry on its return.'

'Were the men he's said to have killed sae important then?'

Rutledge said, curbing his exasperation, '*They* weren't very good men. But they didn't deserve to be murdered.'

MacLeod thanked him and stood aside so that he could continue his search.

But Rutledge said before MacLeod turned away, 'How do you see murder? If your friend is a killer, do you wonder if he will kill again, if circumstances are right?'

'He's no' my friend. All the same, I willna' fear being murdered in my bed, if he's killed once for his ain sake. But if he killed for gain, I wouldna' turn my back on him.'

'Well said. But which is he?' Rutledge replied. Not waiting for an answer, he went to find the companionway to the hold. The wind was still gathering strength, the ferry pitching ferociously.

As far as he could see in the shadowed darkness below was another sea – of gear. It creaked and strained against its tethers, threatening to burst its bonds. Entrenching tools, boxes of cartridges, crates of what appeared to be rifles, other crates and barrels identified only with numbers. Packed tightly, it still offered sanctuary and would require hours to search the lot. And while he was occupied on one side, Rutledge knew MacBride would be inching his silent way around the other, footsteps covered by the sound of the waves striking the hull.

After a moment, Rutledge called, 'MacBride? Can you hear me? Give yourself up and I'll see you get a fair trial.'

There was silence, only the echo of Rutledge's voice coming back to him from the far end of the ship. And yet he thought he could sense the man's presence.

'Did they cheat you, Cameron and Davies and Kerr? Is that why they had to die?'

No answer.

He hazarded an educated guess. 'Or were you ridding yourself of them before they could tell the world that you'd stolen the Duke of Buccleuch's *Book of Hours*? It was you, wasn't it? It had the earmarks of your style. And it made your fortune, didn't it, that illuminated manuscript? You must have had a buyer waiting, to take such an inordinate risk. It's even finer than the Duc du Barry's prayer book.'

Nothing.

I'm talking to myself, Rutledge thought. There's no one here after all. Even the guard set to watch the hold had bolted for the deck – there had been signs of vomit at the foot of the companionway. But he made a final effort.

'There's a witness to say that you killed Cameron. He named you himself before he died. You can't run forever. And what good will all that money do you, cowering in some backwater of the world, fearful of being recognised? You should have left well enough alone.'

As the echo of his last words died away, Rutledge turned to go. And then he heard a weak voice saying, 'I didn't kill Cameron. Or anyone else. Damn it, leave me in *peace*. I'm dying of this seasickness.'

'I can't leave it. I've taken an oath, MacBride. And just because I wear the king's uniform now, I can't walk away from the king's justice.'

'Be damned to the king's justice. I tell you, I haven't killed anyone.'

'Then why did Cameron name you?'

'It's why I ran, isn't it? Knowing the lads had been killed. Put the fear of God into me. Could be he was trying to warn me I was next. He was that sort, Cameron. Do a friend a good turn. We had enemies, the four of us. Business rivals, you might say.'

'Then they left you holding the bag, didn't they? The police are hunting you, not them.'

'Don't you see, it wasn't me who killed those men. And whoever did knows I'm still alive. There must be something he wants. Revenge, maybe? Why didn't the Yard look at that, I ask you? Why are they after *me*?'

'You stole the *Book of Hours*.'

There was a grunt of pain. 'Bluidy coppers.'

'Or perhaps the man who bought it from you thinks you might give him up one day, to save yourselves. That happens. Is he English or a Scot? Did he come to you or was the theft your own idea? Someone knew how to get into that house and out again. Knew where, indeed, the manuscript was kept. Had he been a guest there?'

'He'd not do that to us.'

'If he'd steal from a house where he'd been a guest, he'd turn on you. Think about it.'

'He's not English. He's got no call to fear us. It's someone wanting revenge. If *he* was going to kill us after getting that book for him, why not steal it himself, I ask you?' He vomited again. But Rutledge couldn't locate the sound.

'And get caught by his host? I think not. What's curious is why he didn't kill you when he had the chance. Before you knew he'd killed the others. But he's content to let you take the blame, isn't he? You're right, no one would believe *you* were innocent.'

After a moment MacBride said breathlessly, 'You're wrong. I had nothing to fear there. It was his idea I join the army.'

'And desert? They shoot deserters, did he tell you?'

'He knows France. He made me memorise a list of friends.'

'I could also give you the names of a dozen Frenchmen. Whether any of them exist or not, you'll have to discover yourself. I could give you a list of a dozen more, who would kill you and feed you to their pigs, if I offered them enough money.'

'He's not like that, I tell you. He's a gentleman, and he left France before the Marne was overrun by the invading Germans. He had help. He said they'd help me as well. Let me be, for God's sake. I've done you no harm. This isn't London, is it?'

There had been weeks of backing and filling before the war began. From the June morning when the Austrian archduke had been shot in Sarajevo to the August morning when the Germans had begun their invasion of Belgium, anyone with eyes could see that the war was inevitable. Russia was bent on punishing the Slavs, and as soon as they attacked, it was clear that Germany would march as well in defence of Austria. Like a house of cards, the situation had deteriorated one step at a time, and someone could easily have chosen to pack and go rather than wait and see.

This Frenchman had had money, then – to leave the country with his belongings, to pay for the theft of the *Book of Hours*, to visit a country house full of treasures he coveted.

Rutledge said, 'No one helped Cameron or the others. Someone stabbed those men in exactly the same place with the same sort of knife. Hardly random killings. Hardly revenge, for that matter. Precise, clean – deadly. You could have done it. Your father was a butcher, wasn't he? And how did their murderer manage the killings? Do you think the men stood still and let someone choose his spot? They believed in him. They trusted him.'

Silence.

'Is he a butcher? This Frenchman? A doctor? A hunter?'

The silence had gone on too long. Rutledge was already edging quickly around the piles and stacks of gear, still talking to cover his movements.

'Tell me the Frenchman's name, and I'll ask the Yard to make inquiries, to clear you of the murder charge. And if they get the manuscript back, they may relent on the charge of housebreaking. I can have this ship sealed, and you'll be taken off—'

There was someone just behind him. Rutledge threw himself to one side, and came up braced to fight for his life. Cornered men sometimes found superhuman strength when they needed it.

He found himself staring into the amused face of the Highlander, MacLeod. Rutledge straightened, feeling himself flushing. They were of a height, and as he met MacLeod's gaze, the man lay a finger against his lips and then pointed to the stern of the hold. The opposite direction.

He hadn't been helpful earlier, this Scot, and it was very possible that he was steering Rutledge in the wrong direction now to give MacBride a chance to slip past and go up on deck.

On the other hand, if even with his own acute hearing, he himself couldn't tell where the sounds were coming from, how had the Highlander determined it? He could as easily walk straight into MacBride.

But it was the only chance on offer, and Rutledge nodded his thanks, then made his way as silently as he could through the maze of equipment. He was nearing the end of a narrow passage between two rows of crates, already deciding that the Highlander had led him astray, when he all but stumbled over MacBride curled into a tight knot on the floor, his face twisted in pain. The man flinched but was in no state to run. There was vomit on the floor around him and Rutledge noted flecks of dark blood in the thin pools before he shouted to MacLeod, 'Find a surgeon. Now.'

He heard heels on the companionway, and turned his attention to MacBride. 'This isn't seasickness,' he said, bending down to loosen the collar of the man's tunic. 'Where does it hurt? Speak up, man, your appendix may have burst.'

But MacBride shook his head, sweat beading his pale face.

Rutledge did what he could to make him comfortable, and after a space, MacBride spoke. 'It *is* the sea; he told me how it would feel,' he answered through clenched teeth. 'He warned me.'

'The Frenchman?'

The answer was lost in another bout of vomiting that brought up little but bile and blood.

And then the surgeon was there, arguing with MacLeod as he came down the narrow passage that Rutledge had just followed.

'—is seasick, man, why should I be dragged down here—' He broke off, seeing the cramped body of the ill man and the vomit around him. 'Dear God.'

He was down on his knees, working with MacBride, asking Rutledge questions for which he had no answers – what had the man eaten, when, how long this had been going on?

'He's poisoned himself,' the doctor said finally, rocking back on his heels. 'Or tried to. Here, get him out of this cramped place and to where I can examine him properly.'

'Why should he take poison,' Rutledge asked, 'when we haven't even reached the fighting?'

'A coward,' the doctor said contemptuously as MacLeod and Rutledge between them lifted the sick man and moved him to a wider space by the hull between bulkheads.

But Rutledge shook his head. He said, pitching his voice so that MacBride could hear, 'What did he give you? And how did he know where to find you?'

'—hid me. On property. Helped me. He said enlist.'

Which, Rutledge realised, was the best way of keeping the police searching for MacBride and not for the real killer.

'What did he give you?'

'Herbs. To keep me steady on me feet . . .' He vomited again, and in spite of the doctor's protests, Rutledge began to go through MacBride's pockets. He came up with a small vial. It was labelled 'Motion Sickness' in an elegant hand. Beneath were clearly lettered instructions: 'Swallow one half of contents on boarding, one half an hour out of port.'

Holding up the vial to the dim light, Rutledge could just make out the level of the liquid inside. It was half full. Perhaps a little more than half.

He hadn't realised that MacLeod was still there, standing just out of sight behind his left shoulder, until the Scot spoke. 'A verra' canny man, yon Frenchman.'

And it was indeed clever. So many were sick even on a smooth crossing. Who would take special note of MacBride's case? Most generally survived their suffering, little the worse for wear once on shore. If MacBride had died, it could have been put down to a weak constitution, a bad heart. Would anyone have considered ordering a post-mortem? And if they had done, would they have bothered to look for poison when the body was not found to be diseased? Even if the army had identified the poison, they would likely have reacted as the doctor had done – the man had administered it to himself, to escape the nightmare of facing the enemy. No one would have thought to contact the Yard. It was an army matter. And so the Yard would go on looking for one Thomas MacBride . . .

The doctor was busy, giving orders to MacLeod, who was racing back the way they had come, returning quickly with an orderly and the doctor's medical bag.

It was a near run thing. The more ill MacBride had become from the motion of the ship, the less of the vial's contents he'd managed to keep down. And he had also continued to vomit, unable to swallow the second half. The army's doctor – one Major Wilkins – took charge of the vial and agreed to send word to Portsmouth to contact the Yard. Meanwhile, MacBride would be kept in an army hospital until he was well enough to rejoin his unit.

MacBride's gaze met Rutledge's as he waited for him to say something about taking the patient into custody as well.

But Rutledge was silent until the major had gone to see about transport to the nearest hospital on landing. Then he turned to MacBride and said, 'Give me the name of your French doctor, and the Yard will see to him. They will also retrieve the *Book of Hours*. You'll be in the clear.'

MacBride tried to shake his head and failed.

'You owe him no loyalty, man, he tried to kill you!'

'It's no' loyalty, is it?' he whispered. 'My key out of prison.'

'Then use it now. I'll see you're assigned to my company, and that will be the end to it. That's to say, if you fight as well as you thieve. At least at the end of the war, you'll be free to spend your fortune long after the Frenchman has climbed the steps to the gallows.'

But MacBride was stubborn, and Rutledge began to suspect he'd prefer to kill the Frenchman himself.

'There can be no charge of murder against you now. You'll face one if you desert and go after him.'

But MacBride was adamant. Just then Hamish MacLeod came in to tell Rutledge that France was in sight.

MacLeod must have seen the stubborn set of MacBride's jaw and guessed at Rutledge's dilemma, for after delivering his message, the Scot said something to MacBride in Gaelic, and after a long moment, MacBride answered plaintively in English.

'Francois du Luc. Ramsditch, Northumberland.'

Rutledge said, 'You won't regret this.' He hurried away to give the name to the major, to be sent back to England with the message. Later, as it was time to disembark, he found MacLeod just ahead of him and asked, 'What did you say to him?'

'MacBride? I told him you'd saved his life. And now ye own his soul.'

Shocked, Rutledge said, 'I own nothing of the sort. But he does owe me good service as long as he's a soldier.'

MacLeod said, 'Aye, well, ye're no' a Scot. It willna' weigh on ye, will it?'

And he was moving off the ship with the rest of the company before Rutledge could think of a fitting reply.

PRECIOUS THINGS
Laura Wilson

Laura Wilson published her first crime novel, *A Little Death*, in 1999, and after further stand-alone novels of psychological suspense, she began a series set during the Second World War and featuring London-based policeman Ted Stratton. The most recent Stratton title is *A Capital Crime*.

'You could do someone a bit of damage with that.' That's what Don had said. Fran remembered her husband in Barbados fifteen years ago, lumbering around the display of over-priced marine tat in the resort's souvenir shop. She could picture him quite clearly: beery chops, sun-reddened belly and flat, flip-flopped feet, surrounded by delicate shells taken from the Caribbean sea and glued together to form the shapes of puppies, kittens and rabbits. Don had been irritable because she'd dragged him away from the hotel bar for five minutes.

Now, she turned away from the office window where she'd been staring out at the grey-slabbed, pewter-skied landscape of an October Croydon lunchtime, and looked down at the object in her hand. It was a perfume bottle, six inches long, cone-shaped and crusted with small pink shells, with a sharply pointed mother-of-pearl lid that must, she thought, have been broken off something larger.

'It's perfect for the collection,' she'd told Don in the shop. 'So kitsch.' She'd opened the tester and waved it under his nose. 'Have a sniff.' The perfume was called 'Night in Barbados'. Don had said it smelt like bubble gum, and he was right.

Fran checked a second time to make sure that no one had come into the office, then turned the bottle over in her hands, examining it. She'd cleaned it so thoroughly that there couldn't be any traces now – or nothing visible, anyway. She'd washed it with detergent and a J cloth then gone over

it with an old toothbrush and a cotton bud before bringing
it into work, and she'd inspected it often in the years since
then. If she were the last to leave, or if everyone else was
at lunch, she'd always go over to the display table and have
a look. Not that she expected to find any new and incrimi-
nating marks – it was just a ritual.

This would be the last time. When they announced the
relocation of the department and she had decided, at sixty,
to retire, the thought of never being able to see the shell
bottle again – not being able to keep tabs on it – had worried
her at first. She'd considered taking it with her, because
nobody would mind, but that didn't seem right, somehow.
Besides, it had all happened fifteen years ago, and no one
had ever asked about it. She'd be safe enough.

She'd been back to Barbados since then – last year, in fact.
A deliberate decision, although she'd opted to stay at the opposite end of the island. It was off-season, just like when she'd
visited with Don – hot sun followed by sudden downpours,
even thunderstorms. She'd found out from her guidebook that
the place where the two of them had spent that week had closed
long before. 'Abandoned and ghostlike,' the book said. She'd
hired a car and driven out to see it.

The resort, now derelict, had failed because it was built
in the wrong place. All the successful ones were on the west
coast, with brochure-golden sands, not on the craggy east
coast where the blue waters of the Caribbean merged with
the grey Atlantic beneath steep, rugged cliffs. Don had been
angry about that – blamed her for not doing her homework
before she'd booked it. She'd blamed herself, too, for getting
it wrong. The conditions needed to be perfect, because their
marriage had deteriorated to the point where she'd known
that, if it were to have any chance of survival, they had to
spend time with each other, to rediscover and rekindle, and
that she must be the one to make the effort. Left to himself,
Don, apathetic and indifferent, would have let it drift forever,
or at least unless – or perhaps until – he chanced upon another
woman to take her place.

Now, she wondered why she had wanted to save her marriage
so much. Pride? Well, a bit. Habit? Ye-es, that was part of
it . . . But mainly, she thought, it was because she had been

absolutely terrified of the unknown alternative. She'd told
herself that she couldn't imagine starting all over again. Had
that been actually true, or had she just been too afraid to allow
herself to think about it? Odd that she couldn't remember.

Last year, when she'd returned to the resort, she had
expected to find barbed wire and padlocks and notices saying
'Keep Out' but there weren't any. Instead, the rusty iron gates
set in the breeze block wall sagged open, and the only sign
that visitors might not be welcome was a tangle of branches
piled in the middle of what was left of the driveway. She'd
navigated round it and parked her car beside the concrete
apartments with their faded pink paint. She walked past palm
trees and cacti in dry, crumbling flower beds, and crunched
across the cracked, glass-strewn concrete surround of the
swimming pool, which was empty but for the deep end where
tyres and plastic bottles floated in stagnant, oil-streaked rain-
water. She stood for a while with her back to the lido-style
cafe – roof collapsed in a heap of tarmac and rubble – and
stared at the main building for some minutes before she
managed to pinpoint the room that had functioned as the bar.
Feeling she ought at least to look inside – after all, it was
where Don had spent most of his last week on earth – she
stepped over the crude wooden barrier nailed across the
bottom third of the doorway. A rusting Toyota had stood in
the middle of the floor, its wheels long gone, its dashboard
frosted with broken windscreen glass and an old grey sweater
curled like a sleeping cat on the passenger seat. A giant
spider's web, studded with insects, was swagged like an ornamental fisherman's net across dusty shelves that had once
glittered with bottles of spirits and mixers.

She peered into the room next door, which she remembered as being the hotel office, and saw broken shelving and
a stack of bed frames propped up against a rust-pocked chest
freezer with a huge sticker advertising Banks Beer. She
remembered, then, that the night clerk and his friend were
playing cards on it when she'd come to tell them that Don
had disappeared.

The room smelt of urine and she turned away, wrinkling her
nose, and went outside to look up at the long balcony and the
row of empty frames behind it that had once contained the

doors and windows of the bedrooms. She'd pictured herself fifteen years before, waving down to Don and calling out cheerily, 'Do you want anything from the room?' So conciliatory she'd been, fetching and carrying, making herself useful, courting appreciation, trying to make him want her . . .

Now, in Croydon, standing at the office window and looking out over the staff car park, she thought, that's the real reason I've never told anyone: not fear, but the humiliation of the whole thing.

Alone in the ruins of the resort, she'd ducked her head and forced herself, heart thudding, to climb the stairs at the end of the main building, trying to remember which room it was that she and Don had shared. Somewhere in the middle of the row, she thought. She advanced cautiously, pausing beside each doorway, gazing in at wiring dangling from gouged walls, lino floors coated in brick dust and lumps of plaster, smashed louvre doors. Halfway down, she stopped dead: this was definitely it. In the middle of the floor, someone had arranged leaves and shells in neat concentric circles, and, in the centre, dusty but intact, stood a perfume bottle with a pointy top. She looked, blinked, looked again, then tottered backwards and grabbed the rail of the balcony for support. For a moment, she thought she was going to vomit. They *knew*. The people who'd worked here. They'd left a message. Or perhaps it was a kind of voodoo, or a way of ridding the room of bad spirits, or . . .

Now she was just being stupid. Pulling herself together, she approached the bedroom doorway again, heart battering at her rib cage, she saw that the thing on the floor was nothing like her shell bottle, just an old-fashioned flask of fluted glass. It was ridiculous – how *could* anyone know? It was children, that's all. Kids playing some game.

She took a deep breath and walked into the room. A mildewed double mattress slumped against the wall. Was that the one? Had it happened on there?

It was so quiet. She moved forward hesitantly, almost tiptoeing, towards the en-suite bathroom. The bath was still there, taps ripped out, it's white surface dirty and scabbed with rust. The loo seat was missing and the vanity unit smashed. She picked up a shard of the mirror and gazed at herself, remembering how, fifteen years before, she had stared at her reflection and seen the face of a woman who was no longer loved or desired. A woman who'd put on her specially bought underwear and sashayed into the bedroom, hoping that the satin and lace would compensate for the broad rump, thickening waist and forty-five years. A woman who'd climbed astride her dozing husband, mimicking a sexiness she did not feel, trying to mask her desperation with carnality, to make her movements slow, fluid and alluring . . . who'd slid her hands up and down Don's suety torso, murmuring, 'I want you, darling . . .'

Don, comatose from beer, sun, and a lot of wine at dinner, had told her to get off, but she'd been insistent, pawing at his unresponsive crotch. 'But I want you so much . . .' She'd felt triumphant when he'd rolled on top of her – no endearments, but that didn't matter, the action was enough. Then he'd stretched across to the bedside table and, eyes closed in expectation, she'd heard scraping and fumbling noises and thought, he's taking his watch off like he always does, and that means it's worked, thank God it's worked, oh thank God, thank God . . . Then his knee had nudged her thighs apart and she'd felt his hand between them and tried to relax and be aroused so that she'd be wet and it would happen and he would come and it would be something good between them and shared and the holiday would be a success and everything would be all right again and then . . . *Christ!*

'What's all this about, then?'

Fran jumped. It was one of the removal men. She hadn't realised that any of them were in the office. He was peering at the label on the wall beside a desk covered with bric-a-brac. '"The Table of Precious Things",' he read. 'What's that in aid of?'

'It started as a joke, really.' She pointed to a model of the leaning tower of Pisa in the middle of the collection. It had little Mickey Mouse arms and white gloved hands fashioned so it was leaning on a cane and raising a top hat. 'Somebody brought that thing back from their holiday and stuck it on top of a filing cabinet. Then other people brought things,

and it got to be a sort of competition, trying to find the tack-
iest souvenir. Then people from other offices started coming
in with stuff, and in the end we ran out of space on the filing
cabinet, and this desk was going spare, so . . . here they are.'

The removal man picked up a statuette of a priapic centaur.
'Bloody hell.' Embarrassed, he put it back in its place between
the plastic sumo wrestler and the leprechaun-in-a-snowstorm
paperweight. 'Sorry, love. Look, we're on our break now.
Best make a start on it this afternoon.'

Fran listened to his feet thundering away down the stairs.
It's because I'm old, she thought. I made him uncomfortable. If I were younger – or perhaps just better looking –
he'd have made a joke of it.

A joke . . . Staring at the centaur's disproportionately large
phallus, Fran remembered the agonising sensation of the
thing inside her that wasn't – couldn't have been – Don. It
was a sharp, rasping object that he'd forced up her so that
it caught and scraped her flesh . . . Now, standing by the desk,
she winced and shut her eyes tight as she thought of how
she'd lain quite still, trying not to cry out, until the pain had
been so bad that she'd begun to struggle and begged him to
stop. 'Don, you're hurting me, please . . .' He had been so
heavy on top of her that she'd had difficulty breathing, and
the pain went on and on . . . 'Please, it's hurting – what are
you doing? Please . . .'

'Paying – you – attention – and – doing – what – you –
want.'

'No, I don't, not like that. Stop it!' With a violent effort
she'd shoved him away, slid off the bed and then run, doubled
over, to the bathroom, where she'd knelt on the floor, rocking
backwards and forwards under the harsh white light, her
hands between her legs.

There'd been some blood. She tore off a length of toilet
paper, folded it into a wad, and, holding it in place with one
hand, clambered to her feet, opened the bathroom door and
listened for a moment. Heavy, rhythmic breathing. Don had
fallen fast asleep.

Sore and confused, she stumbled across to his side of the
bed. The first thing she saw was that he was still wearing
his watch. The next was what was on the bedside table. Next

to a scattering of loose change and a Robert Ludlum paperback lay the perfume bottle she'd bought, blood – her blood
– congealing on the pink shells on the sharp tip of its lid.

She'd known then that the situation was hopeless. Don
despised her, perhaps actually *hated* her, and there was
nothing that she could do.

She turned out the bathroom light, then walked round to
her own side of the bed and curled up as near the edge as
she could, her back to him.

'You all right, love?'

'Mmm . . .?' Fran turned. It was Sheila, the receptionist.
They'd become good friends over the years.

'I *am* going to miss you, Fran.'

'I'll miss you, too. But it seems like the right time . . .
End of an era. You know.'

'Yeah . . .'

The two women stood in silence for a moment, looking
down at the display on the table. Sheila said, 'All these
holiday things – I still remember, when you came back to
work, after . . . The moment you walked in, I thought, we
should have got rid of it all.'

Fran thought of that first day back, the stricken looks on
her colleagues' faces. She'd rung and explained beforehand,
of course, about Don dying and his body being flown back
to England. They'd been so tactful, so kind to her, no questions, only sympathy. And she'd settled down, hadn't she?
At first, anyway. Six months later it all had hit her and she'd
had to take time off to recover. She hadn't talked about it
then, either.

'You know,' she said to Sheila, 'when they found Don . . .
It was in the morning. The night before, when he didn't come
back from his walk, I didn't know what to do, because he
used to get so . . . Well, he drank a lot, and it must have been
pretty obvious – to the hotel staff, I mean. I sat in our room
for ages. I was angry, because that holiday was supposed
to be our chance to make things better. We were going
through a bad patch – like any marriage, I suppose – and
I was desperate to make it right . . . Actually, I wanted to
leave him, but I was desperate for us to stay together because

I was frightened of being on my own. Sounds pathetic, doesn't it?'

'Not really,' said Sheila. 'Lots of people feel like that, but most of them don't admit it, even to themselves.'

'I only admitted it to myself recently,' said Fran. 'I was petrified. There wasn't anyone else – for Don, I mean – at least, not anyone I knew about, and no one came out of the woodwork after he died. It was his complete indifference to my feelings . . . I'd almost started to wish that there had been another woman, because then there would have been a reason for him turning away that wasn't to do with me – or not directly, anyway. But I couldn't imagine any other life. I mean, my life wasn't a bed of roses, but it was *mine*, you know? And I'd remember all the good times we'd had. I'd tried to talk to Don about it, but he just *wouldn't*, and there was nothing I could do, and I used to get so frustrated, feeling he didn't want me, except for clean clothes and things like that . . .'

'Here.' Sheila handed her a tissue.

'Thanks.' Fran blew her nose.

'I wish you'd told me before,' said Sheila. 'Or told someone. Fifteen years is a long time to carry all that around.'

'I know. But like I said, I didn't really work it all out until recently. I was so grateful that you never expected me to talk about it. It was all such a *mess*. I was scared, Sheila, and I felt so *trapped*. I mean, we were supposed to be having the time of our lives. I kept suggesting that we should go out and see the island – we'd hired a car – but all Don wanted to do was sit by the pool and get drunk, and . . . I'm sorry, Sheila. I really didn't mean to say all this. You know, even when I'd made up my mind to tell the staff that Don was missing, I was embarrassed. I was sure they all knew he'd just gone off, because they'd seen the way he treated me in front of everyone. I'd seen them looking at me – the pity – and it was just . . . just . . .'

'Hey! Come on . . .' Sheila put her arm round Fran. 'It's all right.'

'When I told the staff, it was about six in the morning. The night clerk said he'd phone the police, but no one seemed to take it very seriously. "Don't worry, madam, he'll turn up . . ." as if Don was a lost dog or something. Then, in the afternoon, they came to my room and told me Don had been found, and I had to go and identify him. He was all grey because he'd been in the sea . . . it looked as if he didn't have any blood left in him. There were cuts on his head, you could see, where he was starting to lose his hair – it was *horrible*.'

'Oh, *Fran* . . .' Sheila gave her a squeeze.

'I'm all right. Just . . . you know. Last day here and everything.'

Face buried in Sheila's shoulder, Fran thought of how, that night, she'd woken from an uneasy sleep before dawn and lain on her back, staring up into the darkness, listening to Don's snores and the sound of the sea. Then, moving gingerly, because she was still sore, she'd swung her legs over the side of the bed, fumbled around for clothes, and dressed herself. She found the key for their barely-used hire car in the pocket of Don's shorts and left. The roads were dark except for a few street lights in the villages. She found herself heading along the coast, to the caves she'd persuaded him to visit with her two days before, not thinking of what she might do when she got there, just wanting to be somewhere away from him. There was a café there, and she thought she would have a cup of coffee when it opened. Then, as she pulled up beside the shuttered building, she remembered that she didn't have any money. The powerless feeling engendered by this small withdrawal of options made her cry.

She drove a little way off and stopped the car beside the edge of the cliff. Sitting in the driver's seat, looking out to sea, her head was a minefield of memories from the previous few years: her increasingly desperate efforts to please Don and engage with him, and, worst of all, the creaky self-consciousness of her failed attempts to seduce him. She realised, then, that he didn't think of her as a person any more, never mind as a woman. She might as well have been a domestic appliance, except that she nagged him and interfered with his drinking. Perhaps, she thought, he'd be happier on his own. Perhaps it was her fault. Perhaps the drinking was her fault, too.

Eventually, she fell into a doze. The first rays of the sun on the windscreen woke her at dawn. She blinked, bewildered, and then remembered where she was. I'm stuck, she thought. She looked out over the sea. All she had to do was to start the engine and drive over the cliff. Just slip the brake and put her foot down. Easy.

As she turned the key in the ignition she glanced mechanically into the rear-view mirror and saw a man walking towards the car. For a moment, she didn't recognise the balding, flabby individual in the shorts and Hawaiian shirt. Then she realised it was Don. I don't know you, she thought. You could be anyone – anyone at all. But you're not. You are *my husband*.

Sheila was rubbing her back. 'You poor thing. That's why I thought it wasn't right to keep all this stuff,' she said. 'Always reminding you . . .'

Fran disengaged herself. 'I'm glad you didn't throw it away. I like it.'

'You even brought something back . . . that was it, wasn't it?' She nodded at the perfume bottle in Fran's hand.

'Yes. I bought it from the hotel shop. I suppose I thought Don would have wanted me to bring it in. I'd told him about the precious things, you see. He thought it was funny.'

'Are you going to take it home with you?' asked Sheila.

'No.' Fran put the bottle down beside a pair of apple-cheeked Alpine toddlers locked in a china embrace. 'It belongs here, with the other stuff.' Fran blew her nose again.

'You *sure* you're going to be all right, love?'

'Yeah . . . just . . . Don't be so nice to me, Sheil. I just . . . I think I'd like to be on my own for a few minutes.'

'OK.' Sheila patted her shoulder. 'Tell you what. Why don't I go and get us a sandwich?'

Left alone, Fran remembered Don tapping on the window of her car. She'd opened it and asked, 'How did you know where I was?'

'It's the only place we've been.'

'How did you get here?'

'Walked.'

That surprised her. 'All the way?'

He shrugged. 'I'm going to look at the view. You coming?'

'No.'

'All right, then.' He turned away and wandered towards the edge of the cliff.

Watching him go, she thought, why is he here? If it was to apologise, why hadn't he? Or at least said they ought to talk about it or something. Perhaps he'd meant them to talk away from the car, but when she'd refused, he hadn't pressed her.

She didn't love him, so it wasn't fair to expect him or want him to love her. But it had been wonderful at the beginning, sharing things, making each other happy. Had they ever been properly happy? Suddenly, she couldn't remember. All she knew was that the slow and corrosive drip-drip of mutual irritation had poisoned their intimacy, that not talking had turned into a habit, and that now the habit of living side by side in isolation was all they had. She wondered then if Don felt as trapped as she did, and as scared.

She got out of the car, shivering in the thin morning sun, and followed him. She called out, 'What's the time?' but the waves must have been too loud for him to hear her. The pain made her grimace as she clambered along the slippery rocks to where he was standing. When she looked down, the long, sheer drop to the sea made her giddy, and she stepped back, hastily. 'I asked you what the time was.'

Don glanced at his watch. 'Half past five.'

He didn't even look at her. She was nothing to him but a set of demands: for the time – *his* time – for love, for proof that he still cared for her, and found her desirable. It's only what all women want, she thought, bitterly. All men, too. It's *normal*.

How *dared* he condemn her to this pitiful, lonely *facsimile* of a life, with no passion and no hope? He wouldn't care if she left him – in fact, she thought, he'd probably be relieved. Was his act of cruelty and degradation an attempt to force her hand, to get her to divorce him? Had he followed her here in the hope that she would say that? My God, he couldn't even be bothered to tell her he wanted to leave her. She wasn't worth the row or the fuss. He wanted her to say it so that he could agree. Well, he could go on wanting. Fuck you, she thought, the surge of uncharacteristic vehemence making her swear. *Fuck you.*

A single, quick shove. In her mind's eye she saw herself

step forward and push him, hard, in the small of the back.
She'd put out her hands in front of her, almost feeling the
cotton of his shirt, the solid slab of flesh beneath, and then
. . . then . . .

Then she took a step back and watched, incredulously, as,
arms flailing, he lost his balance, toppled forward, and disappeared over the cliff.

There was no sound from him, no shout or thud or splash,
just the noise of the waves beating against the rocks below.
Without stopping to think, she ran, heedless of the pain, back
to the car. She started the engine, reversed, and drove away,
fast, down the empty road.

She didn't – couldn't – believe she'd done it. Had he turned
to look at her and slipped? Surely that wasn't possible. But
she hadn't really wanted to kill him, had she? *Had* she? Or
was it an impulse – something irresistible, over before she'd
had time to register it properly, her body acting independ-
ently of her mind.

By the time she'd got back to the hotel she'd convinced
herself it hadn't happened at all. She'd honestly expected to
walk into the bedroom and find him asleep. It was a shock
to find the room empty, but the realisation still didn't come
as she lowered the blinds and sat in the gloom, waiting for
him to return and getting angry when he didn't.

'Injuries consistent with falling from a height,' they'd said.
That, and a high percentage of alcohol in the bloodstream,
was given as the cause of death. Nobody'd noticed her driving
away from the hotel or returning, and the coroner had delivered an open verdict. Given that she had no memory of
anything beyond imagining pushing Don, that had seemed
both fair and right.

Then, six months after she'd returned to work, the nightmares had started. It was always the wrong way round in her
dreams, she and Don on the cliff together – she could never
see his face, but of course it was him. He would start to undo
his watch strap and she knew that as soon as he'd taken it
off he would push her over the edge and she wouldn't be
able to stop him. She'd feel the shove and start to fall, and
then her body would jerk upwards and she'd wake, sweating
and terrified.

There hadn't been anyone else since Don. She'd got used to living on her own, and even, after a few years, grown to like it. Lying in their double bed by herself, she felt safe: no need to pretend or try to please, or risk being hurt or humiliated.

Fran blew her nose again. Funny, she thought, that conversation with Sheila is the closest I've ever come to telling anybody, and when I was saying it, it seemed so true, almost like reliving it even though it wasn't how it happened. Except, in a way, it *was* – she *had* sat in the hotel room and tried to think what to do, and when she'd interrupted the men's card game and told them that Don was missing, she'd believed utterly in what she was saying. She could remember that part quite clearly, but the thing itself – pushing him – had never come back to her.

She shook her head. Even if I told someone the truth, she thought, a psychiatrist or a priest, it wouldn't sound true because I couldn't give any details. And – this was the oddest thing of all – she knew she wouldn't actually believe it herself. That had been the real reason why she'd returned to Barbados last year – to try and recapture it and make it real. She'd kept the fact of that holiday a secret, too, telling her colleagues she was going to visit her sister in Anglesea. Fortunately, the UK temperature had been in the nineties all of that week, so no one had questioned her suntan.

'You still here?' The removal man was back with a stack of flat-packed boxes. 'We'll start with these knick-knacks,' he added, and then, seeing what he thought was a frown of objection on her face, 'if that's all right by you, of course.'

'Fine.' Fran's hand hovered over the shell bottle.

'That your favourite, is it?'

'Yes. You won't damage it, will you?'

'Don't worry, love,' said the removal man. 'It'll be well wrapped up. We'll treat it like the family jewels.'

'The family jewels . . .' repeated Fran. The man stared at her, bewildered, as she started to giggle.